B E S T
WOMEN'S
EROTICA
2 0 0 1

B E S T
WOMEN'S
EROTICA
2 0 0 1

Edited by

Marcy Sheiner

CLEIS
PRESS

Published in the United States by Cleis Press Inc.,
P.O. Box 14684, San Francisco, California 94114.
Printed in the United States.
Cover design: Scott Idleman
Text design: Karen Quigg
Logo art: Juana Alicia
First Edition.
10 9 8 7 6 5 4 3 2

"A Girl's Gotta Have Friends" was published in *Australian Woman's Forum Erotica*, Issue 3. "Branded" was originally published in *Viscera: An Anthology of Bizarre Erotica*, edited by Cara Bruce (Venus or Vixen Press, 2000). "Hair" has appeared in *Zaftig! Sex for the Well Rounded*. "The Language of Snakes" was originally published on erotasy.com in 1999. "Rope Burn" was originally published in *Clean Sheets* in Summer 2000. "Sukreswara" was originally published in *Exhibitions: Tales of Sex in the City*, edited by Michelle Davidson (Arsenal Pulp Press, 2000). "Tic Sex" was originally published in the premier issue of *Blue Food*, Spring 2000. "Wages of Faith" was originally published in *Viscera: An Anthology of Bizarre Erotica*, edited by Cara Bruce (Venus or Vixen Press, 2000). "Waste" was originally published in *The Bust Guide to the New Girl Order* (Viking/Penguin, 1999).

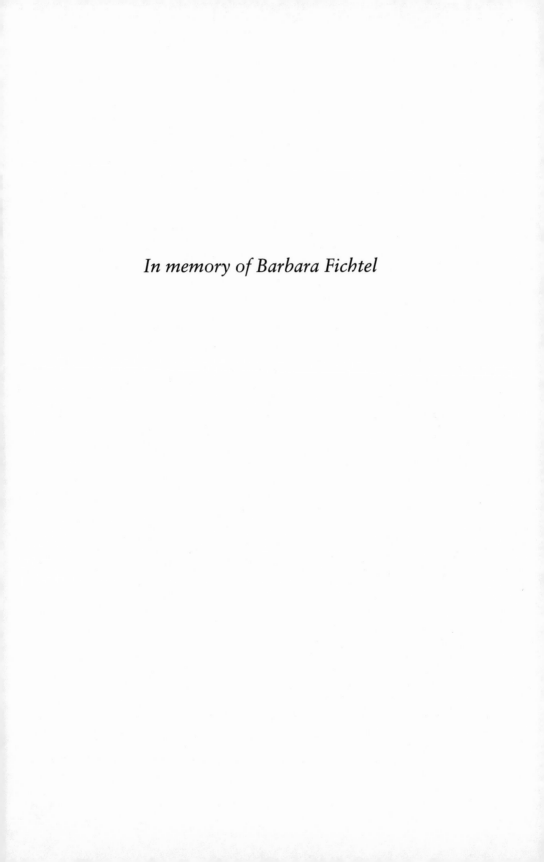

In memory of Barbara Fichtel

TABLE OF CONTENTS

Introduction:
Shadows and Light

I confess: I have a fondness for stories that reveal the darker side of sex. By "darker side" I mean sex that isn't always an expression of love, but that might be laced with anger, grief, revenge, and other emotions not usually considered "nice"—certainly not culturally condoned motivations for lovemaking. In fact, sex stories that deal with dark themes frequently come under vicious attack.

If you think I'm exaggerating, let me tell you about a recent incident that occurred at a bookstore reading of the first edition of *Best Women's Erotica*. Cara Bruce read her story "Lita," in which the female protagonist witnesses the death of a neighbor who falls through a plate glass window while making love. Days later, the surviving partner comes to visit the protagonist and they engage in grief-laden, cathartic sex, with the narrator pretending to be his dead lover. After the reading we invited questions from the audience. One man accused Cara of being misogynistic: he was disturbed, as were several other members of the audience, by a story he saw as somehow condoning the death of a woman. That the story was fiction didn't seem to matter. (Nor that women are knocked off in droves in mystery books, horror flicks, and made-for-television movies on Lifetime.)

The truth is, in real life, complex and ambiguous emotions are frequently expressed through sex—though many people are afraid to write about it, publish it, or just plain admit to it. This is particularly true in the realm of women's erotica, where a kind of political correctness subtly encourages stories in which sex is an expression of love, or at least of kind feelings between partners. Another PC notion is that the woman's pleasure should be central to the story. Well, I don't like *shoulds,* particularly since they leave little room for exploration.

These kinds of constraints were to be expected ten or twenty years ago, when, merely by publicly revealing our fantasies, desires, and experiences, women proclaimed ourselves no longer "nice girls." It was a daring act to sign one's name to a sex story, then as now, and many of us hid behind pseudonyms (a porn tradition that continues to this day). But the genre of women-authored erotica has evolved, and I think we're ready to take the next step: not only to proclaim ourselves as sexual beings but also to tell the truth about the darker side of our sexuality.

As philosophers from Freud to Foucault have pointed out, sex is more than an expression of desire; it is an arena where we human beings confront our shadow side. Some of us run from it, some of us deny its existence, some of us keep it secret. Some people, like the audience at the bookstore reading of Cara Bruce's story "Lita," fervently *wish* we'd keep it secret. Sorry, folks: *Best Women's Erotica* celebrates both the shadows and the light.

After I confessed my affinity for dark-themed stories in the introduction to *Best Women's Erotica 2000,* word spread like wildfire along the sex-writer grapevine. Writers whose dark stories were languishing in their "rejected" files dusted them off and sent them to me. Others who had wanted to delve into this territory but were afraid of alienating editors felt encouraged to take the plunge. Thus the submissions I received for this second edition were staggeringly weighted in that direction and *Best Women's Erotica 2001* includes a proportionately large number of such stories—sprinkled with stories of old-fashioned love and lust, which I hope will never go out of fashion.

These stories depict sex as an expression of rage ("The Survey"), grief ("After Loss," Climbing the Wall"), and a hefty dose of revenge ("Infidelities," "Jack," "Pilegesh," "The Best Revenge"). Complex emotions and circumstances permeate "The Language of Snakes" and "The Mark." "Waste" and "Branded" dare to talk about highly unorthodox sex acts. "Rope Burn" is fraught with otherworldly mysticism and obsession. "Wages of Faith," while not overtly sexual, portrays the eroticism that seeps through religious sacrificial rituals.

I'm an advocate for people with disabilities, about whom I frequently write, so the freshness and honesty of "Tic Sex" just about knocked my panties off. "Tic Sex" turns a socially embarrassing disability into a sex toy, irreverently smashing tired old stereotypes.

Several of the stories inhabit a kind of gray zone between pure romance or lust and darkness. "Contented Clients" buzzes with humor, "Hair" deals with a benign fetish, and "Devotion" and "Sukreswara" defy traditional notions of religious sanctity—an old theme with new twists.

For a healthy dose of what's considered healthy sex, there's "The Heart in My Garden," "A Girl's Gotta Have Friends," "Tara's Stew," and "This Old Bed." Even these stories, though, defy taboos of one kind or another, and reveal insights about the complexities of human sexuality.

If I was thrilled—and I was—by the first edition of *Best Women's Erotica,* I'm beyond ecstatic over this one. Many of these stories delve into territory that's long fascinated me: the connection between religion and eroticism, the desire to be fully possessed by a lover, the sex-death connection, and, perhaps most of all, the ways in which sex is used to exact revenge on a partner who's "done ya' wrong."

If the series continues to embarrass audiences, shock readers, and elicit more daring stories from writers, I'll be delighted. Erotica is supposed to titillate and to serve as a catalyst to real-life sex—and these stories do. But if they also provoke readers' thinking and encourage greater sexual honesty, *Best Women's Erotica* will have served an even more important purpose. As Oliver Wendell Holmes said, "A man's mind stretched to a new idea never goes back to its original dimension."

Marcy Sheiner
Emeryville, California
August 2000

Infidelities

G. L. Morrison

How did I know he was unfaithful? I knew it because I was his second wife. He'd been unfaithful to his first wife—with me. I remember the excuses he gave her: working late, "business trips" we took together, absurdly frequent engine trouble or flat tires.

"She didn't fall for that?" I asked him. He assured me that she believed every word.

I now know that she didn't. I don't. I am just too amazed at his audacity to argue. Now I also know what I didn't know when he and I were making love for hours, pretzeling into impossible, playful, passionate positions and then sleeping, twisted into each other's arms in a borrowed apartment of a friend who was out of town for the weekend while Stephen was supposedly on one of those "business trips." I know that Stephen had sex with his wife, though he told me he didn't. I know it because he is still having sex with me. Tender, guilty, exhausted sex.

Now, six years after our illicit affair has been legalized, sanitized into a state of respectability, I am twice wounded.

My husband is cheating on me with another woman. And all those years ago my lover, the same man, was cheating on me with his wife. I don't know which betrayal I resent more. I should be angry. I should resist the seductions and cut flowers, as short-lived as his excuses. But I don't, because Stephen's a really great lover. I don't know where he finds the energy. Does it excite him to crawl into my bed with the scent of another woman still clinging to him? To kiss me hungrily?... *Yes, Jennifer. He does still kiss me hungrily.*

The other woman's name is Jennifer. Stephen crawls into my bed as little as fifteen minutes after leaving hers. She lives only a few miles away from us. I've never met her. But I know where she lives. Does it excite him to rush into me after making love to her? To twine his tongue around mine so that I can almost taste her? So that the smell of her cunt, still wet on his chin, overwhelms me. It excites me. It doesn't lessen my jealousy, but it excites me. When his kisses have inflamed me enough, I push his head down. His rough tongue patiently tickles the inside of my thighs.

"Quickly," I hurry him. I want some of her juice still on his tongue while he's licking me. Is it me he's thinking of while his tongue wriggles into the muscled cave of my cunt? Is her cunt lightly downed as mine, the hair thinned with age, or is she young and rebelliously shaved smooth? I read his diary but he leaves out details like these. "Jennifer," I heard him say into the phone as he hung up very quickly. (*J* in his diary.) There were only two Jennifers in his address book. One of them I recognized as an eighty-year-old great-aunt. I wrote down the other's address and phone number. *Sloppy, Stephen. Very sloppy.* Which is how his first wife caught us. I wasn't surprised his habits hadn't much changed.

I didn't call her. What would I have said? I've driven by her house, hoping to catch sight of her. My jealous curiosity drew me there. One day when I knew him to be on a real business trip *(Let this be a warning to you, Husbands of the World. It is not that difficult to check.)* I stopped. I got out of the car. I rang her doorbell. She could just as easily have been on the trip with him. She wasn't.

Twenty-something with red braided hair answered the door.

"Hello," I said, cold and defiant.

"Hello," she said sweetly.

"Do you know who I am?" I demanded.

She looked puzzled. She shook her head apologetically. "I haven't lived here very long."

I didn't know what to say. This interview wasn't going at all as I had imagined it.

"I'm Karyn," I said. "Karyn Feinberg."

Her red braid bobbed amiably.

"Stephen Feinberg's wife."

She didn't bat an eyelash. Not a flicker of recognition.

"Are you Jennifer?" Maybe I was at the wrong address.

"Jennifer Reidenbach." She shook my hand politely.

I felt a little foolish. I kept waiting for Rod Serling to step out from behind a well-manicured bush. Should I ask her, "Are you having an affair with my husband?" Should I demand to smell her pubic hair? Would it be the same salty-sweet I licked off his cheek some nights?

Jennifer Reidenbach was looking at me kindly. "Can I help you?" she asked.

"I've lost my..." (Mind. I've definitely lost my mind.) "...my puppy. Have you seen him?"

"What does he look like?"

Like every other imaginary pet. "Brown, furry. About this high. Comes to the name of Romeo."

"That's a funny name for a dog."

"Isn't it?"

Jennifer Reidenbach shook her red braid. "No. I haven't seen him."

"Maybe your husband has seen him."

"I'm not married."

"Can I use your phone?" I asked.

"Sure," the fly said to the spider.

She led me to a kitchen phone. I stared at her pointedly. She left to give me privacy. I hit each of the auto-dial numbers programmed into her phone. One of them was certain to be Stephen's office number or my home. I hung up whenever anyone answered. I didn't hear a voice or message machine that I recognized. That doesn't prove anything, I told myself.

The walls of the kitchen and hallways were covered with snapshots. I looked for pictures of him, of them together. They were all of people I didn't know. I took in as much as I could of her apartment. "Are you a photographer?" "I wish," she said wistfully. "I mean, yes, I am. I'm trying to be."

In spite of myself, I liked her. I went from room to room, looking at the photographs; looking around for some evidence, some telltale sign of Stephen.

"Maybe Romeo will come home on his own," Jennifer suggested.

"What?"

"Your dog. I hope you find him."

"Oh, him. He's the wandering type, seems like he forgets where home is."

"You should have him neutered," Jennifer said.

"That's a good idea," I agreed. Then I saw it—a picture of Stephen, a Polaroid of the two of them at the County Fair. *Last year's* fair!

"Who is this?" I tapped the photo.

"That's my boyfriend, Mark."

"Mark?"

"Uh huh."

"He looks familiar," I told her. My teeth felt sharper for saying it.

"Does he? He lives in Philadelphia."

"Philadelphia?" I choked.

"Yes, he calls me when he comes to town. He comes here a lot on business. But not often enough. You know how long-distance relationships are."

"No...why don't you tell me?" So she did. Every word she said made my eyes a little wider. She was a very young, very beautiful, very gullible girl. He'd told her his name was Mark Smith.

"Smith?" I said. "You must be kidding."

She laughed, a completely guileless laugh. "That's what I said when he first told me. But somebody has to be named Smith, right?"

"Right."

She made me coffee and told me how they met, the last time she'd seen him, every implausible word he'd ever said, how fervently she believed them all, and of course, what a wonderful lover he was. I ground my teeth silently.

"How do you know he's not married?" I asked her.

"Oh," she shrugged the idea off. "I'd know. I want to show you something." She took me by the hand and led me to her bedroom. The bed was covered in tie-dyed silk. The walls were crowded with pictures. Here was Stephen. There was Stephen. Stephen everywhere. It was a temple. The walls were altars and Stephen's face blazed like a candle in every corner.

In one he held his hand out in protest. *No more pictures.* Another was clearly taken in the garden of his mother's house. (What had they been doing there? Where had his mother been? Whose house had "Mark" said it was?) Every piece of the puzzle fragmented into more questions. I was more confused than ever. More pictures were of him sprawled on her bed, this very bed. I looked at the rumpled sheets, smoothed them with my hand. In some he was naked. In some, sleeping. In some he was looking out at her with undisguised lust. It was odd, since he seemed to be looking right out of the picture at me. He seemed to be saying *I want you. Now.* Although I knew it was not me he had been wanting, my clit leaped like a candlewick under the familiar attention of a match.

Jennifer grinned like a child sharing a secret treasure with a friend, which is in fact what she was. I ruffled her hair.

As I was leaving, Jennifer hugged me earnestly. "I hope you get Romeo back. I know how terrible it is to lose something you love."

"Thank you," I said.

"Please come back again."

I grinned wickedly. "I will."

After that, I did what any vigilant dog-owner would do. I kept my husband on a tight leash. I made plans to do things in the evening, couple things, command-performance things like dinner at his mother's. I became good friends with the boss's wife. We had dinner with them once a week. I'd have finagled more if I could but it was difficult to wrench the boss away from *his* mistress—a girl who worked in the office and looked no more than sixteen. I dropped in at Stephen's office unexpectedly "to have lunch together." I was suspiciously romantic and spontaneous. Stephen retaliated by varying his lunch hour erratically and saying, "If I'd only known you were coming," hoping to force me to call and announce my surprise inspections. It was a statistical certainty that one day I would be arriving as he was leaving. That day came. He didn't see me, so what choice did I have but to follow him? What would I do if he led me to her house? Would I burst in on them, catch them in bed, wipe the lust and bliss off their amazed faces, while the lustful, blissful photos stared down from the bedroom walls at us—a jury of our peers? Would I sit frozen in the car while they made love inside? What if I rang the bell and no one answered? Who would untangle her limbs from her lover to answer the door? Leave him for Jehovah's witnesses, Girl Scout cookies, or pseudoneighbors' lost dogs? And when they didn't answer the door, what would I do? Crawl in a window? Break down the door? Call 911? *Help. My husband is making love to a beautiful woman.*

I shouldn't have worried. He didn't go to her house. He went to a restaurant. For lunch. Not a terribly suspicious way to spend one's lunch hour. And oh, how fortunate for me...to be able to "surprise" him here. "Honey, what a nice surprise!" I'd exclaim brightly. I could feel the leash tighten. I hid my face behind a menu and sauntered toward his table. But the chair across from him wasn't empty. Jennifer's hair fell around her shoulders in tight, red curls. They framed her face like a halo. I sat where I could watch them. I ordered something. I ate it without tasting it. I watched "Mark" and "his girl." Jennifer fed him cheesecake with her fork. I noticed she saved him the last bite. Neither of them saw me. Neither of them looked in my direction even once. They left separately. On a whim, I decided to follow *her.*

We ended up at the mall. I followed her from the parking lot, through the stores, unseen. I felt like that character in a Woody Allen movie who turns invisible after drinking a strange Chinese tea. Could anyone see me? Had I eaten something at lunch that might make me invisible? Was I really this stealthy or was I dreaming? I'd felt a little dreamy ever since I'd rung Jennifer's doorbell that day, or maybe even before that, when I first saw her name in Stephen's address book. I had that disconnected, floaty feeling. It wasn't dreaming. It was waking up from the dream, a lie that had been my life. So this was being awake? This half-angry, half-horny, half-grieving, curious, bewildered, excited, half-mad, more-than-a-hundred-percent feeling?

Three teenagers, walking astride, scowled at me. In my reverie I hadn't noticed that I was supposed to have stepped aside for them. At least that's what I interpreted from their scowls. It could also have meant "I hate the world, not just you." I stepped aside. An elderly mall-walker who had stopped to tie her shoe shook her head regretfully. Whether she felt sorry for me or the teens, who knows? But it was confirmed: I was not invisible. I walked a little faster. I caught up with Jennifer. I put my hand on her shoulder.

"It's you!" she said.

The delight in her voice startled me. It also warmed me. She was glad to see me. I was surprised how much I liked that. I felt a twinge of guilt for deceiving her. I hooked my arm in hers and we walked through the shops together like old friends. She must be lonely, I thought, to have taken to me so quickly. Is that why she let herself fall in love with Stephen, believe every word he said? Is that why I had? Loneliness and passion—a dangerous elixir.

I pointed to Victoria's Secret. "Come help me pick out a bra."

Giggling, she followed me into the store. Jennifer was out of her element there. She looked as dumbstruck and embarrassed as if she'd been caught going through her mother's underwear drawer. What gives? I thought mistresses were born with the *Kama Sutra* in one hand and a suitcase of elegant lingerie in the other. Clearly someone had forgotten to tell Jennifer this.

I pulled her into the dressing room. "Help me with this strap."

She buckled the red velvet bra. We both admired my reflection in the mirror.

"What do you think?"

"You're beautiful," she said innocently.

I jiggled in it for effect, watching my velvet-clad breasts bounce in the mirror.

"But is it sexy?"

She bit her lip. "Oh, yes."

I smiled. She was so easy. *Like shooting fish in a barrel, Stephen. Where's the sport in that?* Emotions played over her face in shades of pink. I brushed a strand of red hair out of her eyes, tenderly. She swallowed hard.

"If you think it looks good, I'll buy it," I said.

"Shall I wrap it for you?" the teenage sales clerk asked, sounding as if she assumed I was buying it for someone younger, infinitely hipper, than myself.

"No, I'll wear it." I tore off the tag, handing it and my credit card to the clerk. I whispered in Jennifer's ear, "I love the way it feels. The way I feel knowing I have something so sexy on under my clothes." Jennifer squirmed. I moved away from her as abruptly as I had moved near her. I scrutinized the racks.

"What do you think of this?" I held up a daring bit of lace.

"Oh, well..." Jennifer stuttered. "It's very, um. There's not much to it, is there?"

"Do you think what's-his-name would like this?"

"Who?"

"Your friend," I smiled patiently.

"Mark?" she choked, a cough that ended in giggling. "What man *wouldn't* like it?"

"What man indeed?" I asked.

The sales clerk snickered. She had clearly gotten the wrong idea about us.

"We'll take it. Charge it to my card." I threw it on the counter.

"Oh, no!" Jennifer groaned. "I could never wear something like that. I'd be too shy. I couldn't...it's just not...it's just not me!" She blushed just looking at it on the hanger.

"Exactly why it would be such a lovely surprise." Just not the surprise you're expecting, I thought.

Jennifer continued to protest half-heartedly as the salesgirl rang it up.

"Thank you." Jennifer kissed me on the cheek, shyly, as she took the unwanted package.

The sales clerk snickered her signature snicker. Lesbians were the height of comedy in her small world. As I was signing the receipt, I leaned close to the clerk and purred, "Try it. You might like it."

"What?" Jennifer hadn't quite heard me, but thought I was speaking to her.

"Nothing," I said. I slipped my arm around her waist in a friendly gesture.

Since we were "neighbors" and my car was in the shop, I caught a ride "home" with her. Actually my car was parked in the row behind hers. It surprised me how easily lies fell off my lips now. How quickly they came to me, how confidently I spouted them. *I see the appeal, Stephen.* It's not just sex. It's the ability to be anyone, anyone at all. To make up a life on the spur of the moment and then to wear it like an expensive suit. Chic, well-fitted, and in whatever color you want. What no longer surprised me was Jennifer's unconditional belief in everything I said. She was well trained. She was the perfect accomplice to my lies: so willing to believe anything. Who could resist lying to her?

In the car we talked about music and food and our childhoods. I wondered how much of what I told her was true. The truth sounded tinny to me: small and unbelievable. I retold stories I had told a million times before, but now I heard them with a new ear. Is that the truth, I wondered? Is the way I remember it true? Lying had made the truth enigmatic, a sort of unachievable ideal. What is true? I even doubted my likes and dislikes. Was artichoke chicken with corkscrew pasta really my favorite dish? Or had I simply believed it the first time I told myself it was? Believed it, stopped asking questions, and from then on reported it as the truth.

Every story Jennifer told me about Mark was the truth—the truth as she knew it. She asked me if I had found my dog. I admitted to keeping him on a chain now but that he still managed to wriggle out of his collar and run free. That was the truth, wasn't it?

At her house, I didn't need a lie to get inside. She welcomed me in. She made me feel at home.

"I'd like a drink."

"Herbal tea or Coke?" Jennifer asked. "Or I think I have some orange juice."

"Something stronger."

She brought out a bottle of wine. I took it into the bedroom. I sat in a chair and she sat on the bed. We drank and talked and laughed. All around us, pictures of Stephen/Mark smiled.

Halfway through the bottle I suggested she model her lingerie. There was much blushing and a little protesting. Not as much protesting as I'd expected.

Just enough "Oh, I couldn't" to oil the machine of my "It'll be fun." I was sure that was true.

She unzipped her jeans. Wriggled out of her silk blouse, her red curls bouncing riotously over her bare shoulders. I watched her. I was fascinated—and hungry. Had Stephen watched her like this, shucking off the day's clothing and burdens to reveal this blinding skin? Had he sat in this very chair and seen what I was seeing? The chair's hard back kept me alert, aware of a slight discomfort. Jennifer watched me. It wasn't Stephen she was seeing in the chair; it was me. She undressed slowly. She pulled her shirt over her head like a burlesque stripper removing a glove. Slowly. Her back was lightly muscled, yet classic as a Greek statue. This Aphrodite looked over her shoulder and smiled at me.

I picked up Jennifer's camera from her dresser and checked for film. I snapped her picture. Whirr. Click. She quickly turned toward me, surprised and embarrassed. She laughed and hurried to put her clothes back on. I kept taking pictures. Whirr. Click. She was as beautiful re-dressing. Hopping, half in and half out of her pants, she raised her hand in impatient surrender. It was the same gesture I'd seen in Stephen's picture.

No more pictures.

"Stop," she laughed.

I didn't.

Pants on, but unzipped. Blouse in hand. "Stop, really."

I really didn't. Whirr. Click. I snapped another picture of her crossing the room. I got another, a close-up of her jostling breasts, before she reached the chair.

"Give it to me." She held out her hand for the camera.

"Are you shy?" I snapped another picture. Her red-brown nipple. Her frowning lips.

"C'mon. Give it to me."

"What will you give me if I do?"

Jennifer licked her hesitant lips. "What do you want?"

"I want to take pictures of you."

She took the camera from me and turned it over in her hand. "I'm not comfortable on that side of the camera. I like to see, not to be seen."

"Jennifer, there's so much you don't see."

"Huh?"

"Let me show you how other people see you. How I see you."

I held my hand out for the camera. She looked dubious. I refilled our wineglasses.

"You take my picture," I said, "and then I'll take yours. Fair?"

"Fair," she agreed.

On the dresser where I'd found the camera there was a clock radio. I turned it on. I unbuttoned my shirt, seductively swaying to the music. Whirr. Click. Whirr. Click. I danced for her to the metronome of the camera, the strobe of the flash. I told myself brilliant, exciting lies. I was Cleopatra. My hips could bring a nation to its knees. I stepped out of my clothes. Dancing, whirling for her. I was Salome, only even John the Baptist couldn't resist me. The taste of me was sweeter than heaven. I was a stripper in a filthy nightclub. Jennifer was hordes of men hungry to stick dollar bills—hundred-dollar bills!—into my G-string. I used the chair as a pole, bumping and grinding. I swung my leg over the chair. I was a housewife seducing my husband's mistress. I laughed. No, that fantasy was too farfetched. I was every model seducing every photographer through the raw art of her body.

Walking toward her so that she had to back up to keep me in the frame, I steered Jennifer toward the bed. She backed up until she could back up no further. Whirr. Click. I leaned over her, pressing my navel to the camera lens; blinding the camera. She was mine now. I didn't know if this was how Stephen had her and by now I didn't care. I tugged her jeans off and tossed them on the floor beside her shirt. She was wearing Batman undies. I threw my own clothes on the growing pile. I gently parted the lips that Batman had recently guarded and kissed her cunt. I reveled in the smell of her, not the faraway hinted-at scent mixed with soap that I smelled on Stephen's half-washed face. This was the real smell of woman. An alive, musk-breaded smell. I wanted to swallow her whole.

I'd never touched any cunt but my own. I'd never seen one so close. It was fascinating, elaborate, more stunning than I'd fantasized. The pictures I'd seen barely hinted at the color and intricacy of the flesh that lay open before me. In every way imaginable I was swimming in forbidden, unfamiliar waters. Tongue-first, I dived in. I began licking her gingerly, but encouraged by the noises she was making, I threw myself into her cave with all the enthusiasm of a more experienced spelunker. Though I tired quickly—unprepared for the vigorous exercise this sport required of my jaw—I didn't let up for a minute. I wanted to feel her, to taste her coming into my eager mouth. She didn't disappoint me. There was a sharp taste like metal amid the musk and she came, writhing wildly, so that I could barely keep my mouth on her. Then she turned me over and gave me (or had) a taste of my own medicine.

Curious and tireless as only virgins can be, I licked every inch of her and she nibbled most of me, including territory I never remember having had nibbled before. After hours and orgasms—neither of us bothered to count—I parted her cunt-lips and kissed them more fondly than passionately.

"I wish you could see what I see."

Jennifer handed me the camera. She held her lips open so that I could photograph the velvet inside. I tried to coax her clit into the picture but, overworked and camera-shy, it hid stubbornly beneath its hood. Still she was beautiful, different in every frame. Click. I held the camera in my right hand and took a picture of my finger on her clit, deep inside her. My finger here. There. Two fingers. Click. Click. Jennifer softly moaned until I ran out of film. She reloaded the camera. I held it out to get pictures of us together. She did the same. We agreed they'd be terrible pictures, off-centered, oddly angled, random and beautiful...like our love.

She used the word *love*. It surprised me. *Oh, Stephen. She's so easy. So innocent. So inexperienced that she thinks sex is love.* But maybe it is. How could a liar like me know the truth about love? I remembered what she'd said in the lingerie store: "I couldn't wear that. It's not me!" How would Jennifer know that what we'd done tonight was anything but the real "me"? It made sense that she would interpret my actions as love. She wasn't the sort of girl who jumped into bed with strange women. She wasn't the sort of girl who had affairs. That wasn't *her*.

I didn't ask the obvious: what about Mark? I was sure she'd break it to him gently. If she chose to break it to him at all. Perhaps she intended to cheat on me with him. As she'd cheated on him with me. Which was it? Perhaps she didn't know what would happen next. I certainly didn't. If the new "me" she'd discovered was capable of this, wasn't it capable of anything?

That picture of Stephen leered down at us. The one with the look, the smug look, the I-want-you-and-you're-mine look. I'd wipe that look right off his face.

"Promise me one thing," I said.

"Anything."

"Promise you'll put up a picture of me, a picture of us, right here." I took the leering picture down and put it under the bed. "So I can watch you sleep."

"Whatever you want," she whispered into the small of my neck.

That answered all the questions I might have about Mark. If he ever came into this bedroom again, he'd see what I wanted him to see. That I'd been here. That he didn't know her or me at all. That women are not numbers that lie flat in your address book just waiting for you to call. And what could he say to that? To her? To my triumphant picture?

Love is a fickle religion. The next time I came to her house—if I ever came again—I might find my own face and skin and hers, wet with my kisses, lit like a candle in every corner. Or she might promise me anything and then do as she liked. My picture might come out of the closet like some aunt's tacky, unwelcome gift that you put on display whenever you expect her visit. Anything was possible. Hadn't I just proven that? Her devotion was so believable. But believable is not the same as truthful, is it? What if Jennifer wasn't so simple, so easy? What if she'd played us both, Stephen and me? What if she believed my lies (and his!) the way that Stephen thought I believed his lies? Yes, I laughed, and what if I really *was* Cleopatra?

Liars believe that everyone's lying. After a really big lie, no truth seems possible. Was I lying when I said I loved her? I whispered it again into her soft neck. If a good lie sounds like the truth, then what does the truth sound like?

I let myself out while she was sleeping. The lingerie sat untouched in the Victoria's Secret bag. I pulled out the leering picture of Mark from under the bed and put it into the bag. I took it with me. I called a taxi from the corner. The taxi took me to the mall, where I'd left my car. From there, I drove to "Philadelphia." *You remember Philadelphia, that's where Mark lives.* Fortunately it was only ten minutes away.

Mark...no, Stephen...was waiting up for me.

"Where have you been?"

Oh, what a tightrope is jealousy! Why had I never thought to make him follow me, watch me, wonder where I was when he wasn't around?

"Where have you been?" he demanded, louder.

"Shopping," I said, although the mall had been closed for hours. I hefted the Victoria's Secret bag for effect. Then I showed him that bit of lace Jennifer had thought was too daring. That little bit of covering that was more naked than being naked. And I dared and dared. I turned on the radio. I tuned it to the same station Jennifer listened to. I danced for him. I didn't show the same energy and enthusiasm as I had a few hours before. I was tired. And he was my husband, not a conquered general or a biblical prophet or an intoxicating, nubile, redheaded, new woman-lover. He was just my husband. He was a sure thing. My sure thing. And I was his sure thing. (Though not, perhaps, as sure as he'd thought.) It isn't so bad being or having a sure thing. I knew which wiggle and oomph would get a sigh or a smile. I could predict his expressions before they found their way from his brain to his face. And that was a good thing. I liked his expressions. I especially liked the one he wore now, a heat burning in his eyes as he pulled the lace off me—a little too roughly. It was the same hunger and satisfaction, the same look as in the picture.

We made love. It was Stephen's turn to taste the other woman on me. Did he know what he was tasting? As I was coming, I thought about calling out "Mark," but why spoil a nice moment? The idea was so funny to me that what came out of my mouth was *oh*-laugh-*oh*-laugh-*ohmygod*.

While he was brushing his teeth—what a familiar sound— I put the lacy thing in my underwear drawer. I put that damn picture in there as well. What should I do with it? Hang it over our bed? Or in his office, replacing that irritating cowboy print?

Stephen looked up at me from the underwear drawer, grinning lewdly. I buried him in bras and panties. For now, he was fine where he was until I thought of someplace better.

Sukreswara

Kristine Hawes

I stepped forward as the woman in front of me moved. I was firmly planted in the middle of a human string stretching from the doorway of the temple to the riverbank. This ribbon was clothed in bright white cottons, intricate silks, and the flowers of a thousand miles. The scents of creamy jasmine and dense orange poppies mingled with the pungent aromas of cinnamon, cardamom, tea, and nutmeg. The dark-chocolate faces of the native people glowed against their vivid, fragrant necklaces. Bowls filled with ripe fruits and small metal trinkets rested beside their owners, some of whom sat as they waited for their turn to see Him. To pray on the banks of the river, to seek solace from the god they believed in.

I didn't know if I believed or not. Puttabhi believed; maybe that was all that mattered. I looked down at my caramel-colored hands, gold bracelets tinkling over my wrists. Puttabhi had given me everything I desired. He took care of me as every man of his upbringing would—with fine golden things, a lush home, the comfort of a traditional Indian family.

Everything that seemed lacking in my American upbringing.

Everything except a child.

The line moved slowly as another woman slipped into the sheath of the dark doorway. The humid sun hung above the tiled rooftops. I sighed and shifted the fabric of my sari to cover my unaccustomed skin. Puttabhi said it was my duty to serve Him, to please Him; only then would the child be brought to us. Puttabhi was raised here and his belief grew as he did; it had become part of his very skin. I grew up hearing stories of India, not really believing there was such a place where the Gods spoke to you. Gods didn't speak to us in America. It was too noisy for us to hear. But Puttabhi believed. So we packed our bags and flew from California to Delhi, traveled into the depths of the Valley, Assam and then Guwahati, where His river, the Brahmapurta, begins. Go, Puttabhi said as I stood at the gates of the massive temple. Go make your offerings. Make them until our child is secure.

Every day many people would cross the river to make their offerings in the twin temples. Durga's was filled with the old and young, men and women hoping that She would give them new life, some token to help them succeed. Shiva's temple was different. Hundreds of women waited for their turn to touch, to taste, to breathe in His aura for the briefest of moments: to take with them the essence of His manhood, His seed.

This was my first time. I wrung my slightly shaking hands. I picked up my wooden bowl of oranges and shifted one person closer to the entrance.

The women around me left me alone. They spoke in hushed tones among themselves, the soft murmur of their language nearly incomprehensible to me. My foreignness clothed me, no matter what my face looked like. I closed my eyes and let my body absorb the heat. Twenty more people, and I would be inside. It must happen before the sun sets, I thought; I can't stand waiting all day for nothing. I watched the neophytes walk regally though the courtyard and buildings.

Here, men cared for Shiva and Durga. The men were silent and efficient, their shaved heads bobbing as they moved through the crowd. Arms heaped with limp poppies, roses, and spice branches, they made their way to the inner temples. A light-skinned woman was a wonder in this part of the world; I caught their eye. Some were curious and stared. Others shunned me as a disbeliever. Maybe they could see inside me. They all continued on their way, my face fading in light of their tasks. One man carried a small box filled with pieces of paper and small icons. The priests took these names, made offerings of incense and song. This was not religion. It was a state of being. I envied their belief.

Closer. The crumbling stone around the entrance radiated coolness. I let my veil fall and reveled in the abundant shade. I could smell dying moss and living flesh but could see nothing. My stomach constricted around my spine. What would I ask of Him? What would they ask me to do?

From the darkness I heard movement, shuffling, footsteps. A woman covered her face as she emerged from the shrine and descended the stone stairs. I followed her movements with my eyes, wishing I could follow her. If I did, what would I tell Puttabhi? I turned toward the doors. A young priest beckoned me with his hands. He did not speak because he knew I would not understand. I followed.

The darkness cradled me with cupped hands. I walked slowly until my eyes adjusted to the dimness. A soft hand clasped my wrist and tugged me forward. I could see the priest smiling.

It was all right, he was telling me, his gestures soothing and direct. Do not be afraid. We turned several times and the darkness deepened. I could hear chanting, soft sounds in the distance. We turned once more, into an alcove. There, in the center of a raised dais, stood a glistening stone man, poised, ready to strike. Not merely a man. A God. The Destroyer. Feet planted firmly on the polished floor, a ready display of power and strength. Delicate chains and bells were carved into the ankles of the God's smooth legs. The orange, yellow, and gold of the heaped offerings was reflected in His milky white skin, sheathing His legs in an illusion of flames. His hips tapered up into a narrow waist, almost feminine, encircled with a carved, gem-inlayed belt. Stomach, ribs, chest—intricately chiseled and smoothed—flowed from his waist upward into smooth, rounded shoulders. His arms ascended in a graceful arc toward the ceiling. His dancing hands, thick and oversized, clasped the rays of light that shot through the broken-tile roof.

His smooth, placid face looked down upon me: His eyes set with huge rubies, His lips full and round, His cheeks and nose angled and lustrous. Serene. Complete. He stood glorious and naked before me. Naked, yes, and full of life. His lingam stood straight and proud: explicit, long, and hung with wreaths of purple and red flowers. A flash of heat coated my cheeks and breast. I looked down quickly. Bowls of red ochre lined the floor at the God's feet—bowls of bloody soup.

My heart beat in my ears. I was ashamed of the God's nakedness, but tried to push my shame away. This was a proud God, one who dealt in power—and where was the seat of His power? I could not be embarrassed. I was here to receive some of that power. Puttabhi expected it.

My guide smiled at my wonder and embarrassment. He said nothing as he touched my elbow and pointed to the dais. He motioned with his hands—go, give what you have. I lifted the edge of my sari and ascended the small steps. My offering was one of hundreds. I looked up. The weight of the God pulled me forward.

I knelt, as Puttabhi had instructed me, and placed my bowl to one side of Shiva's feet. I bowed low, touching my forehead to the cool gray tile, and leaned back. Shiva's lingam stood out above my head, within reach. Its length was daunting. All women came here to give their offerings to the God and to the power He provided. Intense sexual power. My fingers unwound from the fabric of my sari and slowly rose. I stopped, looking back over my shoulder. The priest stood quietly, his hands folded.

He nodded once. I let my hand continue. The opaque lingam was cool, cooler than the floor on which I knelt. My fingers brushed the rounded head, tracing the deeply carved line of its ridge. My fingers circled the shaft and my palm flattened as I stroked downward. The glossy spear was polished with soft hollows and minute rises. Desire grew inside my breast. My body grew warm and my sex ached. My hand flowed down the shaft until it descended into the fragrant flowers at the base. I raised my other hand and caressed upward, feeling the strength of His erection.

A body, warm and startling, pressed against me from behind. My nerves jolted but I did not stop. Dark hands covered mine as I stroked the God's solid member. Saffron, sweat, and unwashed cotton—scents assaulted me as I tried to keep my focus. My guide's hands slowed, stopped. I didn't know what to do, where to go. I looked up. The man's mahogany eyes calmed me. He smiled, his teeth gleaming against dusky, mellow skin.

I rocked backward and rested on my heels. He continued holding my hand, pulled gently, and helped me up. His hands were firm and slow as they turned me toward him. I looked past him, ashamed of what I had done to the statue. I realized then that there were two other priests in the dark corners of the room. Watchers. Silent. My embarrassment grew. I looked down at the floor.

The priest's fingers touched my chin and gently raised it upward. His eyes were clear, deep. They held mine steadily as his hands moved downward, resting on my hips. He did not smile. His fingers worked slowly, pulling my sari upward. My breath came in gasps. My sex ached and my heart beat loudly. I could not move. Puttabhi had said nothing of this. Perhaps he did not know; he only trusted in Shiva. I shoved my fear into Puttabhi's trust and held it there.

I wanted to stop the priest's hands but the tension in his eyes held me. My cheeks flushed. His hands stopped moving, the patterned silk bunched up in his palms. My legs were completely bare, the skin of my back and buttocks sticky with drying sweat. Cool, dark air moved around me. Still the priest held my eyes. His hands pushed lightly against my hipbones, pushing me backward. I began panting. What if someone saw me? The priests! What if I shouldn't do this? My feet did not want to move.

The priest felt my hesitation. He whispered something in a very soft voice. I only understood the word *offering;* I had heard it so much while waiting in line. His voice echoed in the dark chamber. I could hear the movements of others within the temple. Would they pass by this room and know? Was this normal? He spoke again, the same words, gently, comforting. I closed my eyes, swallowed, and took a step backward, then another. I felt the statue behind me. The carved tower of milky white and shadow-dark stone loomed above me. I was the lover swallowed. Shiva's lingam pressed against my buttocks. I opened my eyes and looked again at the man who guided me here. I placed my hands on his, holding my sari, and I clasped the fabric tightly. The priest let me go as my body connected with the statue. He took a step backward and knelt. I looked down on him, my heart full of fear. He nodded with a look of serenity.

I moved back. I was too short. I closed my eyes and raised up on the balls of my feet. The polished stone felt cool. The head of the statue's lingam pressed against the lips of my yoni, taking my heat quickly. I tilted my hips backward, spread my legs slightly, and surrendered to the will of Shiva.

My body opened to the strength of the stone God. I concentrated on letting His erection fill my body. My wetness covered the head of the lingam, making the stone slick. I pushed backward, swaying slightly as my yoni opened wider. Tingles ran up my spine; heat brushed against my thighs. Sweat coated the back of my knees and my palms. I rocked forward, then back, moving more of the God's lingam into my swollen sex. I let go of the terror, falling into my breath and heartbeat. The priest's mouth moved, quiet words obliterated by my panting. His eyes glittered, hands pressed together in supplication.

I imagined the God's hands, thick and wide, resting upon me, holding me as I impaled myself on Him. Puttabhi, oh, Puttabhi never had this strength. I rocked forward and back, my moans filling the stone chamber. My priest also rocked in time with me, his chants growing louder. I could not see the other priests; lust had darkened my sight. My knees grew weak, blood rushing through me. Closer I came to the edge. I wanted to feel the God's sex become huge inside me, swelling and opening me, His seed filling me. I let my head fall, my long black hair swaying with my movements. Back. Forth. The stone was hot fire burning through me. I pushed and pulled, forcing the lingam to press against my womb, crying out in concert with every connection. It was enough. I shuddered and let the climax fill my body. I let out a loud moan, head back, shuddering in each wave of pleasure.

The darkness in my eyes was gone. My head rolled forward, covered with sweat. I could not move. Breathing, simply breathing, felt peaceful. Warmth came to me, stood in front of me. The priest. My guide. I could not look at him. His arms surrounded me, guided my release from the statue.

I nearly fell as the smooth stone shaft emerged from my still-quivering yoni, my knees too weak to hold my body upright. I let my sari fall, once again the proper woman. The priest guided me to the edge of the dais and we turned.

The God stood as before; burnt-blood eyes glistened in the twilight, proud body rising to the heavens. The priest and I knelt, bowing to the floor. Acknowledging the offering of self. My sex was warm, flowing, satisfied. The God looked peaceful. Steadfast. The priest simply nodded, whispering lyrical words. Shiva. Pleasure. I did not know.

Puttabhi would be waiting for me at the gates. He would be looking to me for the token of his God's pleasure. Our God's pleasure. I hoped I would be able to give it to him.

The Best Revenge

Emma Holly

Violet could smell his rage.

It called her from the shops and cafés, from the succulent college students and the coffee-flavored businessmen. She quickened her pace, filling her lungs with the hot jalapeño scent. Heads turned as she passed. Her dress was short, her legs long, her hair a raven-dark fall of silk. It lashed the small of her back as she strode out of Georgetown's shopping district, her heels ringing on the crooked, brick-lined pavement. The rumble of traffic faded into the high-pitched whirr of cicadas. Houses rose, narrow and elegant with tiny sculpted yards and ivy-covered walls; young to her, old to the humans with whom she shared this city. Oaks rustled overhead, moonlight glimmering in their summer-full leaves. Though her walk was nearly a run, Violet was immune to the heat. She didn't sweat and she didn't shiver, except with pleasure at the scent that had lured her, Pied Piper–style, from her chosen hunting grounds.

He's young, she thought, her mouth watering as she caught another whiff. Young and virile and hungry for revenge. She ran her tongue across the sharpening edge of her teeth. Somewhere within this enclave of doctors and diplomats, someone had done somebody wrong.

She turned a corner, moving deeper into the residential streets. A group of young men stopped at her approach. They eyed her strapless black dress, the diamonds dangling from her ears, the depth of her moon-white cleavage. She remembered the words of her mentor: *Dress to thrill, my dear. Blending in is for people who intend to belong.* Though none of the men dared speak, their desire washed over her, sweet as a magnolia-laden breeze. Her mouth curled upward but she didn't pause. She knew what she wanted tonight, and it wasn't some beery college boy. She wanted passion, intensity, fury with a capital F. She wouldn't rest until she found it.

She spotted her quarry half a block further on, a shadow inside a ghost-silver Mercedes. Violet liked big cars, preferably with leather seats and manual transmissions. She'd developed a fetish for gearshifts almost as soon as they were invented. Not that she drove herself. That's what servants were for. But she admired the play of masculine hands on that powerful, bulb-tipped rod. Not quite as sexy as a rapier hilt, but it would do.

Grinning, she slipped off her black suede heels and dangled them over her shoulder. The same aura that kept heat and time from marking her brow protected her expensive stockings. With the stealth of her kind, she approached the unsuspecting man. When she reached the passenger side she peered in the window. Tall and broad-shouldered, he wore a dress shirt with the sleeves rolled up and the tie yanked down from the collar. His eyes were masked by a pair of opera glasses, nice gold-plated numbers, expensive but not gaudy. Violet hadn't been to the opera since Mozart died, but for an instant she felt the pressure of a tight, stayed bodice and heard a crisp melody skipping over a backdrop of violins.

She shook herself back to the present. The man's hands were large against the shiny barrels, large and well-kept. Nodding her approval, she followed the line of the glasses to their target: a lighted window at the top of a black-shuttered, three-story colonial. Her eyes stung at the artificial glare, but her vision cleared as soon as she blinked her blood-tinged tears away.

Ah, she thought, *he's a jilted lover.* The window framed a couple kissing like a pair of octopi. The woman was fair and slim, the man dark and athletic. Her leg climbed his hip and his hand was thrust up the back of her skirt, clearly buried in her sex. They seemed not to care that anyone might see. Violet suspected that they liked the idea— probably thought the rest of the world ought to envy their carnal bliss. She shook her head. Most humans had no idea how banal they could be.

She cast a curious glance at their watcher. Here was interest, if not originality. Fury whitened the knuckles that held the small binoculars. Despite the magnification, Violet doubted he could see what she did. This couple had nowhere near his passion. Even with the thrill of infidelity beating in their breasts, they knew neither true pleasure nor true pain. She saw that the watcher had loved this woman, or the woman he believed her to be. So strong was his illusion, he could barely take in the betrayal. He was here torturing himself in order to force the truth through his reluctant brain. In his tooth-grinding anguish, this man embraced life as fully as Violet did. So to speak.

A wisp of thought brushed her awareness: *Fuck you, Lisa. Fuck you both.* The organ that passed for Violet's heart quivered. She couldn't usually hear thoughts, only feelings. The affinity between her and the man must be strong. How delightful. It had been a long time since she'd enjoyed a truly intimate repast.

With a delicate pucker of concentration, she rearranged a portion of her substance and pushed her slender white hand through the car door. She popped the lock and pulled open the door. The man turned as she slid into the air-conditioned coolness, one long, stockinged leg hissing behind the other. The seats were leather, a soft brown calfskin. The man lowered the opera glasses and gaped.

Violet nodded toward the embracing lovers. "Friends of yours?"

"Yes," he said, so bitter he couldn't keep the answer inside. "Both of them." His gaze roved the curves of Violet's body, his male instincts stronger than his shock at having his vehicle invaded. She set her shoes on the dash and smiled.

"Who are you?" he asked.

"Violet," she answered, studying him with eyes born to see in the dark. He was handsome, which didn't strictly matter, though it pleased her. His ash-brown hair waved to his collar. His brow was high, and his bladelike nose shadowed full, finely cut lips. His pewter-gray eyes brooded beneath a thick fringe of lashes. Behind those eyes his life force glowed pure and hot, not so much candle as coal. His warm gold skin formed the perfect backdrop for the blue thread of his jugular.

She was glad she wasn't hungry, not for blood at least, because the way that vein pulsed made her tongue curl out to touch her upper lip. Blood lust wasn't an easy thing to overcome. She'd searched long and hard to find the Second Path, and that had been but the beginning of her struggle. One didn't master esoterica overnight.

"Violet," he repeated, his gaze locked on her berry-red mouth. "What are you doing in my car?"

"I'm looking for a good fuck."

He coughed and thumped his chest. She smelled the starch of his shirt, the sweat of his anger, and a hint of musk: he was aroused. The flesh between her legs fluttered like a ribbon in the breeze. He found his voice. "I have a feeling I can't afford you, Violet."

Amused, she reached out and covered the hand he'd pressed to his heart. "I'm not a professional."

"And I'm afraid I'm not in the mood."

"Aren't you?" Their eyes connected, his gray to her icy blue. She pushed his hand down his smooth shirt front, over his belt buckle and onto the hard, full lift of his sex. Energy pulsed there, and blood. Her hand sipped at the energy, tasting him, savoring the tiny intermittent rush. "You're hard from watching them betray you," she said, "from watching your best friend shove his fingers between your lover's legs."

He tried to pull free, but her grip was strong. She curled his fingers over his shaft and made him rub himself. He swelled under the friction.

"Do you know them, too?" he panted, wanting to make sense of what she was doing. Foolish boy. The likes of him would never make sense of her.

"I don't need to know them," she said, "and all you need to know is whether you want some of your own back."

He stared at her, breathing hard, throbbing hard, thinking: *Crazy bitch, but she's a looker, isn't she?*

"What the hell," he said. "It would serve them right."

She released his hand and turned sideways on the seat, her shoulders against the door, her legs lolling wide. They drew his hands like a magnet. He slid his palms from her ankles to her thighs, warming up, gathering his nerve to jump this long, lean stranger's bones. She tossed her dark hair with an air of impatience. She was warm already. She was hungry. "Come on, big boy. You can do better than that."

"Here? What if someone sees?"

She laughed, mocking him for his scruples in the face of his girlfriend's lack of them. "Yes, what if someone does?"

His eyes narrowed and now some of his anger was for her. It beat at her in soft, delicious pulses. Violet wriggled her bottom and widened her knees. Her nails were long and painted to match her name. She dragged them up the insides of her thighs, catching the hem of her dress to reveal first her lacy black garters and then the bare white curve of her mound. No human woman could shave herself as smooth as Violet, but this man wasn't thinking clearly enough to notice. With two dark nails, she parted the plump, flawless folds of her labia. Her clitoris was as dark as her mouth, shocking against her marble-pale skin. His jaw fell as he watched her tease the hood back. The tiny pearl glistened and twitched. He swallowed hard.

"What's the matter?" she purred. "Cat got your tongue?"

"Fine," he said, jerking his tie lower. "Let's do it."

His fingers flew halfway down the buttons of his shirt, then gave up and dove toward his zipper. He dragged out his cock, a weighty, surging rod, then fumbled in his pocket.

"You don't need that," she said, before he could tear the packet with his teeth. He opened his mouth to protest so she pushed a little with her mind, and then pushed harder when he resisted. The strength of his opposition surprised her, and the fact that his concern was as much for her as for himself. But she couldn't make the connection she needed through a layer of latex. She needed skin-to-skin contact.

"You don't need that," she repeated more gently than she usually did. "Not with me."

He hesitated a moment longer, then fell into her logic the way one falls into the logic of a dream. He wanted to take her bare. He wanted to feel her pussy creaming his cock. In fact, he wanted it more than he'd ever wanted anything in his life. Nodding brusquely, he gripped her waist and dragged her toward him until her head dropped onto the seat. He shoved his trousers down his hips and aligned his body for entry.

She tensed at the approach of his heat. Such anticipation. Her gums ached as her incisors slid free. They didn't always do that, but she was highly aroused. She bit her upper lip to hide them. Her hips rolled and she thrust her knees wider.

"Please," she said. "Hurry."

He aimed himself. She parted her lips. At the first intimate contact they both jolted: the smooth skin of his glans on the hungry mouth of her sex. The touch was a spark that rolled up her sheath and through her womb. He pushed and entered her, thick, hot, pulsing with life. She sighed. Heaven. The current she craved sprang up between them.

So long, she heard him thinking. *It's been so long since I've done this skin-to-skin.*

Her folds surrounded him, clinging to the flares and bulges of his sex, licking him with wetness. He squirmed deeper, reaching for her limits, then pulled back and stroked again. Ah, his pleasure. She could feel it as if it were her own. His balls were heavy, tight with their gathered burden. His cock ached, a sweet, hard pain that speared deep inside his belly. His nipples were tiny, itching stones. She reached inside his shirt to pinch them. He groaned. Yes, that was what he needed, that. Sighing with gratitude, he rubbed his belly over hers, loving the soft, silky give of her mons. If he noticed that her flesh was too cool, too resilient, too perfect, he showed no sign of it.

But he was being far too careful. This was not what she wanted at all.

She grabbed the front of his shirt and dragged his head to hers. "*This* is how you fuck when your lover is cuckolding you not thirty feet away? No wonder she left you." She made as if to push him away, but he cuffed her wrists and pressed them to the door. He was stronger than she'd expected, almost strong enough to overpower her. At least until she fed.

"Yes," she exulted as the heady spice of his anger rose, its energy pumping into her through the juncture of their loins. "Show me how it hurts. Treat me the way you'd like to treat her."

"I'd like to kill you," he said, tightening his grip and slamming in. The top of her head hit the padded door. Heedless, he drew back and shoved again. His emotions poured into her: grief as sharp and strong as blood, not merely for the woman but for his loss of faith.

"Fucking bitch," he said. "I loved you."

Fury roughened his voice. *Lovely, simply lovely.* She laughed and wrenched her hands free, reaching under his shirt to rake his back with her nails. He winced when she broke skin. The battle was joined in earnest then. He dug his knees into the seat, pounding at her as if his life depended on screwing her senseless as quickly as he could. Violet met him blow for blow, scratching him, nipping him. *Let it out,* she thought. *Give me all of it.*

He could not resist the telepathic goad.

"Whore," he said, yanking down the front of her dress. Her breasts bobbed in the open air, moving with his frenzied thrusts. He did not slow, but the sight of her jiggling areolas brought a flush to his cheeks. Like her clit and mouth, her nipples were points of red in a sea of white. He grunted and arched down to suckle one; no teeth to his draw but real, flesh-stretching force. A second current flowed into her from his mouth, as heavy as sweetened wine. She arched, pushing herself at him, wanting more and more and more.

He switched breasts. She cried out at the loss until he anchored again. *Yes,* she thought, *yes.* The force of his rage roared through her, circling from breast to sex, from cock to mouth. She had betrayed him. She must be punished. She must be soundly, thoroughly fucked. Her thoughts had weight for him. He groaned and slammed into her so hard the car rocked on its chassis. She lifted one arm, bracing it against the door.

"Yes," he said, for this allowed him to drive deeper yet. "Yes, bitch, take it." He grabbed her leg and pushed it up over his shoulder. The tendons at her groin stretched. She growled with pleasure. His thrusts were splitting her; they came so furious, so fast. Still latched to her nipple, he wrenched free of his shirt. She touched him then, palming his heaving chest, his muscled arms, the mixture of sweat and blood that sheened his contorted back.

She knew she shouldn't touch him there; knew she risked losing control. But knowing couldn't stop her, and she gathered the dangerous nectar from his skin. She wrapped him close and tucked one blood-streaked finger in her mouth. Sweet copper fire burst on her tongue. Her body clutched. She was going to come. She could barely hold it back. But she had to wait. They had to come together or all was wasted.

"Fuck," he said, stiffening at the flutters of her sheath. Energy gathered round their bodies, not merely his energy but the energy all lovemaking called from the earth. Violet used her art to coax up more and more until sensation flared like brushfire across her nerves. She gritted her teeth and clenched her hands into fists, willing herself to hold on. The power coiled through their mingled auras like smoke in a bell jar. It glowed blue and gold and sunset red. Her partner couldn't see it but she knew it affected him.

He shuddered violently. "Oh, God. Do you feel that? Do you *feel* that?"

She couldn't answer. She could only gasp for air and pray: soon, please, soon. His cock swelled inside her. His breath whined through his teeth. His motions slowed and grew more intense, more directed. He was pressing the sensitive cushion behind her pubic bone. He was killing her. God in heaven, she couldn't hold on.

"I can't stop," he groaned. "I'm going to explode."

"Yes," she moaned, her fists pressed tight to his buttocks. "Hurry!"

The first spasm caught her before she could stop it. Her head thrashed in protest. No, no, she couldn't come alone, she couldn't. She opened a chink in her psychic shield to let him feel what she felt; one last chance to save the moment. Her pleasure hit him hard. His eyes widened. He cried out and then his cock jerked quick and deep and the flood washed over her: hot white waves of light pouring through her thirsty flesh, intoxicating, life-sustaining surges of pure earth force. She reeled at the strength of it. So much energy. So much life. She drank it in and lost her head. She forgot to be safe, to hide, to keep herself to herself. She tightened her clasp on his sex until the barriers blurred and the molecules of her flesh moved through his, just slightly, just barely, not enough to spark the Change, but enough for him to feel. He moaned, a low wondering sound, and they both caught fire again.

Long minutes later, she sighed at the final pulse of pleasure and relaxed into the leather seat. He sank on top of her, a warm, perspiring weight. His head nestled next to hers. He smelled different now, his hot pepper tang replaced by an orange-blossom sweetness. She smiled and stroked his wide, strong back. He'd fucked out his rage, and now he was feeling tender.

Just the same, she didn't expect him to offer her dessert.

With a hum of effort he rose on his elbows and rolled his head to one side. She thought he must not know how inviting that posture was.

"Do it," he said. "Drink from me."

Words failed her. She licked her lips. Her eyes fell to the tempting, beating vein. "How—how did you know?"

"You sent me that picture, at the end, of you drinking from my neck. Didn't you mean to?"

"No. I only meant to make you come."

"Well, you certainly did that." His grin disconcerted her as much as his offer. He touched her upper lip, pressing it against her itching incisors. "You don't have to kill me to do it, do you?"

She shook her head. "No. When we came together, that fed me."

"So take a taste," he said. "You must be lonely."

Her eyes stung. He must be half-dreaming to speak so openly, not to mention so instinctively. On his own, he couldn't have known what it meant to her kind to drink, how that bond was more intimate, more primal than sex.

"Come," he said, stroking the warm gold column of his throat. "Drink."

She didn't need another invitation. She licked him, tasting his salt, the fluids in her mouth numbing his skin for penetration. He shivered and she bit down before fear could spoil it for him. She sipped at him slowly, the way a sleepy infant will, more for comfort than need. He stiffened at first, then maneuvered her on top of him and relaxed, utterly boneless, one leg bent up against the back of the seat, the other sprawled under the wheel. He stroked her long black hair as she fed, and his body undulated beneath her, as if they were fucking again. His blood was a smoky surprise. Given the way she'd found him, she'd expected to taste a young man's vintage: passionate but not mature. Instead, curiosity, sorrow, and sensuality flowed across her palate, mixed with a sharp, ironic humor, like the cleansing tang of lemon after a rich meal.

Clearly, this was an experience worth repeating. Careful for his comfort, she didn't drink long, though she doubted he'd have stopped her. Her feeding triggered the release of natural opiates. So long as the victim didn't resist, the effect was pleasurable. It certainly seemed to be so for him. His sex had stiffened again and his caresses became more erotic. She lifted her head and licked the wounds to seal them. Curling her hand around his neck, she sent a brief pulse of energy through her palm. Then even the bruises were gone.

He touched the pristine skin. His hips rolled beneath her, the ridge of him prodding her mons.

"I'm hard again," he said, marveling at it without showing any inclination to move.

She cupped his erection with her thigh, more replete than she'd been in many, many years. She drew a deep breath. She had to consider what had happened. She had to decide what she wanted to do. This was not her ordinary one-night stand.

She suspected it wasn't his either. He was still with her—not sleeping, not drawing back the way humans will when intimacy goes too deep. He sighed and hugged her waist. She knew she was about to receive a confidence, the human coin of closeness.

"He was my best friend," he said. "She couldn't have hurt me more if she'd slept with a dozen strangers."

Violet stroked his chest. "Don't you think she knew that?"

"She's not like that. She's not cruel."

After all he'd seen, he could still defend the woman who'd betrayed him, an endearing trait but hardly a wise one. She spoke gently. "Some people hide their cruelty even from themselves. They hurt the people who care for them because they need to prove they can."

His shoulders hunched. "Maybe they fell in love. People do. I ought to be able to forgive them for that."

"They're not in love."

"You can't know that."

"I've been around a long time, boy. I know real love when I see it."

His body tightened. "Don't call me that. My name is Ethan."

"Ethan," she said. The name rang inside her, striking some unsuspected chord. Violet and Ethan. Ethan and Violet. She made a swift decision. "Do you want me to kill her?"

"What?" His chest dipped, the air going out of him. "Jesus, no."

"You can't tell me it hasn't crossed your mind."

"Christ." He pushed her off him and sat up, raking his hair in consternation. He thrust his cock back into his trousers. "She hurt me. I was angry. Maybe I took some of that out on you. That doesn't mean I want her dead."

Violet stroked her lips with two fingers, a gesture older than Ethan probably cared to know. She watched him carefully. "What if you were dying and killing her were the only thing that could save you?"

"Then I'd die," he said.

"Are you sure?"

"Yes," he said. "I am."

Every instinct she possessed told her that he spoke the truth. Was it possible? Could he be the mate she'd given up on finding ages ago? A man with the discipline and strength to live as a decent, God-fearing demon? She had the power to Change him if she wished, but did she want a companion? Violet wasn't a romantic young vampling any more. She had seen too much of life.

Tread carefully, she told herself as she pulled her dress into place again. *This is treacherous ground.*

As if he sensed her thoughts, his eyes narrowed. "You wouldn't really have killed her," he said. "You were testing me."

"Perhaps." She gave him half a smile. "There is the other option, of course."

"The other option?"

She walked her fingers up his chest like violet-tipped spider legs. He shivered with nervous pleasure.

"The other option is living well. The best revenge, so they say." She licked her incisors, retreating now but still sweet with his blood. "I could teach you to live well, Ethan, very well indeed."

He stared and scrubbed the back of his head. He shifted on the seat and rubbed his thighs. He started the engine and reached for the gearshift. "I'd better take you home."

"Why don't you take me to your home?" she said.

She caught another flash of his thoughts, silly nonsense about coffins and churchyards. She slipped her hand up the inside of his thigh. He jumped.

"You have shades on your windows, don't you?" she asked.

He nodded and pulled away from the curb, his brow furrowed, his cock stretching like an animal beneath her nails. Her pussy warmed as he worked the stick. She vowed she'd taste him again before the night was through.

"Look," he said, his eyes sliding from the road to her. "That was another test, right? You asking if I wanted to 'live well'?" His fingers made ironic quote marks but his voice shook. "If I'd said 'yes,' you'd have ditched me, wouldn't you?"

Amused, Violet shrugged and stroked his turgid sex. The young man seemed determined to think well of her, but she wasn't certain of the truth herself.

"It was a test," he repeated, even as he rocked into her hand.

Violet squeezed until he ground the gears and cursed. His cock went steely under the abuse. Was she testing him? She tossed her hair. With any luck, they'd both get a chance to find out.

Climbing the Wall
Sacchi Green

Nothing focuses the mind in the body like a vertical rockface. On one side, an infinity of air and light; on the other, the uncompromising rigidity of stone. I clung between these absolutes, toes edged into a slanting crevice, fingers jammed into a narrow crack, weight poised in utter compliance with gravity.

I had forgotten the intensity, the controlled rush; forgotten, too, the exultant surge of horniness. When I could pause on the insubstantial security of a narrow belay ledge I savored the moment. The view of the green valley with the river winding through was all well enough, but Sigri Hakkala's, broad, muscular butt in canary-yellow stretch fabric twenty feet above commanded all my attention.

Why Sigri? Proximity? We'd been casual friends for years, members of a fluctuating group of dykes sharing a rundown ski lodge in the valley. If she'd ever figured in my fantasies, it had been as a mead-companion, a Viking warrior ravaging villages by my side as we bore off not-unwilling maidens. Now I found myself recalling rumors that she'd done some porn films in her starving-student days, and wondering whether her big breasts made it harder to maneuver close to the rock on overhangs. When she splayed her legs wide to reach a new foothold, I ached to slip a hand between her round, powerful buttocks and feel their strength as they clamped together again.

Fantasy fueled by adrenaline. People had been trying to throw us together all week on the theory that the recently bereaved must want to compare notes. We'd been trying just as hard to avoid each other.

So why choose to climb together? The simple answer was trust in each other's competence. This route was only moderately difficult, iron bolts not more than twenty-five feet apart. But when you take the lead with the belaying rope and call, "Watch me," you damned sure need to know that when your partner on the other end answers, "Go for it, I've got you," she has, absolutely, got you, and will hold you if your grip fails or a rock edge breaks away and you plummet down the unforgiving cliff face.

Somewhat less simple to understand was my willingness to let Sigri lead most of the way. She'd raised a quizzical eyebrow each time as I waved her ahead. I couldn't explain to myself, much less to her, my sudden obsession with looking up at her muscular, well-padded body.

Whatever the trigger, this surge of pure lust was both agony and exhilaration, like the awakening of an anaesthetized limb. I understood now why Janet had urged me to go climbing, although she sure as hell hadn't foreseen the matter of Sigri's butt. A year ago Jan would have sabotaged my car, even broken my leg, rather than let me join a climbing expedition; but a year ago Becca's death had been a fresh, gaping wound in my soul, and preservation of my own life had had negative priority. Now I was not so much healed as more or less resigned to living, to giving Janet whatever I had left to give.

Understanding as Janet might be, clearly resignation wasn't cutting it any more. "Damnit, Raf," she'd panted last week, "You just go through the motions!"

"Something the matter with my motions?" She lay sprawled among pillows and twisted sheets, flushed and damp and breathless, looking about as thoroughly fucked as it's possible to get. Her lips and nipples were still swollen, and there were wet spots wherever her ass rested. I like to astonish her with the extremes her body can reach; I take a sort of detached, professional pride in how far I can push her. The problem was that the sweat and slickness were always hers, not mine. I could let her take the edge off, but that was about it, and, in spite of how well I distracted her, she recognized the difference.

"You know what I mean!" It would have been a shout if she'd had enough breath for it. "You used to rattle the windows and make the walls shake!"

I didn't ask how she knew. Becca and I hadn't realized she could hear us all the way down in the basement apartment she'd rented, but once Becca got me going, it wouldn't have mattered.

Now that Becca was gone, I didn't see how anything could ever get me going like that again. It wasn't Janet's fault; I just didn't have it in me anymore.

But maybe I was wrong. Each precise, careful shift along the cliff from hold to hold said "Yes!" to life. The rough scrape of granite against hands, knees, chest, drove home the stark reality of the flesh and its capacity for extremes.

I looked up again. Sigri tilted her head back and her thick, pale braid swung free. I followed her gaze to see a peregrine falcon soaring toward its distant nest, some small, inert creature borne proudly in its talons. Sigri glanced down at me briefly and grinned, teeth white in her tanned face; it was the first emotion I'd seen her show all week. I wondered whether

I'd been turning the same defensive mask to the world. Old friends had braved it to offer condolences, but I was ashamed to realize how hard I'd made it for them.

Sigri moved upward and onward, and so did I. The sun broiled us against the rock for a while, and then a cold breeze dried the sweat and raised goose bumps, as refreshing as a sauna. Except that in a sauna, I could have seen Sigri naked. As I had, in fact, any number of times, but back then I'd been more concerned with wondering just how impressed Becca might be with Sigri's forceful blend of bulk and strength. Not that Becca would ever have let me see that she had eyes for anyone but me.

Now, though, with the rush of my body's reawakening...I mentally slapped my own hands, and imagined how hard they'd get slapped if I tried anything. Sigri was the only woman I'd ever met who could beat me at arm wrestling, sometimes as many as three times out of five.

The members of our group ascending other routes were already disappearing over the top of Cathedral Ledge, but neither Sigri nor I were in any hurry. I felt so alive—would the feeling last once the intricate vertical dance of the climb ended?

Sigri's mesmerizing yellow buttocks disappeared at last over the lip of the cliff, and I followed. When I had retrieved and coiled the rope and slipped off my nylon harness I sank down beside her in the shade of a wind-gnarled pine. The breeze had died down and the afternoon was getting uncomfortably hot. "Drink?" I said, offering my water bottle, since I'd seen her empty her own a while ago.

"Thanks." She leaned her head far back as she drank, which lifted her remarkable breasts, and I found myself enjoying the view a bit too much. And a bit too overtly.

"Hey, watch it, Rafaela," she said, and handed back the bottle. "You know I'm not that kind of girl." There was dry amusement in her voice. A butch with a build like that learns to cope; I was lucky she was going easy on me.

"Yeah, yeah, I know." I flopped back onto the pine needles. "It's just that I've been wondering whether I'm still any kind of girl at all. It's a relief to at least start taking an interest."

She raised a quizzical eyebrow. "I heard you were with Janet these days."

"Right. She's meeting me at the lodge tonight. She's been great; she was great helping out while Becca...while Becca was sick..." Well, at least it was out in the open now. I drew in a long, shuddering breath. "But..."

"I know." Sigri looked out across the valley. "I haven't even tried yet."

It was as if some safe ledge had been gained for a moment. "I shouldn't have worn this," Sigri said, plucking at the canary yellow fabric clinging to her powerful thigh. "It reminds me too much...Julie liked to watch through binoculars, liked me to be easy to spot."

"Becca could never stand to watch me climb. Maybe that makes it easier, I dunno. I wouldn't have come at all if Janet hadn't insisted. I think she wants to jolt me out of something. Or into something."

"That's pretty much what I had in mind for myself." Sigri stretched, and lifted the heavy braid off her neck. "Getting too hot out," she said, shifting into enough-sharing-already mode. "I've been thinking of chopping off all this damned hair. That short crop works for you, but you're dark. I might look bald with a buzz cut."

"Don't do it!" I said. "The Valkyrie look is dynamite. Nobody can carry it off the way you do. Don't tell me the girls aren't lining up to run their fingers through your Nordic gold." I had a sudden mental vision of the thick mat of Nordic gold between her canary-clad thighs, and felt the tension build between my own. Damn, if I didn't get a grip I was going to make a fool of myself.

Sigri's white-toothed grin was more Viking than Valkyrie. "No shit! At first I thought it was just my track record. Twelve years of treating somebody right..." The smile faded and she rubbed her hands across her face. "Twelve years..."

In spite of the bright sun a cloud seemed to pass over us. Then Sigri stood up in one determined motion. "I've got to get out of this outfit and wash off the sweat. See you back at the lodge."

"Wait a minute." I stood and gestured toward the trail. "You know where this branches off toward the waterfalls? 'Diana's Baths'?"

"Sure, but that'll be crawling with people on a day like this."

"I know, but there's another place a little farther on that hardly anybody knows about. Up a side stream, no major falls but some pools and cascades and moss so green it glows. A beautiful spot."

"Sounds like a special place." Special to me, she meant, and Becca. She was right. I wasn't sure I could handle going there myself.

"Yeah, but you're welcome to enjoy it. I'll be staying up here for half an hour or so." I gave her directions, and she set off without any firm indication that she'd use them.

It was a long half hour. The sunlit panorama, the pine-scented air, the graceful wheeling of a falcon pair soaring on thermal updrafts, should have brought me some peace. But peace was the last thing I wanted. What I wanted, with increasing urgency, was to watch Sigri strip, sink into an amber-green pool, and rise with her long wet hair streaming across her full white breasts. Never mind that I knew her taste ran to the delicate, doe-eyed, gamin type, and I had been drawn to sassy redheads who only came up to my chin.

Half an hour I'd promised, and half an hour I waited at the top of the cliff. Then I hiked the distance in what must have been record time, Wagner's "Flight of the Valkyrie" galloping through my head.

A canary yellow beacon flashed at me from a mountain-laurel bush, along with a white, industrial-strength bra. I was going to get the chance to make an idiot of myself.

She wasn't in the water. The stream surged into a small, deep pool between the ice-sheared halves of a great boulder. The larger section loomed high above, while the other had settled with its flat surface a few feet above the torrent; and there, in a narrow shaft of sunlight, lay Sigri.

Several seconds passed as I stood on the thick velvet moss of the stream bank, looking down in awestruck admiration at her expanse of naked flesh, rose-pink from the cold water, spread against the gray rock.

I knew I should leave her in peace. I knew I wasn't going to. Could she be asleep? She didn't seem to be moving. Then, since I was fixated on them anyway, I noticed her buttocks clench, and relax, and clench again, and it hit me like an avalanche.

Sigri was humping the rock.

Or trying to. Suddenly I felt it as though her body were mine—the pounding in the crotch, the desperate need to drive the ache further and further, to meet cold stone with all the heat of a clit engorged past bearing, when even the touch of your own hand would be too desolate a reminder of what you'd lost.

And I could feel, as well, the anguished realization that it wasn't going to work. Stone had revived her voracious appetite for life, but all it could do now was scrape her tender parts raw. My own tender parts clenched in an ecstatic agony of sympathy.

I was naked and thrusting through the water before I knew what I was doing. For a moment I clung against the side of the rock, bracing against the current, then I pulled myself up to sit beside her.

"Raf..." she grated on an indrawn breath. Of course she thought she meant, "Raf, get the hell out of here!" But what I heard was a cry for help. Or, at the least, the climber's call of "Watch me!"

"It's okay. I've got you," I said, stretching out beside her. "It's just you and the mountain, and a slightly softer grade of stone." She didn't resist when I nudged her onto her side. Her face was streaked with moisture, not, I thought, from the pool alone, although rivulets still streamed from her hair. "Go for it," I murmured, pressing my long body against hers. "You know I won't let you fall."

She drew in several long, shuddering breaths. Her nipples, erect from the cold water if nothing else, jutted into me and her opulent breasts overwhelmed mine, their full curves forced toward my face. Somehow I managed to refrain from pressing my hungry mouth into the creamy flesh, sensing that that wasn't what she needed.

What she needed was to ride. I don't mind being ridden once in a while; it can be one of the finer things in life. I let her push me onto my back, surge over me, and work her crotch against my thigh and then my hipbone as I dug my hands into the fullness of her ass. The feeling of each thrust of her well-padded gluteals sent a spasm through my cunt. But this was Sigri's climb; I stayed rock-steady, no matter how much I ached to do more, to catch her tantalizing, swaying breasts in my mouth—until, as her breath came in wracking sobs just short of release and getting no closer, I knew just how much more she needed.

"Trust me," I whispered. Whether or not she heard me, she didn't flinch when I slid one hand between her buttocks, stroking lightly across her quivering asshole. Here? But her body language urged me lower, into her hot, slippery, clinging

Sacchi Green

folds. Here. Here. More. I pressed my fist inward, forward, insistent, not quite invasive, easing off just to press forward again, and Sigri bucked hard between my unyielding hip and my unrelenting hand, until at last she came with a long, vibrating shout of triumph that would have done her Viking forebears proud.

She collapsed onto me, panting hard, and I gently withdrew my hand, leaving streaks of her juices across her flushed skin. Then she twisted away and pushed off from the rock into the deep pool.

As I poised to follow, my whole body throbbing with unslaked tension, she rose from the amber-green water just as I'd envisioned. Long pale-gold hair streamed across her great swelling breasts and droplets gleamed on her rosy, thrusting nipples.

What I hadn't envisioned was the icy light of battle in her fjord-blue eyes.

"Damnit, Raf, now it's your turn! Once you get it off the slate is wiped clean!"

There was no arguing with her logic. Or with my own need. I slid off the boulder and surfaced beside her. "No holds barred?" I asked.

"Give it your best shot!" She grinned and dove and I followed, wrapping my long legs around her haunches, reaching around her sides to cup her breasts in my hands. We came up in shallower water, rib-high, and she turned in my grasp, and it was all I could do not to lose it right then, as first her ass and then her generous belly brushed hard against my clit. But the setup was too good to be hurried.

"No holds needed." I let my arms drop. Slowly I brought my hands up under her heavy breasts, cradled them, raised them gently toward my bent head. Sigri, who could have broken almost any hold of mine and matched me strength for strength, had no choice but to stand without resistance as I tasted her cool, smooth flesh. At first I barely brushed her nipples with the tip of my tongue. Her response was reluctant, but came at last, and a sharp intake of breath told me when it was time to flick the hardening peaks a little faster, still with teasing lightness.

"Hey, whose party is this?" Sigri asked in a strangled voice, but I couldn't answer. My mouth was full at last.

And got even fuller. Her swollen nipples challenged my tongue, surged against the roof of my mouth. When I switched from one to the other I was startled to see that the wet, dark-rose mouthful I'd just left was only about the size of the first joint of my thumb. It had felt much bigger.

And so did my clit, as Sigri's knee forced my thighs apart. I couldn't hold out much longer. But I was ravenous for more.

"It's my party, and I'll eat what I want to!" I muttered, moving down at last from her breasts to her belly, and then the water closed over my head.

I clung to her strong hips, my hands anchored in the sweet finger-crack of her ass. I worked my mouth against her mound, thrusting my tongue through the dense, wet curls until I found what I wanted, and then, thrusting even harder, feeling her clit respond and thrust back at me, and even when my lungs were about to burst I kept on because I could feel that Sigri, too, was at bursting point.

I heard her shout of release even through the water, felt the reverberations through her whole body. I erupted into air and light, gulping for air—and in that moment of helplessness Sigri charged me and pinned me against the side of the boulder, using her greater weight to hold me there.

"Damn you, Raf," she panted, "That's two I owe you now!" She glared at me through serpentine streams of hair and water. As soon as I could make the effort I tried to answer, but all the hard-won air rushed out at once as Sigri pressed her hand hard into my crotch, caught my clit in the vee between her middle and index fingers, and went to work on me.

I didn't have enough breath left for the sounds I needed desperately to make. I thought I would die if she didn't let up. I knew I would die if she did.

"Breathe...hard to breathe."

She slowed the rhythm of her hand just enough to let each wave of sensation penetrate to my core before the next one crashed. Breathing forgotten, I arched into her, straining toward the pressure of her fingers. She flashed her white-toothed Viking grin and teased me a little longer, working my juices, slicker than the water around me, over my throbbing clit, until urgency consumed me and my hips thrust forward into an accelerating tempo.

Sigri had me. She wouldn't let me fall. She pushed me right up over the edge, and beyond, until orgasm surged through me so searing and intense it could have split rock. I thought the reverberations would never subside. Maybe they never will.

We rested for a while on the flat rock where the shaft of sunlight penetrated the green canopy of leaves and needles. In tacit agreement we didn't return to the lodge together. Just before Sigri started down the trail she turned and said, "I still owe you one, but I'll leave it to Janet. You'd better save plenty for her, Raf. Getting your rocks off is fine, but it doesn't take the place of love."

"You bear that in mind, too," I said, and waved her off. I lay back and allowed myself a few precious minutes submerged in the memory of Becca lying beside me in this very spot. It hurt, but with a gentler pain than I'd expected.

Then, deliberately, I thought of Janet, her fierce, protective devotion when I didn't care about living, her prodding when it was time to take up life again, her infinitely responsive body and eager hands and mouth, her unconcealed need for me.

The residual glow between my thighs intensified. Yes, I definitely had something left for Janet. Some surprises, even.

And for Sigri? Sincere wishes for someone to fill the emptiness in her heart, now that her body, like mine, had burst through to life.

Contented Clients

Kate Dominic

Andre was more than a little miffed. I'd been quite specific in letting him know that the matronly outfit he'd designed for me was about as sexy as a burlap sack.

"I want to show boobs, dear," I snapped, dumping the custom-made '50s-style housedress on the neck of the naked, headless mannequin. "Mother's naughty 'little boys and girls' need to be squirming in anticipation of a nice, comforting nipple to suck on, even before I turn them over across my knees."

"As Madame wishes," Andre sniffed, his beautiful green eyes flashing with righteous indignation as he tossed his short blond curls. In a flash of dramatic pique that only a former runway model could master, he turned and swept up the yards of atrocious yellow floral print. He froze in mid-pirouette when my hand snaked out and gripped his slender, denim-covered butt cheek. Hard. I wasn't sure what Andre's problem was today. His costumes were usually exquisite. But I was in no mood for an artistic temper tantrum when I had clients scheduled for that scene in less than a week.

"Madame damn well wishes," I said quietly. "And if Andre has a problem with that, perhaps Madame should call Andre's sweet, smiling lover over to give dear little Andre an attitude adjustment."

Andre looked nervously over his shoulder, his eyes locking on the large bearded man hunched intently over the computer screen on the other side of the room. The only time I'd ever seen Bedford's lips so much as curve upward was when he was paddling the bejeezus out of Andre's ass.

Andre shivered as Bedford clicked onto a new screen, leaned back, and carefully stroked his chin. The latest design appeared on the web page he was updating, and Bedford nodded once, so slowly that the long brown hair tied back at his neck barely moved over the flannel shirt covering his thickly muscled shoulders.

"That won't be necessary," Andre said primly, almost hiding his shiver as he carefully set the discarded material onto a side table. He glanced once more in the direction of his bearish lover. "Shall Madame and I sit down at the other work station and discuss alternative design options?"

"The operative word being *sit,*" I snapped, releasing his ass cheek. I managed to control my smile as Andre politely escorted me over to the computer, offering me a chair before he called up my profile with even more efficiency than usual. From the way his ass was twitching, I gathered that sweet, pouty little Andre's entire snit had been staged purely to let Bedford know that he was hungry for a good, old-fashioned ass-warming. Despite Bedford's apparent lack of attention, I had no doubt that he'd heard every word—and that a very sore and well-fucked Andre would be working standing up for the next couple of days.

It wasn't the first time I'd been an unwitting prop in one of my friends' private little scenes. I doubted it would be the last. I shook my head and bit back a grin as my voluptuous cyber-model filled the screen and a nervous, eager-to-please Andre and I got back to designing the perfect costume for my stable of submissive little boys and girls. Overall, I'd been quite pleased with Personal Fetish Attire, Inc. PFA had provided me with my first dominatrix outfits with almost off-the-rack speed—no mean feat, given my well-endowed size-2X proportions. As my clientele grew, Andre and I worked together to design some very chic leather teddies and harnesses that emphasized my Rubenesque curves for my hardcore "mistress" clients, as well as the flowing drapes of satin and lace that highlighted the ample padding so comforting to my naughty adult children. When I'd branched out into less traditional fetishes, PFA had quietly made some introductions to other clients, for whom they then also supplied costumes. Several of my fantasy scenes had even been Bedford's idea.

"We've got this guy who's really into horror flicks," Bedford had said one fall afternoon. He was lacing me into my new black corset as Andre put the finishing touches on my Halloween vampire costume. "Cleavage" didn't begin to describe the size of the valley developing between my boobs as Bedford cinched me into place. Andre had somehow managed to build in a truly comfortable support bra without losing the sleek lines of the corset. "This dude would think he'd died and gone to heaven if you had your way with him in this costume, Ms. Amanda, especially if you bit his neck a couple of times. Hell, if you let him nurse on these mamas, he'd pay whatever you wanted. And honey," Bedford winked at me as he tucked the lacing ends under the intricately tied knots, "he can afford to pay whatever you want."

In short order, I'd found out that Timmy could indeed afford my services. Frequently. From there, it was a short step to a half dozen men who wanted to be spanked and diapered and fed a cup of warm milk, then held on Mama's large, comforting lap to nurse contentedly on her huge ol' boobs while they went to sleep. That costume was easy, too. I set the scene to be one of "baby" waking up at night, so the seductive peignoirs that, along with leatherwear, were the mainstay of PFA needed only a complimentary pair of feathered satin mules to have baby's hard, horny dick drooling into the neatly pinned cloth-cotton diapers Andre had custom-made for them. At the end of the scene, I'd sit in the oversized rocker Bedford had built and unhook my specially made "nursing bra," one cup at a time, and let baby suckle my huge, dark red nipples until the heavenly stimulation—and the ben wa balls in my pussy—made me explode in orgasm. The sucking, along with my usual expert wrist action, usually had baby creaming into his diaper as soon as he'd sucked me through my climax.

My submissive and infantilist clients were an excellent match for me, as my breasts were about the most sensitive part of my body. After a good session of nipple stimulation and roasting naked backsides, all it took was a few quick flicks to my clit or a well-placed toy to make my cunt gush.

Although my clients paid well enough that I needed to have only a few regulars, I was interested in branching out again. For the first time, I also had a couple of women clients. One of the girls, Cherise, was into enemas. Because of her prior problems with bulimia, I'd had a long talk with her doctor before I accepted her as a client. With his permission, I'd written her a "prescription" for one enema each month, of no more than one quart, administered by the stern, uniform-clad Nurse Harriet, so long as Cherise kept her weight up and stayed completely away from laxatives in the interim.

Cherise had been following her program like a champ since we started, cuddling contentedly into my lap to nuzzle after a long medical session with prim, no-nonsense Nurse Harriet. Andre's costume had combined an extremely short, starched, white hospital skirt with a matching low-cut top that unbuttoned to show a soft, white-lace bustier. Cherise had been so tired after her session and her overwhelming climax that she'd spent the last half hour of our time together dozing in my lap, my nipple resting on her thin red lips as I stroked her hair.

Cherise was not into infantilism, though. Spanking, yes. But at twenty-six, she saw herself more as a naughty high-schooler who needed someone to take her firmly in hand and to teach her to be good and do right—and to help her gain a healthy dose of the self-esteem she was fighting so hard to achieve. After her last visit, I'd told her that next week her mother wanted to discuss her report card with her—most specifically, her citizenship grades. And to be sure to wear her best school clothes and saddle shoes. Cherise had shivered, her face positively glowing as she kissed my hand and whispered, "Yes, Ma'am. I'll be here right after school." Which meant 6:30 P.M. sharp, after she'd finished work and eaten exactly as the doctor's regimen directed.

Part of the success of our session, however, hinged on whether Andre got off his butt and got me a sexy enough loving-but-stern 1950s-middle-class Mom costume for Cherise. Andre hadn't shown me the real design but he told me I'd be pleased. He also assured me that my costume would most definitely be ready by Thursday evening. I assured him that it had better be, or I'd be lending Bedford one wicked fucking Lucite paddle.

As I suspected, Bedford had heard the whole exchange. As I walked toward the door I heard him growl, "Drop yer pants and get over my knees, boy!" followed by the sound of a chair being pushed back, the clink of a belt being unbuckled, and Andre's plaintive, "I'm sorreeeee, Bedford!" I smiled and turned the window sign to "closed" on my way out, locking the door behind me.

Whether it was the hiding Bedford gave him for sassing the customers (for which Andre tearfully apologized into my answering machine) or just his usual desire to create gorgeously sexy attire, Andre outdid himself with the new and improved version of my happy-housewife ensemble. The soft, full, autumn-colored skirt brushed just below my knees, a wide leather belt cinching Mother's ample waist just enough to show her well-rounded hips. A simple beige silk button-down blouse tucked into the waist, veiling but definitely not hiding the cream-colored peek-a-boo satin-and-lace front-hook bra that was, again, wonderfully supportive and comfortable.

Since it was a warm fall day when Cherise was scheduled to visit, Mother wasn't wearing underwear per se, just a butterfly vibrator in a thin-strapped thong-type harness, a lacy garter belt that matched her brassiere and held the tiny control box for the vibrator, and thigh-high seamed nylons. Whether or not my errant daughter was going to discover what was beneath my skirt remained to be seen. A pristine starched white-cotton apron tied at the waist rounded out my attire, along with low brown-leather heels and a pearl necklace and earrings. By the time I took the hot rollers out of my hair and sprayed my period-do into place, I had just enough time to spritz on some White Shoulders before the front door quietly opened.

I walked to the stove and lifted the lid of the hearty vegetable soup that was simmering, picked up a long-handled wooden spoon, and started to stir as I heard Cherise come into the kitchen. I looked up at her and smiled.

"Hello, dear. How was school?"

Andre had outdone himself again. Cherise wore a poodle skirt and a fluffy pink angora sweater that softened the angular planes that were slowly filling out as she grew healthier. When I nodded appreciatively, Cherise blushed and slowly turned around, the careful draping of the thick skirt flowing with her as she moved to show off how her pretty bottom was finally rounding out. Her legs were bare except for ankle socks and saddle shoes, and her fragile, usually pale face was suffused with a happy blush. The three textbooks she carried under her arm added more to her teenage look than her blonde ponytail held in place by a charming pink satin bow.

"School was fine, Mother." Cherise smiled, a truly happy smile, even as she quickly lowered her gaze. I was surprised to realize how much I'd come to anticipate that quiet, shy look. "I got all my homework done, and I had lunch with my friends."

But Cherise was studiously concentrating on the pattern in the linoleum. Her deliberately averted eyes told my mother's intuition that something was up. I cleared my throat and set the spoon down on the counter.

"Cherise, are you wearing lipstick?" I asked sharply, clucking in feigned disapproval. "Young lady, someone as naturally beautiful as you does not need artificial enhancements!"

The creamy red ribbon of color would have been impossible to miss. Andre had no doubt spent hours ensuring that it would compliment the natural blush that slowly suffused Cherise's face. She obediently looked up at me, her blue eyes sparkling.

"I wanted to look pretty today, mother," she said shyly.

"Cherise," I said, shaking my head in mock exasperation. "You are always pretty. This," I pointed sternly at her lips, "is like adding lipstick to a rose. I am sorely tempted to turn you over my knee!"

"Oh, no, Mother. I'm much too old to be spanked."

She moved to the table and set down her books. A bright yellow folded sheet of paper fell out: *REPORT CARD*. Quickly she tucked it under her algebra book. I bit my lip and very deliberately wiped my hands on my apron.

"Nonsense, sweetheart. A pretty young lady like you is definitely still of an age for a good, sound dose of Mother's hairbrush when she deserves it. I hope you're hiding that report card because you want to surprise me with your wonderful grades, and not because of bad citizenship marks again." I carefully unfolded the card. One B, three Cs, and a D were marked in heavy black letters in the academics columns—right across from five bright red Fs in citizenship.

"Cherise!" I said sternly. "What is the meaning of this?"

"Um, I don't know, Mother," she said nervously, shifting her weight from one foot to the other as she peered over my shoulder. "Maybe the teacher made a mistake?"

"Have you been doing your homework?" I demanded, giving her bottom a quick, sharp swat.

"Yes." She quickly stepped back out of the line of fire, lowered her eyes again, and stirred her foot in a nervous circle. "Well, most of the time. Sometimes I forgot."

"I see," I said icily, tapping the card on my fingers. "And the tardiness, talking in class, and lack of participation were also caused by forgetfulness?"

"Um, sometimes." Cherise licked her lips nervously, calling attention to her bright red lipstick.

"Yet you could still remember to put on your makeup."

Cherise clamped her hand over her mouth and stammered, "Just today!"

"Give me the lipstick." I held out my hand. "It had better be almost unused."

Andre knew me well. Cherise reached into her purse, and as she drew out the well-worn tube and twisted up the color, I could see that the contents had been carefully honed down so that only half a stick was left.

"So, now you've started lying as well, young lady?"

Cherise hung her head in shame. Her pert little nipples were hard under her sweater. My labia started to tingle.

"I'm sorry, mother," she whispered. "I won't do it again."

"You certainly won't," I snapped, tossing the report card on the table and turning the soup down to simmer. "You've earned a good, sound bottom-roasting, young lady."

"Mother!" Cherise wailed. She backed up against the cupboard. I shook my head sternly at her.

"Not in here, Cherise." I took off my apron and carefully folded it over the back of the kitchen chair. "I'm going to be taking down your panties. If your crying draws the neighbors, we can't have them looking through the window and seeing your bare, red bottom wiggling all over my lap. We're going to your room."

Ignoring the increasingly loud protestations of innocence and the promises to do better in the future, I took my errant daughter's hand and marched her resolutely down the hall, hurrying her with a few well-placed swats when she dawdled. We entered her room, and I locked the door behind us.

For a moment, Cherise just stared at what was behind the door; it had been labeled "Doctor's Laboratory" the last time she'd been here. I'd changed the room that usually doubled as Mama's bedroom for the infantilists into a teenaged girl's dream, with delicately flowered chenille bedspread, turntable with rock-'n'-roll records, vintage movie posters, and a neat study desk, complete with dictionary, sharpened pencils, and a new, lined notebook. As Cherise looked around the room, I purposefully strode to the window and lowered the blinds.

"It's too hot to close the windows, Cherise. So don't even think to complain that the whole neighborhood is going to hear your spanking. You should have thought of that beforehand. Neighbors or not, I'm going to spank you until you're crying at the top of your lungs. Maybe it will do you some good to realize that everyone knows your mother loves you much too much to let a good girl like you get away with such nonsense."

"Mother!" Cherise seemed shocked, but she could hear the air conditioning running and knew this room was as sound-proof as the rest of the house. However, Cherise's low self-esteem in public was a big source of her problems, and the instinctive shiver that ran up her spine told me how much she was enjoying the idea of "public" proof of her value to me.

I walked over to the nightstand and moved the thick maple hairbrush to the front edge, within easy reach. Then I sat down on the bed and pointed in front of me.

"Come here, Cherise, and lift up your skirt and your slip."

"Motherrrrrr," she wailed, stomping her foot. I'd learned on our first visit how much Cherise enjoyed losing the battle to avoid her spankings. "I'm too old to be spanked bare!"

"Right now, young lady," I snapped my fingers. "And for your insolence, you will now take your skirt and slip *off!*"

With a loud sniffle she shuffled over to me and slowly unbuttoned and lowered her skirt. The delicate white satin slip that hugged her hips was a work of art. When she removed that as well, I needed a moment of reprieve while she carefully folded her clothing and placed it on the nightstand. Andre had outdone himself: pristine white satin tap pants, bordered with Irish lace and decorated with dainty pink but-terflies, framed the softly swelling mound between Cherise's legs and clung to the new fullness of her bottom. I slipped my shaking fingers into the waistband and slowly lowered the exquisite panties, exposing the neatly trimmed soft blond tufts covering her vulva.

"I'm too big to be spanked bare," she sniffed, reluctantly lifting first one leg, then the other.

"Nonsense." I smoothed my skirt and patted my thigh. "Mother's lap is quite big enough to hold you." Cherise slowly lowered herself across my legs, reaching forward to grab a thick handful of the plush chenille bedspread as I pulled her into position. She jumped and twitched as I situated her so that her angular bones were cushioned comfortably over my full thighs. I wanted all of Cherise's attention to be focused on her bottom.

"This is going to be a very serious spanking, Cherise." She whimpered as I slowly slid my hand over the smooth, creamy curve of her bare behind. "I'm going to paddle your bottom until it's so red and sore you won't be able to sit down for the rest of the week." I wanted every inch of her backside awakened and hungry to be touched. I caressed her until she was squirming.

"You will give your best effort, Cherise, in everything you do." I brought my hand down sharply across her right cheek. She yelped, jerking, and I brought my hand down hard on the other side.

"Ow!" Cherise arched her bottom up to meet each slap. "Mother! That hurts! Ow! Ow! *Owwww!!*"

A dozen sound hand-spanks later, her bottom was pinkening nicely. After another dozen, she was sniffling loudly, though she didn't try to move out of the way. I knew that would change the moment I picked up the brush.

"By not doing your best, you're only hurting yourself, dear." I quietly lifted the cool-handled maple brush and, with no warning, smacked it loudly over her right bottom cheek. Cherise howled, and her hand came up to cover her behind. I firmly held her wrist against her waist and spanked her again.

"We'll have none of that, young lady."

"It hurts!" she wailed, her legs flailing on the bed as I began to paddle her in earnest. She twisted and bucked, yelling at the top of her lungs as I covered her entire bottom with sharp, hard swats, up one side and down the other, with the steady rhythm I knew she so enjoyed.

"Of course it hurts," I snapped, stopping just long enough to pull her tightly to me. "Mother is punishing you, dear. I want your bottom good and sore."

Cherise's ensuing howls told me she was really feeling each swat. She kicked her way through another half-dozen sound, hard cracks. Then I paused and set the brush down, cupping her heated bottom and sliding my fingers between her legs and over her labia. Cherise's whole cunt was drenched. She arched into my hand, crying out as my fingertip slid forward to caress her swollen clit. Cherise spread her legs, sniffling loudly.

The smell of her arousal filled my nostrils. My own pussy clenched in response.

"Good girls are always doing their best." I gently pinched her swollen nub, my nipples hardening as she cried out and pressed back into my hand. "They take care of themselves so they are strong and confident." I slid my hand back and squeezed her hot, red flesh, first one side, then the other. "You will remember always to do your best—for yourself, dear, but also because you know that mother will spank you if you don't." I picked up the brush again. "Do you hear me, Cherise? You...will...always...do...your...best!" I punctuated each word with another blazing wallop.

"I will, Mommy! Ow! I will! I will!" After another ten scorching smacks, Cherise's screeches suddenly dissolved in great, heaving sobs. Her body shook as the cleansing tears finally started flowing into the soft, fluffy threads of the bedspread.

I set the brush down and gently pulled Cherise into my arms. "There, there, dear," I murmured, holding her tenderly to my breast. She clung to me, sobbing, as I unbuttoned my blouse. I'd barely finished when Cherise pulled the fabric aside and immediately began rubbing her tear-stained face against the soft, creamy lace. Without a word, I unhooked the front latch. My breasts fell forward and Cherise nuzzled her face against my nipple, taking deep, gulping breaths as she shook and licked. Sensations shuddered through me as her cat-rough tongue dragged over first one side, then the other, outlining and laving the areolas. My pussy throbbed. I lifted a shaking hand and gently stroked her cheek.

"My bottom hurts, Mommy," she whispered, her tongue never missing a beat.

"It's supposed to hurt, sweetie." She tickled her tongue over the sensitive tip of my nipple. "That's how you learn. Suckle Mommy's breast if will make you feel better."

Cherise opened her tear-filled blue eyes to meet mine. Then she smiled, and with a long low sigh, wrapped her lips around my areola and sucked the entire nipple into her mouth like a lonely, frightened child. She inhaled deeply and started to nurse.

I held her close, panting hard with pleasure. Each tug brought exquisite sensations. For a while we just sat there, the only sounds the hum of the air conditioner and Cherise's contented suckling, and my occasional moan. When Cherise's fingers slid down to her vulva, I moved my hand to her thigh.

"Would you like an orgasm, dear?"

When Cherise nodded, I eased her legs apart. She slid further down, spreading wider for me, wincing, sucking hard. Her full weight rested on her well-spanked bottom cheeks and my hand slid into her slick folds.

"Don't fight the pain, sweetheart." I stroked my fingers up and down her slit. She whimpered, her legs stiffening as she leaned more heavily on her tender behind. "The soreness will remind you to listen to me, dear one."

Cherise wiggled uncomfortably a few more times, then looked at me and smiled tearfully. She kissed my nipple slowly. Carefully I slipped my middle finger into her quivering hole and caressed her clit with the pad of my thumb.

"You are truly beautiful, Cherise, from the inside out." Her eyes filled again as I pressed my finger deep, curving up toward her belly. She trembled against me as I found the sensitive spot deep inside her vagina.

"Only a healthy body can feel this intensely." With my finger still inside her, I started massaging her juice-slicked clit with a slow, rolling motion. She cried out, sucking ferociously.

"Take care of your body, sweetie, so it can enjoy the pleasure of a healthy, happy climax." I kept up a steady rhythm, pressing deeply.

Cherise's skin started to flush. "That's it, beautiful. Let your wonderful, young body come like the strong, lusty animal you are."

Cherise sucked so hard that my whole body quivered. Then with a loud cry she arched into my hand, bucking and thrashing as her body convulsed with an orgasm that shook her from her toes to her lips, still latched tightly onto me. She clutched me fiercely to her, sucking her way through a long, rolling climax.

She left me shaking with need.

Cherise slowly caught her breath, her lips falling free of my swollen breast. My nipple was a deep, bruised burgundy against her cheek as she lifted a shaking hand to my face. Her fingers traced the outline of my chin.

"Thank you, Ms. Amanda." Her face glowed. "I feel so good all over." She stared at me, slowly brushing her hand over my cheek while another flush burned deeper and darker over her face. "Um, Ma'am, I was just curious, but..." She took a deep breath but this time didn't look away as she blurted out, "Do you get turned on by my, um..." Even the skin beneath her ponytail seemed to be blushing. I laughed and hugged her tightly.

"Yes, love," I kissed her hand. "Pleasuring you is intensely arousing to me."

"But you didn't...?" Her eyes stayed intently on me as she stammered out her question.

"No, dear," I smiled. "I'll take care of it later."

Cherise nodded and snuggled back into my arms. Her breath was cool over my wet nipple as she sighed contentedly and whispered, "In two weeks, I get my report card from my Greek and Latin tutor. Do you want to see that, too, ma'am?"

The possibilities for those costumes were mind-boggling.

I kissed the top of her head and settled in for a final bit of cuddling. Andre was going to be very busy.

The Language of Snakes
Susannah Indigo

There is a girl in San Francisco who decided to become mute. *My name is bluenote,* she writes, passing her notepad to the tall, bearded man, *and I cannot speak but I can play the saxophone, write poetry with my toes, and fuck eighty-one different ways.*

"Well, those are good things," the man replies with a French accent, sitting down on the turquoise blanket next to this lovely black-haired girl. He eyes the balloons soaring overhead, the crowd of people around the bandstand across the park, the yellow legal pad on which the girl has been passionately writing for half an hour. He tries to look at anything but the unfolding and folding of her long tanned legs and the constant movements of her flimsy dress that kept him at a distance until he could reach some state of gentlemanly control within his jeans.

She looks at him questioningly yet kindly, as though he might be a wounded bird dropped from the sky, looks at him with eyes the color of the Celtic Sea, a piercing blue that moves toward green with the shifting sunlight. She carefully folds and rips off a quarter-page of a legal sheet and writes: *What can* you *do?*

My name is Fabrice, he writes back, *and I am a professor here at the university. I am thirty-seven and originally from Quebec.*

She laughs with the bright sound of a sudden breeze tinkling through tiny silver wind chimes, and places her bronze toes in his lap directly on top of his cock. *That's boring*, she writes, *and I can hear perfectly, you may speak. I meant, what can you actually* do?

Fabrice pets her toes and considers his worth. *Maybe my work?* "I can invent synthetic molecules." *My hobbies?* "I can windsurf...I can build things that last, like furniture." *My passions? I must have some...hard to remember...God I am boring.* He wraps one hand around her delicate ankles. "Why don't you show me how you write with your toes?"

bluenote pulls her gauzy white skirt up her thighs and tucks it between her legs. Fabrice catches a glimpse of black curly hair and smiles at the purity of the day. Placing the blue Pentel roller-ball pen between her big toe and second toe, bluenote props the pad on his lap and begins to write in long sloping curves:

> *I am going mad from roses*
> *softly falling into darkness*
> *stripped of love*
> *drifting*
> *down*
> *to*
> *the*
> *ground*

"Why?" Fabrice asks, wrapping his hand in her long black hair and pulling her onto his lap like a child. "Why are you stripped of love? How are you able to laugh and play the saxophone and not speak?" He feels the undertow beginning, the tug that starts at the edge of a man's heart when he finds a girl in need of his strength, the tug that turns into a series of waves like the rise of oncoming orgasm, and then eventually, willing or not, evolves into a tidal force that can take a man right down to places he'd rather not go.

bluenote curls up in his arms as if she belongs there and considers which story to tell this new man. Usually she waits until after she has fucked them at least five different ways before she gets anywhere near the truth. *I went crazy,* she rarely says, *after my lover Sam left me three years ago. I went crazy,* she doesn't say, *because he left me for something evil I did, and I could not get him back. I am still crazy* she does not add, *because Sam still lives one floor above me in North Beach and I am unable to move to a new apartment, not to mention speak and if I lie very still in my bed at night I can sometimes hear him with his new girlfriend from Colorado who is bright and happy and has children and seems normal. I can hear them loving each other and fucking each other and laughing and dancing and moving through life like real people, and I am only* not *crazy,* she should add but won't, *when I play sad, soulful songs on my saxophone every night just before dawn and I know he can hear me, although he mostly ignores me and only nods to me in passing and doesn't even know that I can't speak.*

bluenote looks up at Fabrice and shrugs, never answering out loud, instead running her tongue lightly across his lower lip, often a better answer than anything words have to offer. Language, it has been said, was given us to camouflage our truths.

"I can do one more thing I forgot to mention, sweetheart," Fabrice whispers through her kiss. "I can make a woman come in five minutes with only my mouth."

Show me, she writes slowly down his neck with her tongue, and she tosses her long pristine skirt over his head like a blanket. Fabrice lowers hungry lips and tongue between her legs and it begins.

Back in her apartment, bluenote begins to strip for him—*this is one of the eighty-one ways, use only your eyes and watch me*—she writes using a keyboard and the big computer monitor close to the headboard before she stands up and slips one thin arm from the white dress. Fabrice sits on the bed and tries to focus, but he is quite distracted by the room that he finds himself in—it isn't the blue netting on the ceiling, resembling a tourist restaurant on the Wharf, that gets to him. It isn't all the fish tanks, or the big rattan basket filled with pieces of cut rope and a book on Japanese rope bondage; it isn't even the wall covered with little white slips of paper from a lifetime's worth of fortune cookies—it's the other wall, the one floor-to-ceiling with snakes.

Don't worry about the snakes, she had written with a laugh when he first entered the room and stopped cold. *They just watch.*

There are some images that a man will never forget. Fabrice watches bluenote put on the music, a slow Leonard Cohen song about dancing until the end of love. He watches her dance, watches the big orange, black, and white snakes displayed like artwork in shaky-looking cages on the wall behind her, and he desperately tries to recall the name and color of every poisonous snake he's ever heard of, all the while smiling at the lovely girl who is offering herself to him.

Images at dusk: sunlight fading, shades of gray, shadows on the wall, lit candles, the thin undulating body of the girl as she drops her dress on the floor near the window, this gift of a girl with the dark hair that flows over her small breasts, this girl standing near him wearing only a white lace camisole and white lace-up sandals. She moves toward him, offering her body for inspection, bending backward in front of him and parting her pussy lips to show him her softness; she holds her small brown nipples out for him, pinching them, watching his reaction.

Come, strip for me, she motions to Fabrice as the song changes, pulling him to his feet and unbuttoning his shirt. He tries to move like she does. As he removes his shirt and she circles around him, the world outside the room ceases to exist. She mouths the song's lyrics: *"I remember when I moved in you and the holy dove she was moving too and every breath that I drew was hallelujah..."* Even with her sandals on, she barely comes up to his chin; he thinks perhaps he could lift her up and carry her away and keep her in a cage of his own, and no one would ever know.

She unbuttons his jeans and runs her fingers down inside, tangling his thick pubic hair and bringing his cock out for her inspection. She smiles. *I forgot to tell you this,* he thinks to himself, *this is something I can do. I can offer you what women say is a very long cock, long and curved, not terribly thick, but a cock that reaches every place that needs to be reached.*

bluenote pauses and motions toward the wall, meaning *it's like a snake.*

A baby snake, maybe, he thinks, suddenly insecure. He turns away from the wall of thick snakes to focus on his next move.

He lowers his jeans, removes every stitch of clothing, and stands naked in front of her, trying to hold her close, but she keeps slithering away, dancing, running her hands through her hair and down her body, dipping her fingers into her pussy and licking them clean. She moves like a belly dancer but she has no real hips to speak of, nothing much to hold onto as she twirls around him and lands at his feet. Looking up at him with those eyes, she begins to climb up his body, wrapping around his legs, kissing and licking her way up and around from his cock to his ass and back again.

bluenote picks up a long piece of rope from the basket, stands close to Fabrice, and wraps it around her leg, then around his leg, weaving them together. "You're tying us together," he murmurs brightly, standing very still and watching the artwork of the rope running around his balls, between his legs, straight across her pussy, and then back down her leg. bluenote nods and stands on his bare toes, looking up into his eyes. wrapping her arms around his chest like a child standing on top of her father's shoes, ready to be walked up the stairs. She motions for him to lift her up slightly, while she raises her free leg up and over his cock until it's positioned between her legs. Her wetness flows over him and he understands that she wants him to enter her and continue dancing with her this way, his cock deep inside of her, deep, deeper, driving her up to his lips every time they move. Moving together in exact rhythm, leaning, turning, spinning, pausing, thrusting; the night will last forever.

There are some things that happen in a moment that take a lifetime to explain. As they lie head-to-toe on the bed, exausted and spent, untied but still entangled, bluenote stretches to get a piece of paper from the nightstand and writes—*I hope you don't mind, but I always sleep with Flow, my favorite snake. He protects me.* Fabrice says nothing, finds no words to protest. Somehow it seems a reasonable thing to do: to fall asleep entwined in the legs of a beautiful young girl you just met in the park—a girl encircled by a snake you'd rather not meet.

At precisely 4:30 A.M. bluenote wakes up Fabrice and asks him to leave. She picks a fortune from the wall as he leaves and gives it to him with a kiss. He pauses to read it in his car:

"You can kiss and fix whatever's wrong but no one stays kissed for very long."

bluenote watches from her bay window as Fabrice drives away in his little black Fiat. Playing "Body and Soul" on her saxophone at dawn, she sees Sam across the street, strapping his duffel bag to the back of his motorcycle. It's hard to tell what Sam is up to just by looking at him—he's the kind of guy who wears the same black leather jacket and packs the same bag whether he's going to Colorado or Japan. Though she hasn't spoken to Sam for almost three years, bluenote has her ways of finding out where he's going and for how long. Sam Davidoff: ex-lover, upstairs neighbor, tall, dark-haired, bespectacled, smart, worldly journalist; Sam Davidoff, cruel, cold, distant, gone; Sam Davidoff: the man who was meant to be hers.

It's not really stalking because he loved me. Besides, I don't do anything bad, not anymore. bluenote reaches into Flow's cage to retrieve a key, the copy of the key to Sam's apartment that she has had ever since the breakup, the key Sam has no idea she still has since she has become invisible to him. She wraps Flow around her neck, picks up a piece of cord from the basket and adds it to her snake-necklace. *He's just forgotten he loved me. There have been a hundred men since Sam, but I can't remember any of their faces, though I certainly can remember the snake and the tongue of the man from last night. It's not stalking, because I love Sam and I would never hurt him. He was going to marry me once.* She goes outside and up the back stairs and quietly lets herself into his apartment.

Rituals and patterns create clarity. There are self-made rules and bluenote follows them. First, she checks Sam's calendar to see what's coming up, then she reads all of his downloaded email to find out how his life is going. *I would never actually hack his password and log onto his account;*

that would be a bad thing. It's bad enough that I gave his cat away and he has no idea. But I was so angry back then. And I did find the cat a good home. She reads the latest installments of both his novel and his play, resisting the urge to edit. Standing up, she strips off her dress, drops it onto his bed, goes to his closet and chooses one of his big white button-down shirts to wear. Leaving the shirt open, she sits on his bed and ties her ankles together and then ties the rope to his bedpost. Flow wraps around her leg, and then she lies back across his big brass bed and begins to remember and dream.

It was our last conversation: Sam told me to stop talking, to stop saying so many words, that none of it meant anything. I stood naked before him and begged his forgiveness, and it all could have been OK, but he wouldn't forgive me. "I'd say I'm sorry too," he said, "but I don't apologize for things I can't control."

I tied myself to his bedpost that night, this very same bed-post, tied myself the way he used to when he practiced all the secrets of Japanese rope bondage on me, when he promised that I would be his forever, when he said that he owned me body and soul and we both liked it that way. I wouldn't leave that last night. I told him a thousand times that I only did what I did because he was gone for so long, four weeks in Japan, and I thought he would be proud of me for taking care of it all.

He wouldn't touch me, no matter how I begged, and he finally just left me there and walked out. He had been back from Japan for almost eight weeks and everything had been fine when this chaos began. I should have just stayed silent. I thought maybe I'd never tell him what I did, but eventually I had to. I decided that honesty mattered.

bluenote strokes her legs, letting Flow wrap around and around her, and tries to relive her last night with Sam, tries to create in her dreams how it could have been.

If I dream it just right it will be different. "I understand why you had an abortion while I was gone," he would whisper kindly to me, "and I understand that you got sterilized while you were at it, because you thought I truly didn't want kids like you don't." He would stroke my shoulders, my face, my tears; he would tell me he loved me anyway. "I understand," he would continue, "that you weren't really being sneaky, that you didn't contact me in Japan because you were upset and scared and thought I might be proud of you even though you know that we agreed you weren't to do anything drastic in your life ever again without discussing it with me," and he would cover my body with his bulk and hold me down on the bed the way I needed him to, and he would tell me over and over again, "It's OK, I love you, Kendall my sweet bluenote, it's OK, it's just an unexpected twist of fate and we can handle it. I love you"...and he would crawl right up into my body and fuck me hard into the bed and all the words would have meaning and I would never again in my life have anyone or anything else inside of me except for Sam.

bluenote begins to come, shivering and shaking and crying on top of the bed with the force of memory and possibilities, but she is sad, as always, to open her eyes and find that it is still only her and Flow keeping Sam's bed warm.

Rituals and patterns create clarity. After she comes, bluenote hangs up Sam's slightly wrinkled shirt, gets dressed, eats a bite of food from his refrigerator, brushes her teeth with his toothbrush and proceeds to scrub his bathroom for him— a small act of contrition. She leaves his apartment and locks the door, tucking the fortune she has brought for him under his doormat—*you will attend a royal banquet and remember what you already knew.* She whispers the only word that still sounds right in her throat—"Sam"—and goes back downstairs.

"You should have a party, Sam," his lover, Annie Braverman, says when visiting him in June. "You're always happy when I have them in Boulder. At least let's have a dinner party— you're a great cook. We could fit six people here—and let's invite that sad-looking girl who lives downstairs, the one you used to go out with, so maybe she'll stop staring at me out her window like I'm poison. She must have a boyfriend she could bring."

Sam and Annie are wrapped together in his deep old-fashioned bathtub, soaking beneath the bath oils and bubbles that Annie never travels without. Sam is holding her leg up in the air and slowly shaving it for her, one of the ways she's convinced him not to be such a guy, not to just shower all the time.

He looks at her hard when she suggests the party. Annie has begun to fill up every available empty space in his life—his bathtub, his apartment, his writing, his heart. Somehow she makes him do things he hadn't even thought of doing. Already, thanks to her suggestion to *do* something about the problems in the world, he's "adopted" three poor kids in Appalachia through some children's group and keeps their pictures on his fridge. She's made him try snowboarding, learn tantric sex, laugh more than he'd ever laughed before—even as a kid—and she's managed to make him acknowledge the word "dream" again, a word he likes to edit out of every story that comes across his desk.

How to tell her? "The girl downstairs is named Kendall, and I haven't spoken to her in several years. I'm surprised she hasn't moved away. All I remember about her is that she was a good writer, mostly poetry, and that she worked at home and was starting to do some kind of research on the Web for a living. She used to have a snake in her apartment, and she used to take care of my cat Maxie for me before he ran away." *What else to share?* "I hardly ever see her. She was a little upset when we broke up a long time ago. Let's *not* include her for dinner. I've seen her with a lot of different men, and I'm sure she's happy. But she was always a little crazy around the edges."

"Aren't we all, Sam," Annie offers, rising from the bubbles and floating up to stretch out and press her bare body on top of his in the water and kiss him softly. "Aren't we all." She turns over, lies with her back to his chest and kisses him with a reverse kiss—a kiss as simple as turning your head and kissing backwards in a way that makes the person you're kissing look and feel entirely different than the basic eye-to-eye kiss. A kiss that starts on the lips and travels to the tongue and then back to concentrate on the sucking of the bottom lip, sucking until the victim is moaning with pleasure. Annie moves down through the water to his chin, to his neck, to his nipples, and she stays there for a very long time, moving from one of his nipples to the other and sucking and biting until they're bright red and standing at an attention that could rival his cock's.

Sam closes his eyes, moans, and runs his hands up through her long, tangled wet hair. "Annie, Annie. Do you know, I'll do anything for you..."

Annie smiles and lies on top of him again, with her back to his chest. She slides his hard cock inside of her, wrapping her strong legs down and underneath him, sliding slowly up and down against his body, fucking him in exquisite slow motion, breaking from another reverse kiss to whisper, "Then a dinner party it is. It will be good for you, darlin'—and besides, I *like* girls who like snakes."

bluenote and Fabrice arrive for dinner promptly at seven on Saturday night, joining Annie, Sam, and two of Sam's favorite editors, Howard and Hannah. Several bottles of wine are offered up by Howard and Hannah. bluenote brings tea and oranges—all the way from China, she writes.

bluenote wears a long red sleeveless dress with big pockets and carries a half-sized legal pad and pen in one pocket. When Annie asks her what kind of work she does, she writes, *I research words on the Net—lyrics, poetry, fortune cookies.*

"Fortune cookies?"

Yes, specialty fortune cookies. I help write them too, but all sayings have to be cleared for copyright. GenX Cookies, Atheist Cookies, Random Song Cookies, X-Rated Cookies (of course), Over-the-Hill Cookies, Chicken Soup Cookies. Even Y2K Cookies.

Annie laughs as she reads bluenote's words and asks about her favorite fortunes, but she notices that Sam is watching and listening from the kitchen while chatting off and on with Howard, who is helping him cook. Sam has been almost completely silent since the girl arrived and Fabrice explained to everyone that she could hear but not speak. As he serves the couscous, Sam is beginning to remember three things about bluenote: that up close she is strikingly beautiful in a fragile-waif kind of way; that she has eyes a man can get lost in; and that everything she says must be examined for shades of the truth.

At dinner, Fabrice talks about his new after-hours work project—researching speech patterns and communication. "bluenote is psychologically mute, a condition more common than I realized before meeting her this spring," he explains. "I figure if my lab can make synthetic molecules that profit rich drug companies, surely I can use the same research skills to help one woman regain her speech."

bluenote laughs and shrugs and rolls her eyes, as if to excuse Fabrice's devotion. She writes a note for him to read to everyone at the table. *I don't need to speak. Everyday language is highly overrated. I can do more interesting things than speak—I can play the saxophone, write poetry with my toes, and fuck eighty-one different ways.*

"Eighty-one?" says Annie, barely missing a beat. "Wow, that's great. I only know maybe sixty-two, and I've studied the Kama Sutra forever. We need to compare notes."

"The number eighty-one," Fabrice explains as though this is important, "is one of those 'magic multiples' of nine—products, sum of the digits, the works. bluenote loves ritual and precision."

"Not to mention," says Hannah, "that 81 is a number that can be turned top to bottom and still maintain its identity."

Everyone laughs away the awkward moment, but Sam stares hard at bluenote, trying to determine how much of this is an act for him and how much might be true. "Kendall," he says, a bit sharply, speaking to her directly for the first time since saying hello at his front door, "maybe after dinner you can entertain us with these things."

bluenote stands up and clears her plate, making herself right at home in Sam's apartment, almost as if she lived there. She comes to him, leans over his shoulder, and writes—*entertain you with the eighty-one ways?*

"No. The music, the fortunes, the poetry, the toes—all the remarkable things you can do." When she presses into his shoulder, her intense scent is immediately familiar to Sam—she has always worn men's colognes, Old English or Brut, which smell entirely different on a woman—and he slips away to pour more wine before he recalls anything else.

I'd be glad to provide any of my talents for tonight's entertainment...but I'm being so rude, bluenote writes, turning toward Annie and the others. *Tell me, what can* you *do?*

Everyone has something to offer. Howard begins. "I can speak some Japanese. I can tango. I won a yo-yo championship in college and can still 'walk the dog,' do 'around the world,' you name it. But, Hannah...Hannah can sing like an angel."

Hannah smiles genuinely, but with a certain distance. "I'm still in process about my singing. Something I *can* do is act like the Red Queen and imagine six impossible things before breakfast every day."

"Impossible things, yes. A good plan," agrees Fabrice, sliding his arm around bluenote. "Personally, I can tell you exactly how many steps it takes to cross the Golden Gate Bridge. bluenote makes me walk across it with her all the time. I lived here for ten years and never once set foot on the bridge 'til I met her. I have to say, she's made me much less boring than I was when we first met."

Even Sam laughs at that.

Your turn, Annie, bluenote writes.

"Well, let's see. I can stand on my head for an hour."

So can I, bluenote writes quickly in response, turning to face Annie and looking at her expectantly, pen poised to respond.

"I can beat Sam at chess."

So can I.

"I can talk with my cats."

I can talk to my snakes, we speak the same language. What else?

Annie laughs and considers. "Well, I can dance with my cat, Zenrose. Sometimes she even leads."

bluenote smiles smugly. *I can dance with snakes. Want to try it?*

When Annie agrees to go downstairs to see bluenote's snakes, everyone else accompanies them, albeit with some reluctance. After one peek at the wall of cages, Hannah suggests to Howard that they really should leave because it is so late and she needs to be fresh for impossibilities the next morning.

Sam stays, entranced by all that he sees. Ropes, the book about bondage, mementos that he recognizes as his; a wall of fortunes on which he reads several of his own statements, including *"Never say you're sorry for things that you can't control"*; two dozen snakes arranged like art on a museum wall. He walks around the room for a long time and finally sits on the edge of the bed and watches Annie and bluenote together.

"They're not dangerous," Fabrice is assuring Annie. "These are called Louisiana snakes, and they only *look* like the poisonous coral snakes." bluenote hands the first snake to Annie, who bravely holds it out in front of her.

"Are you sure?" Annie asks a bit tentatively.

bluenote nods.

"Really?" Annie brings the snake a little closer.

"Of course," Fabrice answers with a laugh. "Believe me, I had the same question when I first came here, but I've learned to trust bluenote completely."

bluenote wraps one of the smaller snakes around each of her bare arms and beckons Annie to do the same. *They're like bracelets,* Annie says to herself, that's all, and follows suit, shivering from her bare shoulders down to her now-bare feet. Fabrice has lit candles and put on music, some kind of West African high-life music, sophisticated but still primal, music that makes dancing with snakes by the flickering light in this strange girl's apartment seem like a sane thing to do.

bluenote hikes up her long red dress and ties it at her hip. She dances over to Sam, twirling, arms undulating high above her head, snakes inches from his eyes, teasing him, rubbing her leg up against his. He doesn't even flinch. She dances to Fabrice, to Annie, back to Sam, and even Annie has forgotten the snakes on her own arms as she watches the way bluenote can move.

Dance with me, bluenote beckons to Annie and they begin together, arms intertwined, hips rotating, bluenote slinking down to the floor and helping Annie tie up her long black skirt at her hip, baring one leg. *One more snake,* bluenote motions, and finds Flow and lets him wrap himself from Annie's ankle up to her thigh. *Dance for Fabrice,* she instructs. Annie tries to move the way bluenote does and twirls around Fabrice, who stands and takes her hand to guide her.

bluenote wraps snakes around her neck, her legs, her waist and returns to Sam. *Do you remember,* she asks him with her eyes, *you were the man who taught me to dance this way.* He sits very still on the edge of the bed. She moves slowly, pressing in between his legs, stroking his cheek, watching him want to get up and leave, but he appears hypnotized and unable to move. *Do you remember,* she asks him with her body, her knee pressing firmly against his crotch, *do you remember how I can make you feel, do you remember the things we tried with the snake, do you remember the things you did to me.* bluenote glances toward Annie dancing at Fabrice's feet with his hand in her hair, and leans into Sam, pressing him back toward the headboard, climbing up over him and straddling him, dancing with her skirt fully lifted, snakes crawling, music pounding, and Sam finally turns his head away to try and clear it and what he sees looped around her bedpost near the pillow stops him cold.

Sam grabs bluenote by the arm and pushes her off him and onto the floor. He holds up the little green cat collar with the brass bell and doesn't say a word. He drops it in her lap and looks around the room one more time; looks in her eyes and sees what he never wanted to know; looks to Annie who has stopped dancing for Fabrice and is watching him closely. He stands up, straightens his clothing, and begins to walk away.

bluenote regains her composure and motions to Fabrice. "Wait," says Fabrice, doing his best to interpret. "Maybe it's time for Sam to tell us what *he* can do."

Sam pauses and turns, with a look that scares even Annie. "What can I do? I can *leave.*" The door slams behind him.

Twenty-nine million cars go across the Golden Gate Bridge each year and well over a thousand people have jumped off it to their deaths. On Sunday afternoon, Annie, bluenote, Fabrice, and Flow stand on the east-side pedestrian walk looking over the railing. Flow is wrapped safely around bluenote's neck, underneath her jacket.

"I used to come here all the time too, when I lived in the City a long time ago," Annie says. "It's the most popular public place in the world for suicide. The Eiffel Tower is the second." Annie holds bluenote's hand tightly. "I considered Paris."

Why? bluenote writes.

"Who knows? It seemed so intensely important at the time. I was miserable. Some man broke my heart. I was obsessed with that loss. I was empty. I couldn't feel anything. Do you know that at least twenty-five people have jumped off this bridge and survived the jump? And that none of them who have been interviewed ever even *tried* to kill themselves again? Most said they regretted it the second they left the bridge. Things change. Chaos subsides. Time alters our existence— one day out of the blue I learned that there was joy in the world and it was mine for the taking if only I would pay attention and reach for it. I guess it's like the song says, *"Once in a while you get shown the light/in the strangest of places if you look at it right."*

bluenote smiles weakly and writes quickly. *Decisions made too hastily seem to be the ones that last. I came here every day after Sam told me to be quiet, and I considered how the cold water might feel. I wore my long cape and sometimes I'd tie myself to that railing over there, always carrying my camera so people would leave me alone. Then I started bringing Flow. How could I jump without him? How could I jump with him? He saved my life. I just stopped talking instead. It makes the world a softer place. Nobody ever yells at you when you can't speak.*

Fabrice wraps his arms around bluenote and holds her tight and tells her he loves her.

It's been harder to keep up my obsession since I met you, Fabrice. You distract me with your kindness.

"I am focused on you, sweetheart, and you will learn to do the same with me. Even if I have to tie you directly to my heart."

Tuesday morning in the hour before dawn: Annie is asleep, but Sam isn't—awakened, he realizes, by the silence—the absence of bluenote's saxophone. He hears a scratching at the door. Sam pads quietly through the apartment, opens the door, and finds his old cat Maxie there, her green collar intact, the key to his apartment hanging from her collar, and a little white fortune attached to the key: *It's never too late for another simple twist of fate.*

Devotion

Natasha Rostova

I never understood the meaning of bliss until I let myself surrender. Every night, candle flames painted viscous shadows on the walls of my cell. They gathered in the corners of the room and flirted with the shreds of moonlight spilling onto the stone floor. The shadows seemed to love the sparse, enclosed space, the single crucifix on the wall, the surface of my woolen blanket. And yet they possessed devotion toward nothing save their own insubstantial alliance of light and darkness. I both envied and pitied them, cherishing my intense dedication to the holiest of unions.

We were an enclosed order, bound by our vows to a contemplative life motivated by prayer and salvation. Our convent walls blocked us from the eyes of the laity and forced us to turn our own eyes inward. The deliberate merging of light and dark had become part of my self-scrutiny. During these late nights, after supper and prayers, after Mother Superior had walked the corridors, I kept two candle flames lit to let the shadows live.

Sleep wouldn't descend for hours, I knew, and I would lie in bed clad in my thick cotton shift, my mind filled with thoughts of spiritual unity. Peace and quietude hovered like a cloud over the convent yet failed to calm the increasingly faster rhythm of my heart. Just moments before, I had knelt beside my bed, my thoughts filled with blessings, gratitude, and words of faith. And now, unmoving, my body reacted on some primitive level to the force of my piety, stimulating my blood with longing. How I craved a full awareness of the spirit.

My soul was the bride, thirsting for the word and love of God, desperate to quench the aridity of secular life. We are one flesh, wrote St. Bernard, one sublime, intimate spirit transcending reality. The mere thought of myself as part of such a union elicited a wave of pure rapture, skimming over the surface of my skin and into my very blood and bones.

I stared at the opaque shadows, their sinuous movements of joining and separation. They fluttered together and drifted apart, yet always dissolved into one. Perspiration broke out on my forehead as my heart brimmed over with the need to capitulate. Humble—I would be humble and obedient, demonstrating my submission through every word and action.

Want pulsed in my veins—a desire so intense that it was as if my body no longer belonged to me, as if I had given over my flesh to someone else as proof of my devotion. As if I had sacrificed myself. A vaporous mist clouded my mind, leaving space only for the purity of sensation. The woolen blanket stifled me. I pushed it aside, then reached up to yank at the tight collar of my shift.

Heat covered me like a cloak. I grasped the folds of the shift in my fists, pulling the thick material up to my hips. As a crest of cool night air brushed against my bare legs, a welcome relief, my fingers brushed against the damp curls shielding my sex. I slowly parted the folds of my labia, sliding my forefinger into the hot fissure. A twinge of physical pleasure undulated outward from my touch like the expanding ripples from a stone tossed into a pond. I stroked my fingers over the slick folds and up to the swollen pearl of my clitoris.

An unbidden thought visited me: perhaps I should be ashamed of my self-pleasuring. But such bliss filled my soul that my compunction quickly melted away. I eased a finger into my body, feeling my inner walls clench and pulse with the hunger that had begun in my blood.

With a moan I pushed up my shift to bare my breasts to the air and shadows. I felt so free—a stark contrast to the iron bars on the windows of my cell and the habit I wore daily. I cupped my breasts in my hands, tracing the tight areolas, sliding my fingers over the warm crevice underneath them. I stroked my palms over the swell of my belly and the curves of my hips, marveling at how the soft, fine hairs on my skin rose at the slightest contact. Lost in pleasure, I didn't hear the door open until a sound from the doorway broke my trance.

My eyes flew open, meeting the startled blue gaze of Catherine, the sister who had arrived here only several weeks ago. I pushed myself up onto my elbows, trying to clear my mind of the lingering threads of sacred and profane desire. "What are you doing here?"

"I came to ask if you would help me make herb poultices tomorrow," she stammered. "They say you know about the medicinal properties of plants." Her eyes darted quickly over my naked body before looking away. "What you're doing is wicked, you know."

Her eyes made my skin prickle. Her tall frame set her apart from the other sisters, her fine-boned features infusing her with an air of controlled dignity. I didn't make a move to cover myself. "If it's so wicked, why does it feel so good?"

"You're supposed to be beyond the pleasures of the flesh."

I gazed at her for a moment, enjoying her discomfort. "You haven't done this to yourself in private?" When she didn't reply, I pushed further. "Or with anyone else?"

Her eyes widened with shock and an unmistakable glimmer of guilt. "No, of course not."

"Don't worry, I won't tell anyone." I allowed my eyes to travel over her shift, wondering what the curves of her waist and hips felt like underneath the thick material.

Catherine's mouth tightened with displeasure. "Don't displace your wickedness onto me."

"Then why is it you keep looking at me with lust?"

"I'm doing no such thing."

I skimmed my fingertips over my hard nipples, thrilling in the shiver that skittered through my body. My eyes met Catherine's again. The air between us thickened. "No?"

"No!"

"Close the door or someone will hear you."

Catherine shut the wooden door with a heavy click, but remained standing where she was. Her hands clenched into fists at her sides. "How did you know?"

"You just told me," I replied. "Who is she? The new novice?"

"You'll do penance for this."

"So will you." My body continued to hum with arousal, like the taut strings of a violin still resonating with vibrations. I lifted my arms above my head, stretching out in a posture of submission. "Are you going to tell Mother Superior, or do you want to punish me yourself?"

Two spots of color appeared like blossoms on Catherine's cheeks. She hesitated, waging the age-old battle between lust and faith. "Your vow of chastity forbids voluntary sexual pleasure."

"What if my sexual pleasure is *in*voluntary?" I asked.

Catherine's eyes darkened to deep indigo. She strode across the small space between us, reaching down to yank the blanket off my bed. She grasped my knees and pushed my legs apart, exposing the folds of my sex.

"Do it, then," she hissed. "Touch yourself in front of me. Prove to me that your pleasure is involuntary."

Her anger fueled my hunger. I splayed my hand over my sex, rubbing it until a waterfall of shivers spilled over me. My clitoris pulsed against my fingers, tightening a ribbon of pressure in my lower body as I began to sink once again into the web of sensations. My fingers delved into my vulva, exploring my womanhood the way I had been taught to explore my soul.

Catherine put her hand over mine, and for an instant I thought she would join me in this pleasuring. Instead she resolutely pushed my hand out of the way, shooting me an acrimonious glare. Her fingers forcefully probed my damp crevice, prying apart the folds so that she could immerse herself in me. I stared up at her, part of my mind aware that the balance of power had shifted, that my taunting challenge had slipped into something far more momentous.

Catherine pushed her finger into my cunt. Her eyes seared me. "You're a wicked slut, aren't you?" she said, her voice trembling with an edge of fury as her fingers manipulated my sex with a definite expertise. I lifted my arms to remove my shift, letting it drop onto the floor. Catherine's hot gaze moved to my breasts. She bent and grasped one of my nipples between her teeth, conveying sheer pleasure down to my loins. Her tongue swept around my areola. I twined my fist through her hair, letting the blonde strands slip through my fingers like polished silk.

As soon as I touched her, Catherine yanked her head away from me. She walked over to the small armoire that held my clothing and removed the belt of my habit.

"Turn around," she ordered.

My heart pounded wildly against my ribcage, but I rolled onto my belly.

Catherine grasped my wrists and tied the belt around them. It took me a moment to realize exactly what she had in mind. Fear cracked open inside me, momentarily submerging my excitement. I pulled against the restraints, but Catherine swiftly lashed my wrists to the iron bedposts.

"Catherine—"

"Shut up," she interrupted coldly. "You know you deserve this."

Her hand grazed my damp back, pressing against the ridges and bumps of my spine. My pulse pounded violently inside my head, leaving me unable to think a single rational thought. Then Catherine's hand slapped my buttocks so suddenly that I let out a startled cry. My body jerked forward, even as Catherine's hand came down hard again. She grasped my hair and jerked my head back, clenching her thin fingers around my neck.

"Virgin or whore, Teresa," Catherine snapped, her breath rasping against my ear. "We both know which one you are, don't we?"

She bit down hard on my earlobe before releasing my hair and landing another slap on my buttocks. I shrieked and squirmed, pulling futilely at the restraints to escape the next blow. Confusion bit at me with sharp teeth, calling forth images of martyred saints and penance. Catherine's breathing grew rapid from exertion as she spanked me again and again. Pain spread like a rash over my buttocks. How I must look, spread out and lashed to the bed with another woman punishing my naked buttocks. My eyes brimmed with tears of discomfort and humiliation.

I looked over my shoulder at Catherine. Her pale skin bloomed reddish, her tight nipples tenting the material of her shift. The sight of her so disheveled, so aroused, caused my sex to surge anew. I let out a moan, writhing and shifting my hips to urge her to delve her fingers again into my swollen vulva.

Catherine ignored my plea and continued to slap my buttocks until agony and heat scorched my tender skin. Finally, the sting of her hand ceased, allowing me a brief moment to catch my breath and absorb the burning sensation. Tears spilled down my cheeks and into my mouth. I could taste the salty flavor of my shame.

The bed shifted with Catherine's weight as she knelt on it, insinuating herself between the juncture of my legs. She pushed my thighs apart. I winced, burying my face in the wet pillow as Catherine's hands spread over my bottom, kneading my sore flesh. Her fingers slipped into the crevice and probed at the virgin aperture of my anus. I had never felt so wholly open and exposed—not even when I gave my entire self over in prayer.

Catherine suddenly leaned over me, curling her fingers around one of the thick candles on my bedside table. I held my breath as she grasped the candle and sat back, dripping a trail of sizzling wax across the expanse of my bare back. I let out a muffled cry, even as the relief of the cooling wax blurred the distinction between pain and pleasure. A ripe need swelled within me, a need to surrender myself to Catherine the way my soul had already surrendered to God. I had never been so keenly aware of my senses, of the need within me and my self-surrender.

Catherine extinguished the candle flame, leaving the cell shrouded in only the light from the second candle. The acrid scent of melted wax filled the air. Her hands on my thighs, Catherine pushed my legs further apart. Rubbing her fingers over my soaked labia, she let out a husky laugh.

"Our resident slut," she murmured. "Perhaps the priests have enjoyed your treasures as well?"

I blushed hotly, wondering just how much she knew of my secret carnal activities. I didn't reply, allowing myself to sink into the luscious pleasure of her touch. Her long, slender fingers probed at the crevices of my sex, and then I felt the candle pressing between my legs. I stiffened in surprise, even as my vulva constricted with anticipation.

Catherine laughed without humor. "It's not the first time you've wanted a thick shaft between your legs, is it?" She inserted the end of the candle between my legs, sliding it over my oiled folds and around my clitoris. The firm wax felt delicious against my sensitive flesh, and I thrust my bottom upward in an unspoken plea for her to push it into me. My blood grew thick and heavy, throbbing in my veins with a craving that went beyond the physical.

"Where do you want it?" Catherine hissed.

I moaned, thrusting my bottom toward her.

"Put it in me," I moaned. "Fuck me with it. Oh, God, please."

With one movement, Catherine slid the candle into my humid passage, filling me, owning me. My body stretched to accommodate the thick rod, my inner walls clenching around it as if it were a man's pulsing erection. I grasped the iron bedposts and strained toward a feeling that seemed to lie just beyond my reach.

I slipped onto my back as Catherine adjusted her position, and then the velvety end of her tongue touched my engorged clitoris. My hips bucked upward as she began thrusting the candle in and out of me, working at my labia with her tongue. Voluptuous pleasure flowed through my entire body, centering in the expanding ache of my loins. Catherine's lips and tongue plied the crevices and valleys of my sex with an exquisiteness that foretold secret delights. Moaning, I writhed underneath her as much as the restraints would allow, my bottom still burning from the sting of her hand, my nipples chafing deliciously against the rough bedsheet.

Slowly Catherine pulled the candle out of me and held it up. She didn't have to tell me what to do. I parted my lips, allowing her to insert the candle into my mouth. The flavor of my own juices mingled with the taste of wax, causing my blood to throb with shame and delight.

Panting, I tried to collect my senses as I hovered on the brink of ecstasy. I wanted to reach up and touch Catherine, but my wrists were lashed to the bedpost. My sore buttocks burned against the sheet but I almost welcomed the pain —it heightened my awareness of my body. I gazed at Catherine with pure lust. She had removed her shift, and the pale lines of her body fairly glowed in the darkened room. I ached to touch her, to kiss her, and an overwhelming gratitude filled me when she bent forward and dangled her breasts over my mouth.

"Suck, slut," she whispered.

Obediently, I opened my mouth and drew one of her pink nipples between my lips. Her body tensed with pleasure as I laved the sensitive tip, circling it with my tongue. I ached to free myself from the restraints so that I could clutch the sweet curves of her hips. I was hers, utterly, my pleasure at the mercy of her whims.

Catherine moved her body further over mine, positioning herself directly over my mouth. I gazed rapturously at the spread folds of her labia glistening with dew, the quivering ring of her vagina. She lowered herself onto me. I closed my eyes, sucking up the evidence of her desire with my lips, tasting her heavenly nectar. I swept my tongue over her labia, grazing her oiled bud that blossomed from beneath its protective hood.

Catherine's raw breathing filled the air. I shoved my tongue into her creamy channel, overwhelmed by the musky scent and taste of her. Catherine shrieked suddenly, her body bucking and trembling as fluids spilled from her delicious cunt. I drank the sweet fluid from her before she pulled away.

Sweat shimmered on her skin as she looked at me, her chest heaving. I pulled vainly at the restraints. My body vibrated with tension and need, demanding full and total surrender to carnality. I gave Catherine a pleading look.

"Please, Catherine. Please."

She untied me. For a heart-stopping moment, I thought she would lie over me and crush her body against mine, that our breasts would press together with lascivious friction and our hips would writhe in the rhythm of lust. I so wanted to touch her.

Catherine, however, picked up the candle and tossed it at me. "Pleasure yourself with that," she said.

Desperate, I grasped the makeshift phallus and plunged it into my body, spreading my legs wide. I pressed the heel of my hand against my clitoris and pumped my hips up to match the thrusts of the candle. Shudders of rapture rained through me almost immediately, catapulting me over the edge. A cry tore from my throat, echoing off the stones and shadows and darkness.

My hand went limp and the candle clattered to the floor. Panting, I wiped my damp forehead with my arm, slowly absorbing the multitude of vibrations still pulsing through me. I opened my eyes and looked at Catherine. A blaze of anger, as fathomless as the sea, flared in her eyes. "Whore," she snapped, turning on her heel and storming out of my cell. The door closed firmly behind her.

The cell seemed to tremble from her departure. I stared at the whole of my belongings—the few articles of clothing in the cabinet, the candle, the holy book on my bedside table. Everything, I had given up everything for the sake of my faith, for the desire that burned within me. And with the satiation of this desire I had attained the union of body and soul.

I leaned over and blew out the other candle, wiping away the shadows and plunging my cell into darkness.

Hair

Hanne Blank

He was older than she. Considerably older. Enough so that more than once, when he'd show up at their restaurant too early, the maître d' would show him to the usual table and inquire, in his discreet upper-class Irish accent, if his daughter would be joining him that evening. He would nod, but he had no daughter. He had no daughter, and no son, and while he had a wife, they had reached a détente a few years into their marriage. That was nineteen years ago. Since then, she had her lovers, he had his, and they were fabulous—if geographically distant—friends. With two offices to maintain, it only made sense that one of them stay in New York while the other remain in Chicago. He hated New York.

Looking through her wallet while she showered, he noticed with an ironic wince that he had gotten married two years before she was born, if her drivers' license could be trusted. He supposed it could. She'd never told him her age—but then again, he'd never asked. He wondered if he'd have been better off not knowing just how many years there were between them.

He hadn't meant to look through her wallet. Sometimes these things just happen. It was sitting open on the nightstand, her phone card still lying next to it from when she'd called her mother in San Francisco.

"Happy birthday, Mom," she'd burbled into the phone before launching into an incomprehensible mixture of English, Armenian, and giggles. She tended to giggle a lot when she talked to her mother, and she tended to giggle a lot each time he tried to seduce her while she was on the phone. It was her mother's fiftieth birthday. She knew he was older than that. She'd never asked by how much. His lips on the back of her knee, applying consecutive kisses up her chubby, satin-skinned thigh, eventually overcame her urge to wish her mother a happy birthday one more time.

Their sex was thickly passionate. It always was. His head nestled between her legs until she pushed him away, not able to take any more, tears covering her cheeks as she half-choked for air. And then as she rested, he rubbed himself against her buoyant breasts, tickled himself under the chin with her arrogant nipples. He buried himself in her hair, and soon it was over.

And then she showered, and he sat there, contemplative, looking at her driver's license. She sang in the shower. He wondered how many people actually sang in the shower like she did, so beautifully and unselfconsciously. The song seemed half-familiar; he thought it was the same song every time.

Fresh out of the shower her hair hung wetly almost to her knees. She bundled it up in two towels. He'd learned to set out an enormous pile of extra towels in the bathroom. It wasn't that the two of them took so many showers. It was the hair.

It had been in the first thing he ever said to her. She was putting her cello away in the green room after the recital, the rest of her quartet yammering with the friends who had come to congratulate them. The dark nimbus of hair that surrounded her might've been a thunderhead. Her A-string had snapped in the middle of the Schubert, and she was still furious. They'd started again, of course, but new strings never hold tune very well, and now the tape of the recital would be useless.

She fumed silently. Not that she wouldn't have fumed out loud, but sometimes it's less satisfying to have your friends tell you it's going to be okay than it is to get your money's worth out of a good mad. And then he came up behind her, his tall shadow on the wall the first thing she saw.

"I hate to be forward," he began, "but I can't think of anything I'd like to do more in this world than walk barefoot through your hair."

The last two latches on her case snapped shut with angry little clicks. "Fuck off," she said, buttoning her coat and shouldering her case, not even pausing to look at him. She bulldozed her way out of the green room, waving sullen good-byes to her quartet-mates. They rolled their eyes. She was like that sometimes.

He pulled up to the curb where she stood waiting for the bus. It wasn't snowing; it was too damned cold to snow. She hated Chicago in December.

"I'm sorry I was such an asshole back there," he called, unrolling the passenger-side window. "Can I offer you a lift to the train to make up for it?"

She peered into the car. Luxurious. Leather seats, heaters on full blast—she could feel the warmth on her face. He looked like overaged yuppie scum, she decided, but the vibe that he gave off was harmless enough. It was bitterly cold and there was a nasty little ice breeze sneaking up her skirt.

"Sure, thanks. I appreciate it. Let me put Justin in the back seat." He got out and opened the door for her to put the scuffed black cello case on the broad bench seat.

"Justin? Why'd you name it that?"

"Justin Case," she replied, with the satisfied little grin that saying it always gave her. He rolled his eyes. She arched an eyebrow, watching him stifle a chuckle. She revised her opinion to "overaged yuppie scum with a small but important clue," and got into the passenger seat beside him. That was why, when he pulled up to the train station and offered to drive her the rest of the way home rather than making her wait for the train, she said yes. And that was why she let him make her laugh on the way to the near–North Side street where she lived. She probably would've let him kiss her anyhow, it being a cold night and her being more than somewhat attracted after all.

She had to admit it—she liked older men. Always had. And he was quite charming, and tall, and his tight black ringlets were spiraled with whorls of magnesium-flare white, not so unlike her father's. So she let him kiss her. And she kissed him right back.

But she noticed a few things, too, about the way he buried his fingers in her hair, and the way that he kissed her neck as a pretense. It wasn't that he didn't want to kiss her neck; it was just that her hair was there too.

Her hair. That astonishing hair. He hadn't wanted her to know that his fetish was so strong. Sometimes these things just happen. She didn't mind. She didn't seem repulsed. She gave him her number.

The drier her hair became, the shorter it got. It never did get precisely short, though. No curl could ever be tight enough to shorten her follicular profusion to anything less than asslength, and that suited her well enough. At that length, at least, it stayed where it was put, a condition that could not be depended upon when it was short enough to have a gravity-defying mind of its own.

He lay on the bed, cock stirring torpidly against his thigh. He watched her walk from the bathroom to where her bag lay on the floor, next to the cello case. No, he thought to himself, that's not right. She doesn't so much walk as roll, or maybe bounce, or simply undulate. Walk, he thought, had too many straight lines, sounded too Euclidean. She was thirty pounds of potatoes in a twenty-pound sack, he mused, pleased in a stretchy leonine sort of way that was as much love as possessiveness, and as much possessiveness as sheer sensual delight. It would never occur to him to call her fat. Her body matched her hair. That hair, outrageously full, scandalously curly, much of a muchness. Dark as sin, lush as Aphrodite's undies, and hot as hell.

"Not now," she complained in a tone that meant she didn't really mean it.

"Yes, *now*," he said, his hands on her hips, his body pressing against the still-damp hair that hung in a mass down her back.

"I'll miss Schenker," she sighed as her nipples were suddenly trapped.

"You'll survive," he replied, pressing into her with his hips, the length of his cock nestling into the moss-damp crevice of her just-showered ass, her hair a coarse raw-silk mattress keeping skin from skin. She wriggled against him.

"I've already missed three Schenker sessions this semester," she murmured as he filled his hands with her breasts and nipped the edge of her earlobe.

"I'll help you with your homework," he promised, the pressure of his knees against the backs of her thighs pushing her down toward the bed. She let herself be bent over, sighing as he spread her legs and knelt between them, his tongue probing her cunt, lips suckling her clit until she writhed, almost coming, as he flicked the sensitive whorl of her asshole.

She could never resist the quick in-and-out of his tongue in her ass. He knew she'd yield, and she did.

Who was he, he thought to himself, to get to peer over the lip of the bowl of Creation? Each time he slid into her he was transfixed, awed. She didn't seem aware of her fecund potential, the quality about her that was so primevally Woman that it made him slightly insane. As his cock slowly drew out from the grip of her sleek wet walls, and the rock-pigeon noises curled out of her throat, he slid back into her and let his fingers wander through the Sargasso complications of her rippling hair.

She's so far away, he mused. Sometimes it didn't seem fair not to be able to enter her with more than just his body, and a thing inside him yawning with want would wail. His hips pounded her harder. His cock battered her cervix and ripped cat-noises from her throat, his hands mauling her breasts. His descent into madness matched her descent into rut.

Yes, he rutted and bucked hard enough when he rubbed himself against her, his hand around his cock, wrapped in a fistful of her hair. He came quickly that way. And she tolerated it bemusedly, realizing that it was his "thing." But it was extraneous to her.

That was where the madness came from. He could be part of her rut but not part of her, stuck forever squinting through the knothole in the outfield fence. He pounded her hard and harder, wishing his way into her womb, into her belly, into the full sweet sweep of her hips. She whinnied like a mare and her ass slapped his belly, full and fine and fat and glistening with funk as she came full force, squeezing him hard, wringing him like a rag.

"I want another," she panted, looking back at him over her shoulder as he shuttled gently in and out of her body. "If you're going to make me miss Schenker, I want another." Her hunger sent a shock through him as strong as if she'd flipped a switch.

"Where do you want it, then?"

"You know where," she replied, her voice shifting downward, rumbling as dark as her earth-colored mane. Honest eyes met his, and his cock throbbed. Her pussy clenched him. He was grateful for the combination of age and madness. As a younger man he never would've managed. In synch he stroked his cock and her asshole, hand on one, tongue on the other. She shivered and bucked, and he pushed his tongue tip against her, parting her just the slightest bit. It was enough to make her moan.

He thought himself lucky for many reasons. The hair would have been enough. But then there was the music she made. And the way she screamed with his mouth on her clit. And the awe with which she took him in her ass, opening to him soundlessly as he pushed slowly into her until he was lodged to the hilt. As if it had never happened before. As if it could never happen that way again. As if she had never felt anything inside her before.

With his fingers on her clit she never asked him to go slow. Not if she was ready, which she was, already on the verge as he crammed his thickness into her tightest and tiniest hole. As he gazed down at his cock, framed and surrounded by the curling tresses that dawdled across her back and over her ass, she moaned and said please.

One stroke in. All the way. And then all the way out. Two strokes in, all the way in, rocking until his balls made sticky contact with the dripping lips of her cunt. Three.

"Harder." He was happy to oblige. She spasmed and whined, her whimpers turning to kitten-mewls when she realized belatedly that he was not yet close to being done. Riding the endorphins, she was almost silent as he built his speed.

"Yes," she said, her voice solemn and throaty. She liked this part of the fuck, where it became raw around the edges, but she wasn't there quite yet. Not quite. And then suddenly she was, bursting with motion and bucking into him with a ferocity that had frightened him the first few times. She called forth his animals, his demons rising, and she absorbed them, slamming her ass back at him. The challenge was to be mad enough to match her terrible hunger. They collided like boars or elk, her need coaxing him until he slammed into her with the entirety of his weight, and she lay pinned, brutalized, beyond herself.

"Pull my hair."

The reins of conscious thought slipped from him as the thick ropes of her hair filled his hands and he pulled her head back taut against her shoulders.

Slamming into her asshole, his cock burgeoned with the force of seed. His balls tightened. His face was red with furious need and the bliss of being inside her. Just where he needed to be. Just where she craved him. Pulling her down onto him. Savage. Not letting her go. Handfuls of hair, handful after handful after fistful, knotted in his hands. Feeling almost criminal, he lunged deep into the body of the woman he could only just admit he loved. He sobbed it out, face buried in her hair.

In the coffee shop, he bought her lunch. She had to go to orchestra and to quartet rehearsal. He had work to do too. At some point.

"What do you think it is that made you finally decide to tell me that you love me?" she asked. Her coffee cup was almost empty.

"Serendipity," he said.

"No."

"No?"

"No, I don't think so," she replied, her fingers finding and slowly spinning one of the long ebony chopsticks that speared the bird's nest of her upswept hair. His fingers followed her fingers, not her lips, and she knew that she was right. She pulled one chopstick from her hair as she stood, tucking it into the pocket of her peacoat as she grabbed her cello case and backpack and turned toward him. He stood up from the table. "No, I don't think it's serendipity at all," she repeated.

She stepped toward him on tiptoes and kissed him full on the lips. He kissed back.

"But I do," he said quietly. Early March sunlight bleached the side of her face. He relished the brilliance it lent to the outermost haze of her curls.

His crow's feet make him more handsome, she thought. Such a lovely man. Smart. Almost a shame that he's married.

His eyes were clear and strong and they followed her hand as she pulled the second chopstick from her hair and shook her head, the hair billowing down around her shoulders. Extending the chopstick, she smiled.

"Pick me up at the bus stop at nine," she instructed. He took the thin ebony stick from her hand. She walked away, not looking back as she hoisted her cello and moved toward the door, its glass opaque with condensation. Her voice wove its way back to him through the clatter of cups and the hissing of steam.

"And don't be late. I want you to pull my hair again."

This Old Bed
Madeline Oh

The bed fascinated Marie the first time she saw it in Auntie Fluff's pastel pink boudoir. Auntie Fluff was as old as God but her bed was a heavenly creation of pink satin, lace hangings, and a brass headboard with rails and chains and more knobs and finials than four-year-old Marie could count.

"It's an Italian bed," Auntie Fluff once said, flattered by Marie's blatant fascination. "Mr. Lapointe had it shipped over as a wedding present for me."

The thought of that bed on a boat floating across the Atlantic sparked Marie's imagination. She wanted to lie under the snowy white sheets and float, rubbing her face against the smooth satin covers, fingering the bumpy lace.

The foot of the bed was as wide as the back of a sofa, and covered with pink satin. Once, when no one was looking, seven-year-old Marie sneaked in and sat astride the satin padding, pretending she was riding on a magic bed, shivering with goose bumps as the satin rubbed between her thighs.

Marie was a sophomore in college when Auntie Fluff died. Her jewelry was meticulously divided between her great-nieces. Her impressive stock portfolio and house were sold, the proceeds split between her many surviving nieces and nephews. Marie's married cousins claimed the silverware, crystal, and china.

No one wanted the bed. Except Marie.

"That old thing!"

"A bit big for a dorm room, isn't it?"

"You can't be serious!"

She was. Completely. Her summer earnings paid for a storage lockup when her mother refused to keep the bed in the house. Marie often thought about the bed while lying naked with Mike or Josh or Alan. She no longer believed the bed was magic but still sensed it held secrets and memories. She longed to be fucked on satin, surrounded by lace and polished brass.

Once she was gainfully employed Marie spent a good chunk of plastic money to restore and reupholster the bed, and she installed it in her apartment. Auntie Fluff's bed attracted a lot of attention—raised eyebrows, smiles, and slow whistles, to say nothing of enthusiastic lovemaking. But as time went by, Marie wondered if her expectations and dreams were as unrealistic and implausible as her childhood conviction that the bed was enchanted.

Then she met Luke, handsome and bed-worthy, with dark eyes that hinted of wisdom and experience. On their first date, Annie was ready to be conquered, but Luke seduced slowly. They had long conversations, walked by the river, went to Friday-evening gallery hops, and talked on the phone far into the night. He would not be hurried; he seemed to want to possess her mind before he took her body. Meanwhile she had to be content with wild kisses and heated touches.

Until the night he finally entered her bedroom.

"Good Lord!" Luke stopped, pulling Annie against him as he stared. "You never told me."

"Told you what?"

"That you sleep in a bed like this." His lips fluttered along the base of her neck, easing up to her jaw. Insistent fingers unbuttoned her silk blouse before slipping inside to capture her breast. She shivered as his fingers tightened on her nipple. "You like this, don't you, Marie?"

She'd have answered if she were able to. She did manage a little groan as both his hands scooped inside her bra. She hadn't even gotten her shoes off and here she was, shaking. It had obviously been far too long since she'd...He stopped kissing her and let his hands drop.

"Don't stop!" Afraid she sounded desperate, she whispered, "I was enjoying that."

"I know," he said smugly. "I wanted you to." His eyes shone darkly as he eyed Auntie Fluff's bed.

"You like my bed?" Marie asked, hoping to get him into it. Soon.

"My dear." Luke ran his hand over the padded satin. "I like what you'll let me do on this bed." He moved to the headboard and ran his fingers down the brass rail. "I never dreamed you were offering me this."

"Is the attraction me or my bed?" She'd never heard of a furniture fetish, but who knew?

"It's what *we'll* do on this bed."

"You approve?"

"Approve!" He chuckled, slow, sexy, from deep within his belly. "I'm delighted. Why didn't you drop a hint?"

"That I had an antique bed?"

His eyes widened as he looked from the bed to Marie. He seemed to be thinking. A slow smile turned up the corners of his beautiful mouth. "You don't know what this is, do you? To you it's just an antique." He paused as if considering his next move. "Come here."

"I'm here." Marie rested the flat of her hands on his chest, feeling the heat of his skin through his navy silk shirt.

"I'm going to show you what your bed is intended for." Luke's lips came down to her face. Marie pressed against him as she opened her mouth. Lips, tongues, and mouths met in a wild frenzy. Marie heard a moan she recognized as her own, and then forgot everything but the taste of his mouth and his hand easing her blouse off her shoulders. Maybe it fell to the floor; perhaps it vaporized. All that mattered was the thrust of his tongue, his fingers easing down her zipper and holding her steady as she stepped out of her skirt.

Her bra disappeared. Soon she was on her back, sliding across the satin sheets. His mouth closed over her breast and she felt his kiss right down to her groin. His hand smoothed over her belly.

"So hot. So ready," Luke whispered.

Why argue with the obvious? Marie ran her fingers through his dark hair and held him close. "Kiss me again."

"Of course." He planted a slow kiss on her navel. His fingers played with the warm flesh above her stockings. Marie spread her legs—or, rather, they spread themselves. She sighed as he touched the inside of her thigh. Shivered as his fingertips brushed her pussy. She closed her eyes, letting her body melt into the sensation of his touch, whimpering in disappointment when his hand moved away.

"Don't stop. I want more," she murmured.

"You'll get a whole lot more. I promise. But first..." He helped her sit up. "Let me show you something."

He reached over and pulled one of the brass chains toward her. "Look. Bondage chains." He swung the end to and fro, watching her reaction.

"You're kidding!" She was shocked and excited. "It isn't. This bed belonged to my great-aunt!"

"And no doubt she enjoyed herself in it."

Marie thought back to the long-lost photo of Auntie Fluff and the tall, almost legendary Mr. Lapointe. Surely not!

Luke went on. "These chains once held satin or velvet manacles. The rails are for attaching straps or scarves. And as for that beautifully restored padded foot, it's perfect for disciplining an unruly lover."

Marie shivered. "You're imagining things!"

Luke shook his head. "No way! And I'm not imagining your excitement." His hand pressed her mound through the lace of her panties. "You're wet." He licked his fingers. "And horny for what I can give you."

"What might that be?"

His eyes darkened. "Pleasure," he whispered. "If you'll let me..." He paused to remove her stockings. His fingers barely touched her skin as he rolled down the fine mesh nylon. He kissed the inside of her bare ankle.

"What are you doing to me?" Marie asked, her chest heaving.

"Just getting you ready," Luke replied, easing off her other stocking. She waited for the same sweet kiss on her ankle but this time he lifted her leg and kissed behind the knee. It almost sent her into orbit.

"We really must use this old bed as it's intended," Luke said, circling one stocking around her wrist. "Agreed?"

"You're not tying me up!"

"I won't." He paused. "Just one stocking around one wrist. That's the only knot I'll tie. Promise." He kissed the soft skin above the knotted hose. "Now lie down."

Afraid, but incredibly aroused, Marie settled back on the pillow. Luke brushed the hair from her forehead, stroked the curve of her cheek down to her jaw, and trailed his fingers down her neck to her shoulder. His mouth closed over her nipple as he held her arm over her head.

"Easy," Luke whispered, holding her arm steady. "I've threaded your stocking through the rails. Here's the other end. Hold it." Marie's hand closed over the end of the stocking.

She pulled and felt the pressure on her left arm. She relaxed, and her other arm went slack. "See? Only one knot. Hold onto the other end. Let go when you want to be free. You're in control."

Was she? Did it matter? She was hot and desperate and he hadn't even taken her panties off. Would she last? Yes. She'd last forever if she could feel the slow tease of his fingers between her breasts and his warm kisses on her belly—and lower.

"I want you inside," she whimpered.

"Soon, Marie, soon. You're not ready yet." Luke eased himself up the mattress toward her. "Close your eyes." His hand brushed over her forehead and his thumb and finger lowered her lids shut. "Good. You'll feel more if you can't see."

She surrendered, lying in the dark, grasping the end of the stocking for all she was worth, waiting for his next touch. Her toes. He kissed them one by one with deliberate precision.

Something soft and smooth trailed up the inside of her leg and then down the other, carefully skirting where she wanted it most. "What's that?"

"Keep your eyes closed and I'll do it again."

Marie creased her eyelids shut. She felt a soft fluttering across her breast and belly, like the movement of a bird's wings or the softest summer breeze.

"Like that?" he asked. She nodded, her throat too tight to speak. "Good. You like the sensations in the dark, don't you?"

Why try to deny it? His hands eased her panties down. She was naked: when she'd last looked, he'd been completely clothed. She saw the image clear in her mind's eye. She was nude and spread and he was dressed. Marie's cunt gushed.

"Ouch!" Her shoulders rose up as he pinched her arm. "That hurt!"

"Just a little." He kissed where his nails had nipped, soothing the pinpoint of pain. "Better?" She nodded in the darkness and then jerked again as he pinched her thigh. He continued pacing his pinches to her yelps, and then caressing the hurt away with his lips and tongue. Her free hand tightened on the stocking as she braced herself for the next nip. His hand moved to her mound, cupping gently until her hips arched. She whimpered as he parted her labia and held the soft folds open as he...did nothing. Was he still there? Yes, she could feel his fingers holding her open, but nothing else—no kiss, no touch. She was twisting up inside with need. She thrust her hips, hoping he'd take the hint.

"Patience," he growled.

"I want you inside, Luke." She was begging, and she didn't care.

"I know you do. You're wet and glistening. I've never seen a cunt as red and horny as yours."

Her face had to be just as red. No lover had ever spoken that way to her. Suddenly, he was gone.

"Luke!"

His voice soothed her panic. "I'm not going anywhere, baby. I can't fuck you with my pants on."

Marie relaxed, listening to the soft clink of his belt buckle and the rasp of his zipper. Soon the mattress shifted under his weight.

"Raise your hips," he said into her ear, pushing a pillow underneath her. "Good girl." He kissed her belly. "Now I can see you better. I love a cunt like yours."

And then he touched her.

She almost screamed with relief, but it wasn't nearly enough—just a brush of his finger. He persisted, slowly feeding her need until her hips moved in rhythm. She was close to coming but wanted him inside.

Then again, unbelievably: nothing. Bereft, she clenched her hands and all but ground her teeth in frustration. "Why did you stop?" she wailed.

"You're not ready yet."

"I am! I am!"

"Patience."

Marie wanted to spit. To scream. This was killing her. Gradually the tension in her body eased and her breathing slowed. Just when she relaxed he sent a trail of kisses up the inside of her thigh, stopping close enough to her clit so she could feel his breath, but nothing else.

"What do you want next?" Luke asked.

"Suck me!"

"Where?" Couldn't he figure that out? Marie groaned, turning her head on the pillow and arching her hips. "Tell me where you want my lips," Luke insisted, "and I'll kiss you there."

"On my clit and in my cunt."

"A pleasure."

And pleasure her he did. His fingers opened her. Wide. His breath came warm where she needed him and then his tongue touched her. He lapped her, the full flat of his tongue covering her. Slow, teasing licks from her ass to her clit. Each lick took minutes and turned her mind to mush. She was covered, consumed, devoured.

His tongue plunged deep inside her with slow, stabbing movements that sent her head back and her hips up. In and out he went, mimicking the movement of a cock—his cock. That was what she most needed. Sweat ran between her breasts and her right wrist ached from hanging onto the stocking.

"Come into me. Fuck me!"

"Like this?"

His fingers penetrated her. She was filled. Stretched. Marie shuddered with satisfaction as his fingers moved in and out. Sweet friction drove her closer to climax as his thumb slowly worked her clit up and down.

Her instincts took over. She was climbing, nearing the edge, her heart and breathing racing. But nothing hurried Luke. The same steady movements pulled her higher and higher, like an eagle about to spread its wings. Panting, she arched her back and rocked her hips. She was climbing, spiraling up and up. She screamed. Her body soared and she came, again and again, until she collapsed, a shaking heap on the bed. The stocking fell out of her hand—or was it pulled? Luke's arms surrounded her and she tasted herself on his lips.

"You haven't come," she said.

"Not yet. I will."

Marie opened her eyes and blinked in the light. He was smiling.

"So, you want me to fuck you?"

She doubted she could take any more. Her body was still rippling from the last time—but how could she refuse? "Yes."

Luke entered her fast and hard, drilling her with his power and raw male sex, working his need inside her and pulling her back with him. She wouldn't have thought it possible, but she was coming again and again, like short staccato bursts of repeating fire. She was vaguely aware of his groans and the heat inside her as he climaxed. She kept coming until, finally, she collapsed under him.

"You were superb," he whispered. He tugged her left hand, untying the stocking and gently massaging her wrist. "You held this too damn tight."

"Did I?" Her hand could have dropped off and she wouldn't have noticed.

"Stockings are no damn good. Next time I'll bring proper restraints."

"Next time?"

"Oh, yes. There's a lot more you need to learn about this old bed."

Tic Sex
Debra Hyde

The first time I hid Richie's Halperidol he went apeshit on me right there in the kitchen.

"Where are they—Bitch cunt! Cunt face!—Where?"

Naked, I sidled up to him, caressed his chest, and ground my groin against him. An instant erection rose in his pajama pants. Richie was right about one thing: I was a bitch cunt. Especially when I wanted it.

"Come on, Richie," I urged, "I'll give it back. Just make love to me first."

He glanced up to the ceiling, rolled his eyes upwards, then back and forth four times. As he lowered his head to meet my gaze, Richie nodded violently four times. He was working in fours today.

"Come on," I continued, "you know I like it."

Richie sighed. "And you know I hate my verbal tics. They ruin things for me."

"Not all things," I countered. I took his hands and placed them on my tits. "I like having sex with you and your tics. I'm the freak here, not you."

His hands, callused and rough, covered my little breasts, and my soft flesh encouraged him to squeeze. Four times, of course. His fingers found my nipples. He toyed with them, pinching them lightly, alternating from left to right, one, two, three, four.

Richie ate eggs the same way, in fours.

"Tit shit, tit shit," he muttered. Already he was aroused enough that he spoke instead of barked. Focus does that; it dulls his tics. I reached into his pajamas and brought out his thick meat. I slipped to my knees and took it into my mouth. I sucked and tongued him and broke his focus.

"Dick licks! Oh God! Dick licks!" He groaned, then sputtered four more "dick licks." I tasted pre-cum.

"Yeah, baby, I'm licking your dick. Like it?"

"Bitch mouth!"

He liked it.

I kept at it, sucking and nibbling and tonguing him until "dick licks" degraded first into rhythmic grunts, then into normal moaning. By the time he reached that point I was wet and ready. I pulled away from his dick and looked up at him. Richie looked down at me, plaintively, and asked, "Why?"

"Because I like how you talk dirty to me."

"You are sick," he decided.

"Yeah but the sex is great, isn't it?" To prove my point, I lay down on the kitchen floor and spread my legs. "Come fuck me," I invited. Richie stood there, wondering whether to scowl and stamp out of the room or fall to his knees and take me. So I helped him decide. "Right here, on the floor, Richie. Everybody does it on the kitchen floor at least once."

Everybody does it. That did it. That normalized my request and normal appealed to Richie. He lowered himself to his knees and then onto me.

"Fuck floor." Jesus! "Fuck floor!"

114

I took him by the dick and guided him to me. I parted the lips between my legs as I brought my other lips to his cheek. I kissed him lightly as the tip of his cock nudged at my threshold.

Richie pushed into me hard, but it would take three pushes for him to access me. Three, not four. Richie compensated with four massive, full-body jerks, which righted things enough for him to start fucking me.

"Squish, squish," he muttered as he screwed me.

"Yeah, I'm wet for you," I agreed.

Richie quieted then. The rhythm and focus of fucking made the tics recede.

But I didn't care by that point. Richie's verbal dirt had worked its magic on me, and I grunted and went at it like the sex pig that I am. I clutched Richie's ass and pulled him into me, encouraging him to pump me hard and fast. I bucked, giving better than I got. Richie grabbed my breast and pinched the nipple hard enough to make me thrash and squeal and come. That was all he needed. Richie slammed into me and came, snorting like a wild animal.

Soon after, his cock limp enough to slip from me, me wet enough with juice and jism to slick the floor, we rested in a tight embrace. The stillness of lying close made Richie's tics reemerge and he shuddered and jerked several times in my arms. As he yelled "Cunt fuck!" explosively, I realized that the tics were mimicking his orgasm.

Yeah, cunt fuck for sure.

Cunt fuck, cunt fuck, cunt fuck, cunt fuck!

Tara's Stew

Michelle Bouché

Tara enjoyed making her displeasure known to the entire household. How dare they hire someone else to cook in her kitchen! She banged the shiny pots as she put them away, slammed the smooth metal of the icebox door, and glared fiercely at anyone who paused at the doorway. For the last five years she had owned this kitchen, loved it back to radiant life after the old cook had allowed grime and decay to build up around the edges. She'd nourished the family, too, brought them back to vibrancy after years of bland heavy food had caused their taste buds to surrender.

She remembered the day back in 1952 when she'd decided she would rule the Beaumonts' kitchen. Serving dinner in her crisp black-and-white maid's uniform, she overheard the Missus announcing her decision to pension off the old cook. Tara spoke up right at the table, surprising everyone—including herself. The Missus agreed hesitantly. Some vague reference was made to a trial period. Tara just smiled and squared her solid shoulders, confident she could engage them in her passion for sumptuous food and flavors. Later, walking home in the light of a full moon, she thanked the spirit that had prompted her to ask for her heart's delight.

She threw away the hated black-and-white maid's uniforms and spent two weeks' pay on three new, sparkling-white chef outfits with matching linen aprons. Then she proudly marched into the kitchen and conquered it. At first it was reluctant to yield to her fierce and loving care, but within a month the place glowed with new life. Pungent herbs grew in the window boxes; warm fresh bread cooled on the racks, and mysterious concoctions bubbled on the stove. These aromas contrasted sharply with the clean tang of bleach and lemon. The family, never before inclined to linger in this realm of the servants, took to finding excuses to dawdle there, to breathe deeply the now-magnificent air, rich with basil and cilantro, orange zest and seared meat, and sumptuous coffee laden with milk and cinnamon. But her stew was their favorite dish. They always took seconds, not caring if they suffered for their gluttony. Hearty yet tender, the stew was exquisitely delicious. Many a night the women complained that they would have to let out the waists of their dresses.

Despite their grumblings, they couldn't help but indulge themselves at her table. Keeping Tara happy became important. They humored her by painting the kitchen a dazzling white and even put in a fan that twirled from the ceiling, diffusing the luscious smells throughout the house. When Mr. Beaumont rewarded Tara with her own little cabin behind the big house, she smiled and waltzed her rounded figure gracefully through the kitchen, dancing the dinner into a pirouette of tastes to excite their palates.

That night she'd stood outside the door of her new house, reveling in the light of the full moon. Tara opened her nightgown up so moonbeams could caress her breasts as she whispered words of thanks to the beautiful orb shining down on her. It filled her soul. The waves of light beat in time with her heart. She wept as she seldom allowed herself to, magnificent tears of joy, grateful to the family for fulfilling her secret desire.

Since then she'd continued daily, weekly, monthly to tease out the tangiest of flavors, the juiciest of fruits, the most succulent recipes to feed her family, as she thought of them.

And now, for the young Miss's big party, they had betrayed her, cast her aside.

The Missus, obviously flustered, had called her into the parlor to talk about the menu. This surprised Tara, since the Missus usually liked to sit at the little table in the kitchen, sipping her sweet dark coffee and reviewing Tara's plans for special occasions.

Tara refused to sit in the unfamiliar territory and instead leaned against the doorframe, her arms tight over her ample bosom.

The Missus fidgeted. "Now, Tara, Cherry's coming-out party is going to be bigger than anything we've done since you've come to us. We know what a burden it will be for you, so we are going to get you some help. Clara Sue, we've had her before. She has family members who will come special for that night."

Tara shrugged and nodded. Clara Sue would do. But that wasn't what the Missus had called her in for. She fluttered her hands in the air under Tara's silent gaze. "Cherry's daddy wants this to be the biggest, best coming-out party ever. He's hired a band and even a real bartender, though of course the children won't be drinking anything hard. Mr. Beaumont went so far as to hire a man to come in for you. He's a chef all the way from New Orleans."

Tara stiffened. She couldn't be hearing this right.

The rest of her employer's words came out in a rush. "Mr. Beaumont says it's good business to bring someone in from the outside, and Cherry wants something really fancy. And all the best families are fighting over this man. Studied in one of those fancy schools down in New Orleans. It will be really good for Cherry's social standing to have him coming in to help you. I know it will be an adjustment, but it might be fun. Of course, we'll be depending on you to make your best desserts. Mr. Beaumont says no one can touch Tara's desserts." Hearing the Missus say they had hired this *man* to come cook for the party hit Tara like a slap in the face. She had been working on the menu for Miss Cherry's party for weeks—and all for nothing. After all she had given them! She stood up to her full height and glared down at the quivering woman.

The Missus, apparently seeing the impact of her words, tried to take the sting out. "This way you don't have to work so hard. He can bear the brunt of the work. See, he already sent a menu for you to look over. I think you'll love it."

Tara didn't speak. She simply took the menu and left to prepare lunch.

In the weeks that followed, the family didn't linger much in the depths of her kitchen, nor did they complain about the bland food they had to leave uneaten on their plates. Young Miss Cherry came in once to apologize. Tara just turned her bottomless eyes on the girl and waited until she ran crying from the room. They must have told that chef man about it too, because with each menu change he sent, a little token was included. Once, tissue-wrapped ginger candy, another time, dried rose hips. Finally, a jasmine-scented hankie edged with lace, and a written thank-you for allowing him to assist in her kitchen. She sniffed at each gift, tossed them on the windowsill, and refused to release the anger burning in her chest. That he'd chosen jasmine, her own scent, tormented her. How could he have known?

She ordered and stored the food he requested, things she seldom used. She took care to shine her kitchen to its highest polish. Late at night she reviewed cookbooks for the parts of the menu she would carry, determined to prove that she didn't need him.

The week before the party, she got on her knees in the damp, dewy grass and prayed to the moon. "Help me, Grandmother. Someone is invading my life. I'm sure you have a purpose for this, but I don't know what it could be. I've worked hard, Grandmother. Don't let me lose it all."

Would the moon forsake her? No, not when Tara needed her support so much. The Beaumonts' house had become her home in these last five years. She would hate to leave. Surely the moon would respond. It always had, ever since her grandmother had initiated her into the old rites. But she had been lax. It had been a long time since she had come to the moon like this.

She got her answer when the moonlight filled her as her grandmother taught her it could, its power throbbing deep inside her. As always, she felt it pounding in her bones, in her heart, and in that sweet place deep between her sturdy legs. Confident that the big house was quiet, she stepped behind the jasmine bushes, stripped off her gown, and lay in the grass. The moon made love to her, kissed her breasts, stroked the wetness between her thighs, cradled her in its warmth. Moaning and writhing, grasping the moonlight as her lover, she climaxed, peaking once, then again.

The prayer and the lovemaking completed, she lay in the lush velvet grass, confident for the first time in weeks that she would hold her own. Exhausted, she crawled to bed. She looked forward to a good night's sleep—the first since she'd gotten the news about the invading chef.

She waited for him, fear pounding in her chest. Trying to control it, she wiped furiously at the squeaky-clean counter. The maids assigned to help her ducked their heads and made up excuses to avoid her. Remembering last week's foray into the moonlight, she shook her head, frightened by the power of what she had felt and done. The moon had never touched her so deeply. Would it show her the way to defeat this man?

Then the Missus came in to introduce him. "Tara," she said, her hands fluttering. "This is Mr. Charles."

Tara stared at the small, compact black man. He winked at her. His brash laugh filled the kitchen, filled her ears. She reminded herself that she couldn't afford to like him. When his gaze traveled up and down her body and he gave her a brilliant appreciative smile, heat rose in her cheeks. She was appalled; the heat threatened to spill over into her heart. Something loosened inside her.

He swept his eyes across her kitchen and whistled through his teeth. "I don't see many kitchens this well kept," he said to the Missus. "I don't know why you hired me. You've got your own chef right here." He turned back to Tara, again giving her that brazen appraising look. "I'll learn a lot from you, Miss Tara. I've heard of you clean down to New Orleans. They say your stew is the sweetest-tasting thing you could ever get your mouth around. It'll be like getting paid to train under one of the greats."

She tried to push away his flattery, the look, the little emphasis he had put on the word *under*, but her heart thumped, and her mouth puckered from sudden dryness. Licking her lips, she chose not to respond. Instead she watched him closely, relieved when he shifted his attention back to the Missus. He obviously knew how to handle women. Teasing the Missus gently, he soon had her blushing like a youngster and giggling behind her hand. Finally, she allowed herself to be ushered out of the kitchen.

Mr. Charles turned back to Tara. He wore a crisp white jacket and black pants that hugged his narrow waist and caressed the roundness of his backside. His shoulders were broad on his small frame. She guessed at a well-muscled chest and arms under the jacket. His hair was cut sleekly against his head, a good choice for hot kitchens. He had oiled it shiny. She licked her lips again then shook her head, trying to rekindle her anger at this invader.

He watched her watching him. She saw a gentle hunger in his laughing eyes. Not a predatory all-consuming hunger, but the hunger when your appetite has just been whetted, when the saliva flows watery in your mouth and you can barely wait to be satiated. A lazy smile spread from his eyes to his mouth, exposing gleaming teeth, dazzling in the dark planes that made up his face. She squinted at him, trying to block out the glare of his smile. He beamed up at her like the rays of the hot sun searing the jasmine bushes.

For a minute he simply radiated heat and desire. Then he eased back and began talking, soft and gentle, as if to a skittish colt. "Now I know I'm interfering here in your territory, but you know these rich folks, even when they got the best already, they find it hard to appreciate what they got." His gaze fondled her body again. "And I can see they got a lot here to appreciate." He took a step closer. "If I thought I would be a threat to you in any way, I would walk out that door. But Missus Beaumont there has got her heart set on that menu she had me send. And it would be a shame to waste all that food."

Casting his eyes to the floor, he stroked the gleaming countertop, making small circles on the tile with his thumb. "I sure would like to work *with* you, Miss Tara," he said softly. "Nothing makes me happier than cooking with a beautiful woman who's an artist in the kitchen." He kept his head down but moved his eyes up to watch her. "And from what I hear, you're known all over these parts as an artist. Mmmhhhmmm, what I hear you can do with food." He raised his head and looked at her full on. "And when I think about what we could do together, why it just makes my mouth water. Nothing like dancing the food to life with another artist, Miss Tara." He bowed genteelly from the waist and reached for her hand. "Will you dance with me?"

She tried to put him off with a scowl. But he just smiled. Reaching into his pocket, he fished out a small box tied with a lavender ribbon. He presented it to her, holding out his hand flat and steady, waiting patiently, giving her time to come to him. Glowering, she hesitated before reaching out to take the present. Did he really think he could buy her off so easily? Resolving to give it back, whatever it was, she pulled on the bow and removed the lid. A beautiful little stone winked up at her. She reached out a finger and stroked it, the fire of a cat's eye dancing in the light.

"It's a moonstone, Miss Tara. Now I know it's a bit on the extravagant side, but my last big party was for a jeweler and he let me have a choice of a few things as a bonus. This one was small, but when I saw it, well, I don't know why, but I just thought of you, Miss Tara. Let me help you put it on."

Stunned, she allowed him to pick up the necklace and step behind her, draping it around her throat. Tara could feel his breath on the back of her neck and smell the sweetness of his cologne. Her heart began to pound.

"Come on, Miss Tara. Let's step out into the light and see it. 'Sides, I think you promised me a dance." Charles whispered the words into her ear, and Tara felt the heat of his presence behind her. Sweat broke out on her forehead. She stepped towards the door, more to cool off in the breeze than to accede to his endearments. Dizzily she tried to make sense of it all. He'd brought her a gift from the moon! How could he have known? Could the Missus have told him? But the Missus didn't know about that part of her life. No, this must be the answer to what she had prayed for. But was it what she wanted? Reluctantly she allowed him to pull her into a twirl.

He held her close, his feet swift and sure. Then he was waltz-
ing her around the kitchen and out the door. They danced in
the sweet clover grass where just days ago she had lain with
her legs spread, an offering to the moon. She closed her eyes
and let him lead, faster and faster.

She floated in his arms, becoming weightless and small, her
body molding to his rhythm. The sun beat down on her, radi-
ating from him as intensely as it did from the sky. And then
somehow he was behind her. Holding her close with his arms
around her, hugging her, he hummed a tune as he rocked her
back and forth in the morning breeze. A trickle of sweat rolled
down her neck toward her cleavage, caressing the pendant.
He smelled spicy and musky, a little peppery. She inhaled
deeply. His body fit behind her solidly even though she stood
inches taller than he and forty pounds heavier. She leaned into
his swaying, allowing herself to relax a bit, to surrender to the
sun, and the heat, and the man. Sighing, she relinquished her
anger and chose to follow the path the moon had offered her.

"You sure are a great dancer, Miss Tara," he murmured.
"We're a team now, and if you'll let me join you, together
we'll create a feast like nobody's ever seen."

She settled more deeply into him, not worrying that her
bulk would overpower him. A soft moan escaped her. For a
small man he had great strength and agility. She felt his balance shifting slightly with her, letting her know he was in
control, that he was confident in his ability to lead this dance.

"Miss Tara," he whispered again, his spicy breath tickling
her neck. "The Missus thinks I came here to cook for her
party, and I can do that. But I would rather make this dance
with you, this whole night a joy to behold, like it must have
been for the good Lord when He was creating the world.
Only there'll be two of us, so we'll get more gladness out of
it. Why, I expect He'll see us and be downright jealous at the
way we'll dance together." He ran the tip of his tongue lightly

along the edge of her ear and the last of her resistance drifted away with a shiver. He planted a kiss in the hollow where her neck and shoulder met. "Let's make this food a part of our dance, Miss Tara."

I'll pay for this, she thought. But the moon glowed high in the sky and she could feel it tickling the jewel. Earlier she had noticed how the moon and the sun were both shining on her through the window. Together they had raised her temperature even before Mr. Charles had danced his way into her kitchen. The heat had forced her to open the top button on her uniform this morning. And now it encouraged sweat to run down the crevice between her breasts.

The dual light of moon and sun joined the female and male together. It caressed her face as his hands began to caress her body. She drank in the light. She closed her eyes as his hands stroked her arms, her waist, and then her breasts. She made up her mind to let the moon guide her. They said that the moon was the force behind the tides down at Toledo beach. She could let it be her force. He would be her sun. The gleam of his smile and the heat of his personality mingling with her dark yellow glow, all this would warm the night.

Finally, when she thought she could stand this ecstasy no longer, she pulled away. But she turned back quickly to take his hand. "We got work to do," she said. Once she'd made up her mind, it was easy. The power of the moon remained with her, pulsing in the stone, making her movements liquid as she scrubbed and peeled vegetables. He seared the meat and broiled the canapés. She liked watching his quick, efficient movements. His hands deftly turned radishes into beautiful little roses to decorate the plates. The carrots became swirls of orange cascading around trays of succulent pineapple, honeydew, and mango. His strokes with the paring knife as he slit the fruit open were sure and sweet. She admired how each dish got its due—a pat here, a caress there. He kept up a running banter throughout, not seeming to care whether she responded.

She found herself smiling at the way it all seemed to be choreographed. Each of them twirled around the other, working, moving closer and then farther apart. Brushing past the other casually, raising the heat each time. The friction created a spark so hot the kitchen seemed to swell in an effort to contain it. He watched her knead the bread dough, swirling it around in her fingers, working it to the peak of perfection. She allowed it to rise, and rise again. It was the only time that he was quiet. The moon surged within her and she knew they were equals; each had gifts to bring to the other.

She listened while he explained the exotic foods as he worked, turning each lecture into a love song. When he talked about the artichokes he stuffed, he warned her about the outside bristles, how they could prick the skin. "But if you're patient, you get to savor the sweet meat on each leaf and deep in the core." He showed her how to gently scrape off the flesh with her teeth.

She was dripping by the time the meal was served by the silent maids in their black-and-white uniforms. Every pore of her body was open to him, ached for him. It was late. Now the moon poured in through the darkness that had settled over the landscape outside, shining on her dark skin and singing through the stone on her breast. He had faded a bit too. His once-clean white jacket was mussed and stained. The top button lay open and his skin glistened with sweat.

He pulled the dessert from the oven and motioned for her to bring over the chocolate sauce. Islands of meringue swam in the depths of black cherry richness, bubbling temptingly around the edges. Carefully he placed a serving in each dish. Then she drizzled the chocolate in lazy, seductive swirls. Each pass with the spoon was an invitation, each turn of the dish an answer. When the last one was done they stood silently, poised on the edge of the moment, swaying slightly with exhaustion, the soaring heat of the kitchen, and their desire.

She took charge now, dispatching orders to the maids about serving the drinks and cleaning up. Then she reached for him. She took him to her cabin through the moonlight that graced the stone path. The moon encouraged her, pushed her, pulsed in time with her heart.

She left the door open and drew back the curtains. She wanted to see him in all his glory. And glorious he was. She sat on the bed and watched as he slowly unbuttoned his jacket, undid his shoes, and took off his socks, tucking them neatly inside the splattered black footwear. Then he removed and folded his pants, hanging them over the foot of her bed. She liked how neat he was, his body as tidy as his actions. His underwear and his smile gleamed white in the reflected moonlight and then only his smile remained. He spun in the light of the moon, humming that same tune he'd sung when he'd asked her to dance.

She stood to remove her clothing, but he stopped her. Kissing her slowly, his mouth moist with sweat and desire, he took over. He blew on her neck; it was cool and hot at the same time. He stepped behind her, unzipping her damp uniform and pushing the dress down over her shoulders. He nuzzled each shoulder before dropping the dress to the floor. It had been too hot to wear a slip and she was conscious of being exposed. She worried suddenly about her size as his hands roamed over the front of her while his mouth and tongue roamed her back. His thumbs circled her nipples through the cloth of her bra and she arched abruptly, caught by the depth of her arousal. He unhooked the cloth and allowed her breasts to swing free. He moaned a little, kneading her breasts as she had kneaded the bread dough.

Stepping back, he broke the connection to unpin her hair. With his skilled hands he began brushing it, using long gentle strokes with her grandmother's brush. Then he brought a cool cloth and ran it across her body, rinsing away the sweat. She shuddered slightly. No one had tended her like this in a long time. Finishing, he washed his own body. Then he took her hand and turned her around, appraising her in that way he had. Then, in the same singsong voice he'd used to tell her about the artichokes, he described her body, comparing her breasts to the sweetest honeydew melons he could imagine, dark, heavy, rich. He inhaled the smell of them and his tongue traced her nipples. Finally, he popped one into his mouth and sucked, his tongue searching and probing.

"Just like our cherry dessert," he said, and switched to the other dark mound. His hands were on her panties; he slid them down her thighs and allowed them to pool around her feet. "Come, Miss Tara. Dance with me." He pulled her out the open door into the moonlight, and in the shadow of the blooming jasmine they swayed on their feet for a while, drinking in the light of the moon and the kiss of the gentle breeze. The gleam of his smile and the jewel on her breast sparkled. Then, as if planned, they danced into the bedroom. His lips met hers again. She returned his passion, sucking on his tongue, biting his lips. They hungered. They wanted to devour each other.

She couldn't say how or when she ended up on the bed, only felt herself falling onto the feather mattress as she had fallen into his eyes. Tara looked up at him. He stood, caressing her body with a look. She reveled in his admiration.

"We just need one more thing," he said, and, grabbing her old robe, he sprinted across to the kitchen. He returned with the last of the chocolate and triumphantly drizzled it across her body, murmuring that she deserved to be garnished. She squirmed and squealed with pleasure as he licked off the sticky sauce. He compared each part of her body to an exotic food and told her how he would lovingly prepare it. She was flowering, changing beneath his hands, his tongue, and his words, rising like sweet dough. Finally she could stand it no longer and brought him into her, wrapping around him, kneading him with her strong muscles. They climaxed together, fiercely. The moonlight caressed them as they lay in the dying heat.

Tara wriggled her toes in pleasure, stretching like a contented kitten. She loved the way her orgasm passed through her body, traveling down her legs and settling in her feet. His weight descended on her slowly; she felt the slackening in his muscles, the looseness as he gently slid out. She inhaled his peppery, musky smell. The fragrance of his sex, tinged with the scents from their work in the sultry kitchen, was delicious.

He slept, snoring lightly. But she couldn't. She spent hours going over each step; the food birthed together under their joint parentage, the sensuous smells, the ability to anticipate the other's movements. She hugged all these memories to her heart as she wanted to hug him. Instead, she stroked his back lightly so as not to disturb him. She wanted this moment to go on just a bit longer before she had to face the kitchen alone.

The new day was coming on fast. Their loving had lasted most of the night. The sun's morning rays nibbled on the edge of the horizon. The moon hadn't yet gone down—nor had the pounding in her veins ceased. Suddenly she hated the sun, cursing it for bringing her this sweet morsel and now coming to take him away from her.

He responded to her caress and snuggled his head down on her chest. She smiled at him. He was so small yet so perfectly formed, like a miniature god nestled in her arms. She liked the image of holding God. Overlooking the blasphemy, she thought about what a good lover he was. She yearned to have him tease her again with his tongue, taste her ears and neck, nuzzle her breasts, and feast at the sweetness between her legs. She heard again the sweet phrases he had spoken, how he planned to work his magic and skill on the banquet that was Tara. Beneath his touch and fingers, words and tongue, she felt beautiful. He appreciated her size and muscles, her meatiness and strength, her artistry both in the kitchen and in bed.

A small tear rolled down her cheek. It had been too sweet, like the pain in your head on a blistering summer day when you sucked in that first huge mouthful of ice cream. You wanted it so badly that the shock and pleasure reverberated throughout your body and focused on one nerve in your head. The anticipation had been like that. She had known somehow that the sweetness of the night would turn into the painful cold of the morning. But she couldn't have stopped herself. Nothing else would do but to drink in as much of him as she could. She clutched this ache to her too, allowing the tears to roll down her cheeks and neck, to wet the pendant, now cool on her chest. Silently she sobbed, not wanting to disturb him, not wanting this moment to end.

He shifted slightly and his face moved closer to her neck and found the small pool of her tears. Instantly he was awake. He assessed her with hooded eyes. Would he get up, begin the going-away process?

He smiled his big brash smile and propped up his head with one hand. With the other he traced the tracks of her tears. "Miss Tara, no need to be crying now. We made us the sweetest dance last night."

She smiled, trying to hide the fear creeping through her stomach. He moved down, closing his mouth over her tears. He kissed and licked them away. When he rose again a seriousness rested behind the light in his eyes. "Seems to me there is some bitterness in those tears. Is this going to happen every time we dance?"

She searched his face, checking for any falseness in his words. What did he mean, "every time we dance?" She couldn't reply—just looked at him, frozen, wondering.

He laughed, yawned, stretched his arms over his head and rolled away from her. "You aren't much of a talker, Miss Tara," he said. Stretching some more, he rolled back to her. His fingers traced a pattern on her stomach. "But I like that. You're like a wonderful stew—pretending to be simple, just hearty and filling, yet really subtle and deep. Well, it's okay, Miss Tara, I'll talk enough for the both of us." He blew all over her body, chasing away the sweat. "Making a good stew takes time, you know. You've got to tend it well, stir it up. Add a little spice now and then. And you want to make sure never to burn it." He stopped and looked deeply into her eyes. "I never ruined a stew in my life, Miss Tara. And I won't leave this one unattended. I already told Mr. Beaumont that we would need to come to an understanding about my staying on here." He hesitated. "Of course, that is if you'll have me. What do you say, can I add a new ingredient to your stew?"

She let out her breath and smiled up at him contentedly. He grinned at the change in her. He cocked his head to one side for a moment then reached down to kiss her, a slow velvety kiss that tasted of salt and sweat and chocolate and lovemaking. Tears welled up again in her eyes and he kissed those too.

"I can see I won't have to worry about this ever being bland," he laughed. "Plenty of spice here." His lips found hers again, his tongue probing deeply inside, lingering as he mixed their juices together. He finally pulled away and they both gulped for breath.

A ray of sunshine broke through the window and splashed across them. It lit him up from behind like the god she had imagined him to be. She caressed his cheek, the moon's promise beating securely in her heart and in the gem on her breast. Finally she spoke.

"What would you like for breakfast, Mr. Charles?"

Rope Burn

Anne Tourney

This place is still raw, the channel between my thigh and pussy. Pink, moist, and rickracked by the hairs of a ghost rope. When I touch the tender strip, the skin stings. The pain calls up a vision of a woman spinning naked on a long cord, her legs spread in a ballerina's arc, fingers grasping the highest knots. I can't reconcile that vision with what I've learned about Mary June. I don't imagine her as a suicidal woman but a sexual one with a fascination for the promises of rope.

A fascination like mine.

I went to Mary June's house to work through a dry spell in my master's thesis. I told myself that I needed silence and distance, but what I really wanted was for time to stop. Two years of graduate school had taught me that I knew almost nothing about my thesis topic, the interwoven coils of rural American family life. Most of those strands in my own past had been torn, either by spite or circumstance. When I thought about my own frayed relationships I wondered where I had found the nerve to write about strangers' bonds.

I chose a town within driving distance of the university, a town known for its orchards of crooked apple trees. The house sat uneasily at the outskirts of the little community, leaning on its foundations as if it expected to be forced to flee. A long scrabbly field separated the house and barn from the main road. As I drove down the rutted path, I could see my landlady standing in the open doorway, her arms crossed over her chest. That stern silhouette sent a wave of guilt rushing through me. It was a guilt I couldn't explain, hot and absurd, like the backwash of someone else's shame. She frowned at my tank top and shorts as I hauled in the books that would keep me company that summer.

"Didn't expect you to bring a whole library," my land-lady said. She led me through a parlor—I had an impression of yellowed lace and sepia shadows—and down a narrow hallway to the bedroom that would be mine. I set my box of books down on the floor. Dust rose in a soft exhalation, as if a restless spirit were welcoming me.

"Maybe I could store some of my books in the barn."

She shook her mule-gray head. "The barn is full of rusted machinery. You'd get tetanus just looking at that mess."

But when I glanced out the window I saw light spearing through the cracks in the barn's wallboards, suggesting that there was open space inside.

"Has this always been a guest room?" I asked.

The room's former occupant had left no imprint; all sensuous memory had been stripped from the room. The paint on the windowsills had flaked away and the wallpaper seemed to have been torn off by hand, leaving only a few shreds of yellow fluttering against the plaster. *It's only twenty-five dollars a week,* I reminded myself. *For twenty-five dollars I can tolerate bleak décor.*

"My girl used to stay here. My boy stayed in the room opposite." With a jerk of her head the woman indicated the closed door across the hall.

The words *girl* and *boy* threw me. Was my landlady referring to farm help or to a daughter and son? I tried to imagine her spare, hard body carrying children. As a would-be sociologist I felt as if I had some kind of responsibility to ask about her life, her family, but her dry words invited no further questioning.

"No visitors after dark," she said. "And no drinking." Then she left.

I had the dream on the very first night, the dream that would wake me almost every night I spent in that house. It was always one step ahead of my consciousness, jumping out of my grasp whenever I tried to remember it. But I know it recurred because I always woke up in the same state: paralyzed, bound. Feeling absolutely alone yet strangely safe. Once the fog of sleep cleared I wondered what was holding me here in this room, which offered no sensory comfort, no release from its emptiness. Why didn't I just leave?

On many nights I heard the woman of the house turning fitfully in her bed, as if she shared my anxiety. The floorboards creaked as she padded down the hall to the bathroom; the heavy porcelain toilet seat clinked as she sat down to relieve herself. I could hear the sounds her body made, hear her sigh, hear her splashing water on her hands. What would happen if I walked out into the hallway to meet her? If I opened my arms to her, would her stony flesh soften against my body?

Days in my room were dim and airless, like abandoned mine shafts. I spent hours watching the stretch of blowzy weeds that lay between my window and the battered, naked barn. The structure was broad and tall, with secretive windows set high on its peeling face. One afternoon, when I was exhausted from avoiding work, I snuck outside to have a look. I could feel the landlady watching me from the kitchen window, probably thinking what a nosy fool I was. The gravel bit into my bare knees as I crouched down and peered through a crack in the door of the barn. When I saw the interior, I forgot that small discomfort. I almost forgot to breathe.

The barn was as empty and numb with light as a church without pews, except for a woman who hung—naked—from a rope on the ceiling. She drifted like a trapeze artist, her thighs curved around the shaft of the rope, her head thrown back. Her vulva was opened coarsely by the rope's weave, her damp lips sucking the thick strand. With one graceful surge she lifted her body, cunt clinging as she rose, and whirled slowly in the pillar of a sunbeam. The tips of her long barley-blonde hair tickled the cleft of her buttocks, and my skin tingled in sympathy. She played games with the rope, made love to it, licking and caressing the cords. Embracing a knot at the base of the rope with the soles of her nude feet, she bent and straightened her knees in a sensual plié.

The sight of that slow-motion, self-loving dance was agonizing. I wanted to feel that rough, prolonged friction, too, all along the velvet canal that started between my breasts and ended between my ankles. I wanted to arch backwards like her, arms fully extended to hold my weight, head flung back, eyelids flickering under the dust that trickled down from the eaves.

Who was the woman? I hadn't seen her on my few trips into town. Even if I had, she might have been disguised as a shy country wife, or an overpainted cocktail waitress. I watched her face flush, her muscles tighten. As she reached the orgasm she thought was private, her body quivered all along its length like a bow after the arrow leaves. Ashamed as I was for watching, I could hardly stand the excitement of it. I closed my eyes, wondering if I was losing my mind, but when I looked again the vision was as tangible as my own flesh.

The woman's shoulders sank, her entire body trembling from her orgasm. My trance ended. I scrambled to my feet and raced back to the house. In the kitchen I collided with my landlady, who had been lingering over a sink full of dishes.

"There's someone outside," I panted. "Someone in the barn." My face was hot, as if I'd participated in that intimate dance.

The landlady stared. In her eyes I saw myself being measured up.

"No one has been in that barn for nine years."

"But I saw a woman. A woman about my age, with long blonde hair. She was hanging on a rope—"

The landlady's face crumpled. A moan leaked from her mouth. The glass mixing bowl she had been drying fell to the floor, bounced once, and cracked.

"Leave my house," she hissed.

Mumbling apologies, I fled.

Still flushed from the erotic dance I'd seen, I was too full of heat and longing to realize how deeply I had shocked the woman. I didn't know what to do with my desire. I wanted to find someone to pound it out of me, a crazy man to fuck me till my pulse finally slowed. I had come to that house, to that slumbering town, to finish something that I had to do in order to become someone better. But in four weeks I'd written close to nothing. I'd given up ambition as easily as a healthy habit.

I wandered up and down the town's main drag all afternoon, stopping at a pool hall near dusk. There was only one other female in the bar, a mountainous woman whose bosom spilled across the table where she sat. A shot glass rested, thimblelike, between her breasts. A lean man, maybe thirty-five, sat beside her. His face was unexceptional until he smiled at me. I saw in his eyes the light I was looking for, a glint of dementia. I imagined his face rising up from between my spread thighs, saw his mouth devouring me like a jackal. He beckoned to me, and I sank into a seat at their table.

"You from around here?" The man leaned closer as he spoke. His brown skin smelled of wind-dried sweat. His eyes were as pale as new nickels.

"I'm just here for the summer. I'm renting a room at the farmhouse on Mullen Road."

"That was Mary June's place," the woman said. "Did you hear that, John?"

Without responding, the man got up and went to the bar. He returned with a glass of amber elixir and offered it to me.

"Who's Mary June?" I sipped the whiskey. Heavy and smooth, it plunged straight through me, making my cunt tingle. The man called John had long creases down his tanned cheeks; I wanted to trace those salty grooves with my tongue. His lean hands caressed his beer bottle as if they were entertaining ideas of their own.

"Who is Mary June?" I repeated, my voice thick and slow.

"That's the wrong question, honey," said the woman. "The question should be who *was* Mary June."

"And what's the answer?"

"A pretty girl who died of shame."

"Women don't die of shame. That's crazy."

"It sure is," John agreed. "It's crazy and wrong. Mary June never felt a moment of shame in her life."

"Did she have long hair? Blonde?"

"Blonde and shiny, like grain piled up in the sun. All the way down to her waist. Sounds like you've seen her."

"I couldn't have seen her if she's dead."

"Why not?" John shrugged, as if the dead had as much right to make themselves seen as anyone else.

"I don't believe in ghosts."

"I didn't say you saw a ghost. Maybe Mary June just left a piece of herself for someone to find."

I made a scoffing noise, a snort that made me sound bolder than I felt. A cold awareness was spreading across my skin. My body knew Mary June's story before I had even heard it. My body experienced her climax on the rope. My body did not care if the girl who did that ropedance was a flesh-and-blood mortal, a hallucination, or a phantom.

As I was absorbing what John had said, one of his firm hands came to rest on my thigh. His fingers slipped under the fuzzy hem of my cutoffs and tugged at the edge of my panties, still sticky from that bewildering vision in the barn.

"Come for a ride with me and I'll tell you who Mary June was." John stood up, his hand gliding along my leg. Mesmerized, I stood up too.

The woman swayed in drunken clairvoyance. "Careful, honey," she cooed. "You don't even know who he is."

"Who are you?" I asked, my caution blurred by desire.

John grabbed my waist with both hands and pressed the length of his body against mine. His wiry muscles reminded me of the braided strands of a leather whip. He bent his head to whisper in my ear, and his smooth lips grazed the lobe.

"I'm the local expert on Mary June," he said, with a softness I found both startling and sweet. "You might even say I was her brother."

Mary June used to sneak out of her bedroom while her mother was watching Johnny Carson to take long rides in men's cars through night country, headlights off. Mary June wore short chiffon skirts that flew up around her waist in the spring and stuck to her thighs in the summer. She left her panties either in her laundry basket back home or balled up under the seats of her lovers' cars. Cars were her favorite place to fuck, her legs spread in a reckless *V* while her lover bucked inside her. She always laughed while she was making love, even when she was coming, as if she were trying to make up for the silence she kept inside her foster mother's house. Eventually her laughter drove the men away and they spread the rumor that Mary June screwed like a mad hyena bitch. Only her brother knew how to make the laughter stop.

Mary and John had arrived at the farm on Mullen Road on a summer day, just before harvest time. Two weeds plucked from a foster home, the girl and boy held hands as they confronted the woman who would be their guardian. Though they weren't related by blood, the children were tied together by coincidence and desperation. Both had been assigned the surname *Smith*. To escape the anonymity of this name they added their birth months, becoming Mary June and John March.

When the children weren't laboring on the farm, they invented games that involved one kind of prison or another. Mary June loved these games, seeking places in the woods where she could act out her dreams of being bound in coils of rope. She became a prisoner of Martians, evil cowboys, or— her most cherished fantasy—a corrupt county sheriff. The threat of law pleased her, gave her a sense of ritual and weight.

As she and John grew older, familiar games turned strange and the rope took on a life of its own. John learned how to make Mary June moan, even cry when the pain was especially sweet. But pain became a weak substitute for the contact that Mary June craved. None of the horny boys in their muscle cars could do for her what John March could do—if only he would enter her.

Although he refused to touch Mary June's berry-ripe nipples or her swollen pussy, John was the only one who could make her cunt dissolve in a shuddering meltdown. All he had to do was watch her peel her flimsy dress off then wrap her nude body in intricate knots. Tighter, tighter he pulled the rope, until her tender flesh burned. When she lay on her back in the deep woods, her wrists and ankles bound, Mary June never laughed. She was paralyzed by an arousal edged with fear—fear of wild animals, of other men, of the possibility that John might leave her there with her fear and desire and no place to put them.

"There's no blood between us," she pleaded. "We're only brother and sister by accident. Why can't you just get inside me?"

"It's an accident that the whole town believes in," John March said. "If you want me to make love to you, you'll have to leave with me."

But Mary June would not leave the farmhouse. Although she had never called her foster mother "mama," a bond had grown between the two women that John March would never understand.

As he spoke, John March drove me through the humid night. His hand found my thigh again, dipped down to the silky hot patch, and rested there. We rode past the orderly shadows of the orchards, past the farms that lay beyond them, to the place where the woods began. He stopped where the road ended and helped me out of the car. My knees were wobbly, my shorts slippery from the pleasure his voice had been giving me. The darkness swelled with an outcry of frogs, the occasional warning of an owl. John led me through the trees. I couldn't see anything but the white curve of my outstretched arm, but he somehow recognized a trail.

"Strip," he said hoarsely. "Strip like Mary June did."

I stumbled out of my shorts and giggled as my arms tangled in my T-shirt. John stood behind me, watching me twist out of my panties. I held my hands together behind my back so he could tie the rope around my wrists. He pushed me to my knees and tied my ankles, too, with the rope running upward to encircle my neck. A mosquito landed on my breast and pierced the wrinkly skin of my nipple. I flinched. The rope responded instantly by squeezing my throat.

"Hold still, prisoner," John whispered. His chapped palms cupped my breasts, gently squeezed. I moaned, but I was afraid. If I moved, the rope would strangle me. I thought I could hear Mary June's ghost-breath in the darkness, and I understood why she hadn't laughed. The hands massaging my breasts grew rough. I whimpered. The rope was already chafing my wrists. I wasn't aroused anymore, only frightened. When I heard John unzipping his jeans, I panicked; my body jerked, and the rope tightened around my throat. For a moment my breath left me. When it came back, I screamed.

John knelt beside me, gripping me by the shoulders. "Shush, shush," he murmured into my hair. When my muscles were soft again, he untied me, but the sensation of the rope never left my skin.

"How did Mary June die?" I asked.

John wouldn't tell me. Instead he described the time Mary June had revealed that she had learned how to do something extraordinary, something she'd seen herself doing in a dream. John told me how Mary June's body looked, slim and golden, when she performed her "circus act" for him in the barn. He watched her, his cock leaping inside his jeans, while she twisted on the rope in a spectacle of aerial freedom, bellowing like Tarzan one minute, soaring like a Balanchine dancer the next. When she descended they tumbled into a hot rut, all haste and gratitude. After they had dozed awhile in the August light, he turned her over on her back. If he could make her come over and over again, he thought, until she couldn't speak enough to protest, he could carry her off the farm. But just when he had teased her with his tongue until she was as weak as a new lamb, so limp that he could have lifted her with one hand, their foster mother found them.

John March was driven out of the house. Mary June was allowed to stay, but she was no longer free in any sense. She hid in her room, door locked, while her mother called her vile names through the keyhole. The foster mother knelt down the way Mary June used to when she was sucking a lover's cock, but instead of hot love there came icy words, words that froze her daughter's blood. Without blood there was no desire. Without the rope there was no freedom.

"I'm not going back to that woman's house," I said.

"You don't have to go back," said John. "One thing Mary June never learned was not to stay where she wasn't wanted. She could have left with me. But she wouldn't leave that woman."

"What finally happened?"

John was silent for a moment. "Mary June hanged herself. Our foster mother found her in the barn."

"Hanged herself," I echoed. Now I understood why I had shocked my landlady so deeply. I had seen an enchanted creature dancing on a rope, but my landlady had remembered a suicide. "Did she really do it out of shame?"

"There's no way Mary June was ashamed. She was proud of the way she was. Proud of her pretty titties, her sweet-tasting pussy. She didn't care what people said."

"Why did she do it, then?"

"How can anyone know? No one knows but Mary June. All I've got to go on is a theory."

"What theory?"

"Mary June hanged herself because she was somehow tied to that old bitch—more tightly than she was ever tied to me."

John's voice trembled. He caught himself before it broke.

This time John tied me differently. The rope snaked around my wrists, knees, and thighs, but left my vulva exposed, the lips spread like split fruit. I shivered as a night breeze sucked at my inner flesh. John's tongue was hot when it dove into the cleft. *I don't know this mouth,* I thought, but it didn't matter because Mary June had known it. His tongue searched the whorls of my cunt, hunting my clit, and his fingers gripped my thighs until I felt bruises blossoming. The rope burned my skin as I squirmed. John slid upward. His face gleamed over mine, predatory. I felt his cock drumming against my belly, but when he slid into me I wasn't ready for its girth. I screamed again—not with fear this time. My instinct was to clutch his back with my arms and legs, but they were bound. I was nothing but open mouth and open cunt, taking the beating of his chest against mine.

"Just lie there," he muttered through clenched teeth. "Nothing else you can do."

Nothing else. Was that what Mary June thought the last time she felt a rope against her skin? I could see her with that rope, alone in the barn, the weight of the body slight compared to that of her sadness.

I wasn't anything like Mary June. When I came with that crazy man, I forgot what I was like at all, but there was no sadness in me. Only burning pleasure under fiery skin, and the thunder of all my captive pulse points. The more I struggled to fulfill my orgasm the longer it was delayed, until the climax turned into a slow, swollen river. My lover bit my nipple, forcing me to peak.

I screamed for the third time as his cock hit my core. I couldn't clutch his back, couldn't raise my head to bite his neck—I went crazy that night from not being able to seize him the way he seized me when his body turned iron in one heartbeat, and his shout silenced all the wild things in the forest.

When you're tied like that, your will is taken away, and your accountability. You're roped to your desire. You can't turn away from it any longer. There's nothing else to turn to.

In the morning I returned to Mary June's house. I didn't have a choice. My books were there, and my notes—all the small things that made up my life. When I saw the house from a distance, standing at the end of a sere stretch of brown land, I thought its frame was leaning even more dramatically. The structure wasn't preparing to flee, as I had first thought; it was ready to collapse. For the first time I noticed all the remnants of farm life that surrounded it: the empty barn, the ramshackle livestock pen, the unidentifiable skeletons of broken tools.

I tried to imagine how two orphaned children would have seen the place when they first arrived. An abundance of space and life, a host of animals to care for, and at the center of all that, a woman who might be won over if the boy and girl could figure out how to pry open her padlocked heart. I could see how the farm might have thrived for a while. With the children's help the livestock would have grown fat, the small crop of grain would have flourished. But when Mary June left, withdrawing her heathen sensuality from the earth, the land hardened itself against the old woman in the house. The livestock sickened. Wherever life had proliferated, it withered.

My books, papers, and clothes lay heaped in open boxes in front of the farmhouse. One of my lacy bras lay on the gravel, embedded in the rocks as if someone had ground it down with a sharp heel. My books had been thrown facedown into the boxes, splayed open so that their spines had cracked. I knew the woman in the house was watching as I unpacked my things, brushed away the grit, and repacked them. I saw the flicker of her hand pushing back the curtain in the parlor. I took my time getting my books stacked just right, my clothes neatly folded. I picked up my bra and blew the dust out of the lace eyelets with deliberate puffs of breath. I hoped she would think of Mary June as she watched me. When I was done, I stood up straight and stared at the parlor window until her shadow finally backed away.

I'm in the car now, driving back to campus, to my old life at the university. I have all four windows rolled down, my thighs spread so that the breeze blows down the hem of my cutoffs, licking the secret raw space. In the seat next to me lies the rope John March gave me. It's coiled like a Celtic symbol, its ends disappearing in the endless loop. Its patterns, its cross-hatched strands are etched on my skin, as meaningful as the intersection of lovers, mothers, siblings.

This is my Mary June rope. I imagine it's the same rope she used for her slow, spinning dance in the barn. Who's to say it's not? The strands keep their dusty secrets wrapped up tight, but I learned some of those secrets from Mary June: how desire can hold its opposite; how captivity can bring you more freedom than you ever thought possible.

The Mark

Helena Settimana

I can make my mark within thirty seconds of the warning whistle blowing and the doors sliding shut behind me—that is, if there's someone to make. I like to play during rush hour, at the end of a long day when all the office folk are returning from their anonymous little cubicles in the towers of the city. I work best when it's crowded, packed like the proverbial sardines in a can: that's when it's safest and the most fun. If I'm wrong and a mark turns out to be no good, I can get away, or maybe he won't know who is at him because it's so crowded. Either way it's a rush.

It's my thing, but sometimes, like the other day, I work with Jay, my partner in this little game. It turns him on to get in on the action. Turns me on too. I mean, that's why I do it, right?

I look for the type who's most likely to let me do a little business. I don't do the derelicts, and not too often the blue-collar types. I have standards to uphold. I mark the guys who look like they've got the big-digit jobs in finance or are lawyers, accountants, traders. Some look like they hold the collection platters in their churches on Sundays and help little old ladies cross the street. Guys who live their quietly desperate lives with little complaint but deep down yearn to kick over the traces, throw off the yoke. They have dogs named Sandy and 2.2 kids and wives who are perfect and groomed or (I would like to imagine) cold and distant. Or drunk. Or messed up on Valium. Anything to make the game OK. Jay doesn't care about conscience. He just wants to watch.

I spotted him right away. This one was a little different; black and as big as a linebacker, wearing a camel topcoat. Tailored, natty even. I could make out his trousers and jacket. Dark brown, finely textured wool made him look sort of monochromatic. French pleats in the pants; I made a little wager with myself that he was wearing boxers underneath.

Jay and I squeezed through the stacked commuters until I could slide in beside him. He had one hand on the pole to steady himself and the other hanging limply by his side. His briefcase was held unsteadily between his feet—mahogany-colored brogues, expensive-looking. The grasping hand was decorated with a chunky gold chain and the cufflink showed. It had a garnet stone set into it.

There's something in the faces of these guys who let me at them on the trains. I can see that this guy is one of those who might fancy himself a player, but he's pounded his round peg into the square hole of domesticity and the nine-to-five workday.

Jay pressed up behind me. More people squeezed onto the train at the next stop and I moved closer to the guy in the camel coat. Jay was moving his hips subtly against my ass, with the train rocking all of us back and forth. He snaked one hand up under my jacket and around in front where it brushed my breast, and then pinched one nipple, hard. I could feel his hardness, his heat through his jeans and my skirt. I felt breathless, wanton, and daring.

Another stop, and the whistle blew, shooing one load of passengers off and ushering another on board before the doors slid closed again. Jay whispered in my ear, "Is he the one you're gonna do? Better hurry before we get to his stop."

More people crowded in so that I was now almost nestled under the big guy's uplifted arm. He was looking down toward his feet. Jay was becoming impatient, kissing my neck a bit, putting on a show for the passengers, pushing at my rear insistently. The train lurched as it rounded a bend in the tunnel and I fell against Mr. Camel-coat. I was right up against him. I got up my nerve, wriggled my hand in close, and brushed it down the front of his trousers. Slowly. I felt his body tense up and I held my breath, praying that he wouldn't freak and grab my wrist before I had a chance to get out of there.

Nothing.

Encouraged, I ventured a slow return up the front of the guy's pants. He straightened up and stood a bit taller; that was all. I applied a bit of pressure—not really a grab, just pressure, to test the waters. The big guy cautiously pushed back. I cupped my hand and placed it squarely over his fly. Curled my fingers around his nuts.

I wanted him to feel me, to know that it was more than his imagination. I was holding him firmly by the balls. He was erect under those nicely made trousers. I had won my bet with myself. Boxers. I bit my lip.

Jay's hands were on my thighs, and he hiked my skirt up a bit. He pulled it up directly in front of him, standing so close as to block the view of just about anyone except for Joe Camel. He was so tall—"Joe," that is. I could see him out of the corner of my eye, looking down at us and then around a bit and then down at me again, as if to confirm that, yes, I was the most likely candidate among the passengers to be stroking his cock through those smart French-pleated pants.

The beauty of playing this game in this city is that everyone is so fucking indifferent to what's going on around them. No one looks at anyone else on the train. No one speaks to strangers. Jay was grinding his cock on my ass. It was rock hard: a diamond-cutter hard-on. I wanted to jump all over it; let it all out and come before the game was over, screaming for all I was worth. But screaming is not an option in the game—everything becomes internalized, that's part of why it's so intense. Last one to come wins.

I was heavy between the legs, aroused. If anyone could see this going down...well, I expect that we would still proceed unmolested by our fellow travelers. Best they'd do is shoot us a dirty look, maybe cluck a little. Besides, they're Canadian, and way too polite to intervene. I stake my reputation on it.

Mr. Camel-coat had made a quarter-turn toward me, which made it a bit awkward to keep a hold on him with my left hand. I ventured a glance at his face, which had turned a remarkable shade of purple—aubergine. He had weird eyes—hazel, almost green. He looked around desperately—everywhere but at me, at us. He was enjoying it, but he wanted it to be totally anonymous, totally out of his control, out of his responsibility. Jay wouldn't look either. He was rolling his hips and jabbing his cock into my hip. It actually hurt.

Camel-coat's mouth was open a little bit, the pink tip of his tongue just visible, and there were little glassy pearls of sweat on his upper lip and forehead. He was still not going to make eye contact. No way. This guy would die before he did that. Naw...this ain't happening to him. *No way. No how. Aw geez*...I could hear him telling his friends later, "You'll never *believe* what happened to me on the way home from work..."

The train swayed into the next station and the three of us froze, locked up, while the crowd shifted and rearranged itself around us. As we began to move again I felt Jay's joint burning against me; his big ol' stump promising me something more. He was whispering to me, telling me not to lose it, not to give it away.

How brave would I be? Jay was intent, standing behind me with his hands gripping my shoulders. I moved a bit so that I could face the big guy, shoving my belly squarely against him. If there's one thing that turns me on it's the hot pressure of a cock straining through clothing against my abdomen. It's as if I have a hot wire running from my bellybutton to my pussy. Maybe it comes from the days of high school dances, where the most exciting thing that could happen was to have your partner pop a woody on the dance floor while the DJ played "Stairway to Heaven."

I pushed a little closer and brushed my tits on the buttons of Joe Camel's coat. My breath caught and my pulse roared in my ears so loudly it drowned out the racket of the train. I rolled into him and he pushed back, grinding in short sharp arcs, like he was desperate to come but afraid of being too obvious.

I shot him another glance and caught him trying to do the same, only to look away sharply as our eyes were about to meet. His mouth was open a bit more, and there was a thin line of moisture running in the cleft of his lower lip. I was overcome. My fingers explored the outline of his dick and worked their way to his zipper. To my delight he let go of his hold on the pole and shrugged off his coat, throwing it casually over the crook of one arm so it hung down in the front and obscured my hands from view. The train lurched, causing him to flail for a handhold again. The dress shirt he wore under his jacket was stuck to his chest with perspiration. Up close I could see his tiny, coiled black chest hairs through the translucent fabric.

I was inside the guy's pants, fishing for the opening in his shorts. His cock was burning hot and a little damp from perspiration and the slow leak of fluid from the tip. I removed my hand for a moment and paused, looking up at him, daring him to look back. He tried: his cat eyes hooded and dark-rimmed; irises, pupils darting beneath their screen of lashes. I licked my fingers deliberately and watched his face convulse before slipping back inside and closing my fingers around him. He increased his pressure and rhythm on me at the same time. I caught the scent of myself; earthy, spiced, musky—I knew he could smell me, too. The head of his cock was slick and I pulled, unfolding its length and drawing it slowly out into the open, where I could rub it against my belly. I could only see a bit; the rest was obscured by the coat. He wasn't cut, so the head peeked out of its hiding place a little paler than the skin around it. I gripped it tightly and made small circles on the head, pushing my hand down sharply so that it popped through my closed fist. One, two, three, four, circle, one, two, three...

Jay was in my ear again, suddenly all attention, murmuring, "I love you baby, make him come for me baby, you get him, you *get* him, you *got* him! Make him come, make him come on you."

I was dying for this huge, shy man to look at me. I stared right up at his face, drawing an imaginary line in the sand, daring him to look—I mean, really *look*. His back arched, and his mouth twisted into a feral leer, but those heavy eyes avoided mine. I would not look away. His cock get thicker, harder, hotter and by his look, well, I knew he was finished. He bit his lower lip, jabbing up into my fist and I jabbed it right back at him. Jay devoured the back of my neck, telling me how he was gonna rip a hole through his chinos if he couldn't get a piece damn soon. He hissed soft encouragements, daring the guy to blow and warning me to hold out.

The guy looked at me.

In that moment, Mr. Joe Camel, ordinary guy in a natty brown suit, back arched in obvious throes of orgasmic pleasure, opened his weird olive eyes and stared at me.

The train came to a rocking halt in the station. I pumped that guy near to death. I felt his knees buckle a bit, standing up close and private like that, and he made a sound like a muffled bellow, an invisible hand clamped over his mouth. Ribbons of jism sailed through the air like ticker tape to alight on my blouse, skirt, and that natty dress coat of his. An alarm sounded somewhere in the distance. As the whistle blew, Jay jerked hard on my arm and we fled like thieves out the doors. I glanced back through the windows of the compartment at the tableau we had left behind.

Scandal and disbelief registered on the faces of our fellow travelers, their mouths frozen in little "ohs" while the man with the camel-colored coat tried desperately to cover his dying erection. It nodded at the thinning crowd. The train lurched into motion. We raced down the platform and up the escalator.

Bursting into the cool evening air, laughing like lunatics, we headed for an alley where I would gladly let Jay win the game.

Waste

Lisa Glatt

Skipper and I are having problems. He's dissatisfied. It's all there in his face, in his flushed, unshaven face, all the problems we are having, all his dissatisfaction. He bites his lower lip and scrunches his eyes together and doesn't even look like Skipper.

We've been together for six years with good sex two to four times a week and decent conversations, then last Sunday morning over coffee and bran muffins his face changes shape; he's hard to recognize. Really. And he looks at me and blurts out that he's never been happy with me, that I've never made him completely happy. He says that I've never fully satisfied him, sexually, that is. I tell him that he's the best sex I've ever had and besides that, there's love here. Right, I tell him, right? And Skipper looks over my head, out the window, maybe at the oak outside the window, and says nothing.

Later that same Sunday Skipper returns from grocery shopping and I'm standing in the kitchen pouring wine into glasses, wearing his favorite black teddy. I help him unpack the groceries and feel silly putting away milk and onions and cheese in such an outfit. Skipper sets the toilet paper on the table. I hand him the razors and soap. It's fine, he says, you look great. But his face looks weird, like he doesn't mean it.

We sit on the couch, drinking. Skipper doesn't look any more familiar and I don't feel any less silly. This was a bad idea, I say.

What can I do? What do you want me to do? I say, and as soon as the words leave my lips I regret them.

You could pee on me, Skipper says. If you loved me you would pee on me.

Skipper thinks all our problems stem from the fact that I refuse (have always refused) to pee on him. If you did this one thing for me one time, Skipper says, you'd see that it's OK, you'd see me love it, and that would make it OK for you— better than OK. Skipper says that he's never loved anyone as much as he loves me and that he's never asked anyone else for urine. And that's why, Skipper says, he's never been peed on. It doesn't occur to Skipper that the other women he slept with, but didn't quite love, might not have peed on him either; I am the only woman in the world selfish enough to refuse him.

Debra would have peed on me, Skipper says nostalgically.

Then why don't you ask Debra? Why don't you call Debra right now, this minute, and ask her? I say.

Because I didn't love Debra the way I love you, he explains. I didn't trust her the same way.

Maybe you should have, I tell him.

Pee isn't such a big fucking thing to ask for, Skipper says. And he puts his wine down and walks to the den.

A couple of days later I'm eating lunch at Sam's Seafood with my best friend Claire. Claire has just finished telling me about her new lover, Lilly. Lilly, Claire says, is the most gifted woman in the world. Lilly, Claire says, is the most generous. No one gives like Lilly, she says, winking. Good, good, I say absently, and I must look upset—maybe my face too is changing shape under all this pressure—because now Claire won't let up. What's wrong with the two of you? she keeps saying. And I surprise myself when I blurt out, Skipper wants me to pee on him, he's always wanted me to pee on him. I tell Claire that Skipper's blowing this pee thing out of proportion, that he's blaming my refusal for his every unhappiness. Claire is trying not to laugh. She raises the napkin to her mouth and pretends to wipe something away. And the laugh is there, there in her napkin.

Is this funny? I say. Claire, what the hell's so funny. Skipper's face is all skewed up into a stranger's face, he wants my urine, and you're laughing.

I'm sorry. I'm really sorry, Claire says.

I tell Claire that I can't pee on Skipper, that I can't imagine my life without him but I can't imagine peeing on him either. If I peed on him, I say, I wouldn't be able to look at myself, talk to my mother on the phone, or pee the same way ever again.

Claire puts the napkin in her lap. She leans in. Maybe there's something else wrong with the two of you, maybe Skipper's using this pee thing as an excuse to leave you, maybe it's symptomatic, she says.

He really wants me to pee. He's wanted it from the beginning. You just don't know, I tell her.

The waiter pops out of nowhere and sets two bowls of creamy soup in front of us. He smiles oddly at me, like he knows, like he stood somewhere listening.

Can I get you anything else? he says. Perhaps some water?

I think I see a smirk. We're fine, I tell him.

Did he hear us? Do you think he heard us? I ask Claire. Who?

The waiter, did he hear what we were saying?

Don't worry about it. It doesn't matter.

But if he heard...

Claire interrupts me then and says, You can't worry about what people think. You just can't. She picks up her spoon and says, I read about a man once who would only have sex with his wife if she barked like a dog. Imagine, barking like a dog—for your husband. This is different, I say.

Maybe, she says.

The first year Skipper and I were together, I thought he would grow out of this urine thing. I thought it was more a fantasy than something he really wanted. The night he brought it up, we were in bed, my head on his stomach. I was looking at the wall, noticing the cracked, yellowish paint. If this room's going to be our room, I said, we should paint it. What do you think of one red wall?

Red walls drive people insane, he said. It's been proven.

What about a rose color then—a pale, pale red?

Maybe, he said. And moments later, with his hand in my hair, he asked, What do you think about urine?

Urine?

Urine.

We were at that stage in our relationship where I wanted so badly to be loved by him that I said things not necessarily reflecting my own feelings—things meant to please, to entice, and to mystify him.

I've never thought much about it. What about it?

Do you think it's ugly?

Not really ugly. Necessary, I said, urine is necessary.

Do you think it's sexual?

I'm not sure. It might be sexual.

And later, watching him sleep, watching his tough jaw, his barely open lips, I remember thinking, this man wants my urine. And I was oddly flattered—that he would want even my waste. I thought him not a freak but an enigma. An enigma, however, I would refuse and refuse and refuse. An enigma I am still refusing.

Had he insisted that night, I might have crouched and let go, might have balanced my eager hips above his stomach or crotch and given him that. But he didn't.

After lunch Claire and I stand outside Sam's.

Is this about control? Claire says. Is this about staying pretty?

You don't understand, I say. It's something Skipper wants that I don't want just as badly.

It'll be OK, Claire says, holding my shoulder.

He's growing a beard, I say.

I thought you hated beards, she says.

"I do."

I suppose it could be worse. Skipper could ask me to kill someone. Or he could ask me to tie him up and stick pins in his feet. Or he could ask me to bark before sex, bark like a dog. Demeaning, that's what barking like a dog is. And I suppose peeing on him isn't half as ugly as him wanting to pee on me. You don't want to pee on me, do you? I asked him a year ago. No, he said, I just want to be peed on. Still, I'm not about to pee on anyone, not even Skipper.

Skipper says that I won't pee on him because I'm worried about society, what the world would think if I peed on him. He says people are miserable, that they shoot each other on freeways, torture each other in dark rooms, judge each other for bad reasons, and all he's asking for is a little pee. He says people think and worry too much about what others are doing in bed, and the reason, he says, is because they're so dissatisfied with their own sex lives and worse, he says, they hate their bodies and their bodies' functions.

Peeing, Skipper says, is a glorious function, and you're too fucked up worrying about the world to enjoy it.

It's just not sexual to me, I say. It's waste, I remind him. You've been poisoned, he says.

When I was in college I dated a bartender named William. William was six feet tall with brown curly hair, and older— nearly thirty. His hands were smooth and tan, the fingers long and elegant. I sat at his bar one night and watched him pour drinks; I was excited by those fingers.

I was twenty and all my friends had boyfriends. I wanted a boyfriend. I wanted more than anything for William to be my boyfriend.

On a Friday night I went to William's apartment to watch movies. He'd promised me a musical and what I got was a lengthy porno film. Near the end of the film a naked woman lay on wet grass, in the middle of a meadow maybe, and a man in an orange cape approached her, carrying dynamite. The woman had yellow hair that fell across her cheeks. Hair like straw. And the man stood above the woman, looking down at her, at her naked body, at her straw hair. He said one word. Open, he said. He stuck the dynamite inside the woman and began to whistle. He lit the dynamite. The dynamite sizzled and crackled and the man continued whistling.

I sat on the couch next to William in my short black dress, watching him watch the woman, watching him watch the dynamite, listening with him to the sizzling and crackling. When the woman blew up, the caption read: The Big Bang. And William laughed and laughed, a big, deep laugh from the bottom of his guts. I hated him then. I felt the hate on my face. It was hot and scarlet; I thought he could see it. I tried hard to wipe the hate off my face, hoping William would like me. Would touch me. Would be my boyfriend.

He started grabbing at me, at my neck and hair, at my skirt. And I was dry inside, all dry, no matter what William did with those elegant fingers. And I remember thinking: we are ugly and deserve each other; we deserve this. And I helped him with my zipper.

When I tell Skipper about William, Skipper shakes his head. This urine thing is not about violence, he says. I don't think sticking dynamite inside a woman is sexy. Don't confuse me with that bartender.

There are lines I don't want to cross, I say.

I am not that bartender.

I know, Skipper.

I don't want to hurt you.

The man in the movie whistled, I tell him. I think it was "The Star-Spangled Banner."

On Saturday night Skipper and I have dinner at Claire's. With Claire and Lilly. We eat bread, salad, and pasta. White sauce. Claire is glowing, there is a red ring all around her. I look at Lilly and wonder if she knows Skipper wants me to pee on him.

I watch Claire watch Lilly.

I watch Lilly watch Claire.

Skipper leans toward me. Part of love is objectification, he whispers emphatically.

I drink glass after glass of wine. Every glass is a preparation. I'm ready for a fourth. I follow Claire to the kitchen. I ask her to open another bottle. She's wonderful, I say, you've never looked rosier. Do you like Skipper's beard?

I think it looks good, she says. But you hate it, don't you?

I'm going to pee on him tonight, I tell her.

Are you sure? Is that OK for you? If not—

Tonight, I interrupt her, is pee night.

Pee night, I repeat.

Why are you drinking so much?

Preparation, the peeing person must prepare, I say, and I laugh, all the way back to the table, I laugh.

On the way home, in the car, I am not laughing. I am looking out the window at the road, at the black trees. Skipper has one hand on the wheel and one hand on my thigh.

What if I wouldn't fuck you—what if I loved you, lived with you, did everything sexually for you, but wouldn't fuck you? Would you stay with me, would you be satisfied? he asks.

Yes, I say.

But would you miss it, the fucking part? Would you want me to fuck you?

It depends.

Would you try to talk me into fucking you?

Yes, I tell him.

We are in bed. The pillows are fat against the headboard. The sheets are white. Crisp. Skipper is naked. I wear a blue silk gown. I am kissing his neck and ear. He is touching my hair, moaning softly.

What do you think about urine? I ask him.

I lay him down on his back. I drink the glass of water I've brought into the bedroom. I drink it down, simply, easily. I set the empty water glass on the nightstand. Skipper is breathing hard now, astonished. I am crawling on top of him, enjoying this. I start to lift off my gown.

No, he says, leave it on.

I pull the gown up, gather it at my waist. I crouch above his stomach, near his crotch, and let go.

As the hot urine falls from my body onto his, down the sides of his body, on the white sheets, I am overcome with anger. I try to stop peeing, I try for the sake of us to stop, to stop this peeing, but I cannot.

And moments later, Skipper is on me, moving inside of me. The gown is wet and tight and tangled about my waist. I am looking at the empty water glass. Skipper is looking at my cheek, kissing my face—grateful. I feel his beard, his red and brown beard, his new beard. The room is pungent. My gown is pungent. Thank you, Skipper says, thank you. And as I move with him, loving him, I am leaving him. I will leave him. It's as sure as anything.

A Girl's Gotta Have Friends

Tracey Alvrez

Organ music drones quietly from the front of the church. I am uncomfortable in my ruffled crimson gown, waiting for the beautiful bride behind me to stop fussing with her dress. Closing my eyes, I wish feverishly that I were anywhere but here. My tongue is sticky as I lick my dry lips; my hands feel strangely moist and I wipe them against the stiff organza.

Will she go through with it? I glance over my shoulder. Faith is looking at me, her eyes unfathomable under the white net veil.

"Ready, Nina?" she asks.

"Lead on, MacDuff," I reply.

Turning back to face the aisle, I wonder if she is remembering, like I am. Or perhaps she is worried that her fiancé Rogan, stiff and neatly packaged in his rented tuxedo at the pulpit, will realize on their wedding night that she is no longer a virgin. And that it's my fault. Faith Johnson has been my best friend since kindergarten and it was I who helped her lose her virginity—so to speak.

I stand on the hard wooden floor of the vestibule and wince as the first notes of the bridal march chime out into the gloomy interior. At the linen-covered altar, Faith's groom stands in a shaft of sunlight, looking every inch the prince who has found his princess.

At that moment I hate Rogan McIntyre with blinding purity. He looks so calm and confident while I wait by his future wife's side in an itchy meringue of a dress, fretting that our friendship will never be the same. We glide down the red-carpeted aisle. My teeth ache as I smile at Faith's friends and relatives, people I've known for most of my life. People who would be outraged if they knew what Faith and I had done last week.

The final notes die away when we reach Rogan and his best man.

"Dearly beloved..." the minister begins.

I don't want to listen to Faith vowing to love and honor Rogan until death do them part. Instead I remember how Faith and I first met in the kindergarten sandpit. She was so blonde and delicate. Even then I succumbed to the urge to protect her—it took two teachers to pull me off the little shit who'd kicked sand in her eyes and made her cry.

I remember staying over at her house on the weekends, playing with her dolls. Faith always gave me the one with beautiful long hair while she generously took the one with a ragged bowl cut and one arm (courtesy of her younger brother).

Then as teenagers. Holding her hand when she got her ears pierced, my frown daring the assistant to comment on Faith's tears. Losing my virginity to David Brown at sixteen and rolling on her bed afterwards, laughing as I recounted in gruesome detail how I'd expected great wrenching pain, and how disappointed I was by David's tampon-sized cock.

Later, when David unceremoniously dumped me, I cried in her arms. It was then that she announced she was going to her marriage bed a virgin. She startled me out of my melancholy.

"But Faith, you don't want to marry someone only to find out later he's hopeless in bed, do you?"

She shrugged and smiled that mysterious, trademark Faith smile. "If he's hopeless in bed I'll have to find some other means of satisfaction, won't I?" And as far as I knew, Faith had never let a boyfriend get beyond a quick fumble beneath her tee shirt. She would smile indulgently at my attempts to break her resolve with detailed descriptions of my bedroom and backseat pursuits.

"There are other means of sexual satisfaction besides bonking your brains out, Nina," she would say primly.

So I bought her some strawberry-flavored edible knickers for her twenty-first birthday. I wonder now if she ever used them—and with whom.

I look down as Faith's nephew passes in front of me, bearing a heart-shaped ivory cushion. Two rings are tied on it with gold ribbon. A chuckle sweeps though the congregation as Rogan struggles to free the rings, and again as Faith tries to force the gold band over his knobbly finger.

"Do you, Faith Maria Johnson, take Rogan James McIntyre to be your lawful wedded husband?" the minister's voice intones.

I bury my nose in the fragrant bouquet I'm holding and drift back in time again. It was no surprise after our long years of friendship that Faith asked me to be her bridesmaid. I accepted happily. She and Rogan were a perfect couple, and I knew that he was devastatingly in love with her.

Things would have continued just fine if it hadn't been for the hen party ten days before the wedding. By the end of the evening, which included numerous shots of Jim Beam, Faith asked if she could crash at my place for the night.

Arms wrapped around each other's shoulders, we staggered the short distance from the bar to my flat and collapsed in a giggling tangle on the living-room carpet. We lay side by side staring at the ceiling, listening to Stevie Nicks sing about Sara.

"I always wondered if she was a closet lesbian," said Faith, muffling a burp.

I grunted noncommittally and concentrated on the ebb and sway of the walls. Then the sweep of her blonde hair tickled my collarbone as she leaned over me and whispered, "And I've always wondered what it would be like with a woman. Have you?"

That snapped me halfway sober in a second. I rolled my cheek off the carpet pile and looked her in the eye.

"I thought you wanted to remain a virgin for your beloved Rogan," I said, finding it easier to evade the question than to admit the truth.

She smiled and said, "I do. You haven't got a penis, have you?" One of her hands ran lightly down my body from breastbone to crotch. "Nope, no penis there. I guess I'm safe."

My heart rate sped up from a drunken plod to a frantic thrum. When her lips touched mine I thought the blood would sizzle right out of my veins. Faith unbuttoned my blouse. Her tongue teased my nipple jutting through the confines of a lace bra and sucked it hard into her mouth. Soft fingers slid under my skirt and panties, and the pad of her thumb traced the slick crevice between my legs. All the time I was crying "Oh God, Faith!" over and over and thinking to myself as we stripped off our clothes, *At least in the morning we can blame it on the alcohol.*

When I awoke the next morning she was gone and my head throbbed with the aftereffects of guilt and Jim Beam. Still, I wanted her again. I stumbled into the kitchen and put the coffee on. The door opened as I carried the cup to the table and Faith walked in carrying two paper bags.

"I bought us breakfast. Fresh croissants, yum."

An overwhelming feeling of relief swept over me. At least she hadn't gone home. But memories of the night before tumbled like bricks through my gut. We sat opposite each other and buttered the croissants.

"Faith?" I said finally. "About last night?"

Faith looked up from her croissant, a smear of butter glistening on her lips. Her tongue darted out and licked it off. My gaze slid to her shoulder. All I could think about was her lips sucking, the waves upon waves of pleasure as she buried her mouth in my wet...Then she was beside me, cupping my face in her hands.

"Last night was wonderful, hmmm?"

She stroked my hair and kissed me until I remembered *exactly* how wonderful last night had been. Until I had forgotten any lingering inhibitions about dining on my best friend for breakfast.

"...man and wife. You may kiss the bride." The last of the minister's words are received with cheers and whistles from the back row of the church.

Rogan's rugby-club wankers, I think uncharitably, and then sigh. Bitchy thoughts are a pointless exercise. It's done now. I watch Faith walk back down the aisle, a married woman.

Outside the sun shines in blatant disregard of my feelings. I stand and grimace at the camera with the rest of the wedding party before being hustled into a gray BMW by Faith's grandmother.

"Don't look so sad, Nina," whispers her grandmother.

The scent of lavender and talcum powder emanating from her makes me want to sneeze. I paste another of my fake smiles across my lips and say, "I'm not sad, Mrs. Atkinson."

She pats my hand. "Of course you are, dear. I know how close you and Faith are."

I bloody hope not, I think.

"It's natural for friends to drift apart a little when one gets married. But there's no need to be upset. Things will settle down once Faith returns from her honeymoon and you'll be back to bosom buddies again before you know it."

Bosom buddies. I smile weakly and count down the minutes until we arrive at the reception. Lavish platters of caviar and bottles of expensive champagne chilling in ice buckets on each table have redeemed the exorbitant fees paid by Faith's parents to the Oakleigh Golf Club. I manage to choke down a few forkfuls of poached salmon before excusing myself from the bridal table. When I stand up, Faith grabs my wrist.

"Are you okay?"

"Fine. I just need to pee," I whisper and attempt a smile, but my lower lip trembles.

Her thumb strokes the skin of my inner wrist. A warm flush flares across my cheeks and my upper breasts. I pull away from her questioning stare and ease past the closely set tables of laughing guests to the empty hallway.

I'm fine. Just fine, damn it, I repeat over and over to myself as I hurry into the ladies' room and pull the door shut behind me.

My reflection looks back at me without sympathy: a young woman in a garish dress, her mousy hair tormented into a stiff bouffant, the carefully styled strands around her face only emphasizing the wet streaks sliding down her cheeks.

The door hisses open behind me.

"Faith?"

She stands in the doorway. Seeing my tears, she says, "Don't cry, Nina. You'll smudge your mascara."

"It's waterproof," I sniff, dabbing under my nose with a strip of toilet tissue. "I came prepared."

She comes in and shuts the door. I hear a faint click as she locks it. I turn away from her and honk wetly into the tissue. Her dress rustles against mine as she wraps her arms around my waist and rests her cheek on the bare skin of my back. We stand like this for a moment, but when her hand drifts up to cup my right breast I pull away and back into a corner of the bathroom.

I expect her to react with hurt indignity. Instead she smiles.

"You don't want me anymore, Nina?" she asks, making sure I see her gaze drop to the rigid outline of my nipples through the gauzy fabric.

"Faith," I say, injecting a warning tone into my voice. She sways towards me.

She tugs at her white lace bodice and frees one rose-tipped breast. Two fingers slide scissorlike over the tightening nipple, squeezing and manipulating it until it stands erect like a newly formed bud.

My mouth is devoid of moisture but my taste buds have a cellular memory of the sweet and salty tang of her skin. Shock waves of remembered passion flood through my system. I grab her shoulders, intending to push her away, but suddenly my hands have all the strength of overcooked fettuccine. We end up with our arms around each other, our lips mashed together, our tongues dancing slowly in perfect synchronization, and our fingers fumble under meters of white lace and crimson organza for soft, moist flesh.

Finally I unhook her fingers from under my satin panties and pull away.

"Faith, we can't."

Her breath, fragrant with the tart scent of champagne, puffs on my flushed face.

"Why not?"

"It's wrong. You're married."

"Shall I stop then?" she asks, playfully leaning forward to nibble on my collarbone.

I try to think of a smart quip, but words fail me.

"You see," she says, "the secret of a lasting marriage is for each partner to have outside interests." She continues kissing her way south. "Other hobbies, other friends, separate from their spouse." Her tongue flickers over my nipple, melting my resistance and logic. "Rogan knows how important friends are. He knows I would never suggest he give up his rugby-club mates, and he insists that I spend at least one night a week out with the girls."

"With the girls," I echo weakly. The air catches in my throat as Faith vanishes under the voluminous folds of my dress.

"I don't intend to give you up, Nina darling," she says, tugging my panties down to my ankles.

I moan at each soft sweep of her tongue, and before the throb of an oncoming climax fuddles my brain, I hear her pause and murmur against my thigh, "A girl's gotta have friends."

Amen to that, I think, and I sink to the floor in a pool of crimson organza.

Wages of Faith
Michelle Scalise

Mama's voices were whispering to her again. I could tell 'cause her eyes were a little out of focus, like she was trying to read scriptures in the dark, and she kept licking her lips, running her tiny forked tongue along the bright pink slash of her mouth. Soon the Spirit would be screaming inside her and she'd have to let it out or go crazy.

Daddy sat in a folding chair three seats down from me, crossing and uncrossing his long legs. He was doing his best not to sweat in his wool suit but it was eighty degrees outside and the double-wide trailer that served as the Church of the Holy Union couldn't afford air-conditioning like that fancy Baptist church down in Layettville. I used my tambourine to fan myself until Mama gave me a look.

My sister, Mary Lizbeth, seemed like a gift from heaven in Grandma's wedding dress, her long brown hair pulled back with a red ribbon Mama had taken from the Christmas box. She sat there, calmly tapping her foot on the carpeted floor as if angels were singing hymns in her ear. Daddy leaned over and spoke to her.

"You make us proud, honey. This is your day. I don't care what that Walker girl says; your Mama has always known you were the chosen one." He turned in his seat and glared at Mary Lizbeth's best friend, who sat three rows behind us with her family. The Walkers had bought their daughter a new white dress for the occasion and made sure they were the last to enter the church so everyone could admire it.

The Walkers should have known better. The whole congregation knew that Mary Lizbeth would receive the Most Holy Union.

I was five years old when Mama, seven months pregnant, started speaking in tongues. The Spirit emerged so strong in her that first time that she bit her tongue down the center trying to control the gift. But the voices couldn't be silenced. They bled from her mouth and wept from her tired brown eyes.

Daddy slept on the sofa after that, though sometimes late at night I'd wake up and see him knocking softly on their bedroom door asking Mama if he could come back. "I am a vehicle for the voices now," she'd say.

There were times I wished she hadn't been given the gift— like when she'd start shaking so bad we had to hold her down. "The serpent's poison is my wine," she'd scream, spittle flying off her lips like a dog gone mad.

"She has too much faith," Daddy would explain.

And over the years she demonstrated it. Even when my brother was bitten handling the rattler and lay dying on the church altar begging for a doctor like a heathen, she never lost her belief. "He was a faithless child in the eyes of the Spirit and he has shamed us. But my Mary Lizbeth will be our redeemer," she announced, and never spoke my brother's name again.

Every five years we gathered at church for the holiest of holy days, the Day of the Union. All the young girls of the congregation between the ages of eighteen and twenty would arrive like brides at their wedding, nervously giggling as their daddies patted each other on the back and claimed their daughter would be the chosen one.

A few years back Mama made a halfhearted attempt when my turn came, but she knew it wasn't to be. Mary Lizbeth was her special child. Afterwards I was so angry I let Jimmy McCoy take the virginity I had so proudly guarded for the Holy Union in the back of his father's truck.

A slight breeze carrying the scent of dying lilacs drifted through the church windows as the music started. The women's tambourines jingled like a thousand wind chimes. I beat out the rhythm slowly at first, swaying my hips to the voices as they rose closer and closer to the Spirit. Hymns pounded the walls as if begging for release. Mama shook in her trance, humming a strange song only the gifted could hear.

Brother Everett stepped up to the altar, white robe starched neat as a linen tablecloth. His eyes, burning fierce with conviction and piety, sent a tingle rushing up my thighs. He smiled and stretched his arms out toward the congregation. "Brothers and sisters, the Spirit is with us this evening."

Mama mumbled incoherently and waved her worn bible in the air.

Brother Everett knelt behind the pulpit and drew forth a wooden hinged box. The air vents on top formed the word BELIEVE. The serpent's rattle hushed the church into a frightened kind of awe. The pastor placed both hands on the box and closed his eyes. "The Most Holy Union is upon us once again and we give thanks." Brother Everett's voice softly wrapped around us. "We are in need of a rebirth. The Spirit demands obedience from his flock."

I could hear Mary Lizbeth as she swayed to the angel's song. "I believe, I believe."

Mama wept and gave praise.

"The gospel tells us that 'In my name they shall cast out devils; they shall speak with new tongues; they shall take up serpents.' And we must believe, brothers and sisters." The pastor's voice rose, the words spoken so fast they seemed a blur as the church members yelled their amens and the serpent shook the sides of his box. "All but those to be chosen take your seats and pray with me."

Twelve girls remained standing. Mary Lizbeth looked down at us and smiled, so sure of her holy stature.

Brother Everett reached into the box and seized an eight-foot-long diamondback rattlesnake. His breath grew harsh as he gripped the serpent. The rattler curled its brown, rough-scaled body up the pastor's arm like a loving pet, twisting slowly up to his shoulder and looking out at the congregation. Its rattle vibrated with a frantic, angry tapping on the ground, as if doubting us all.

I clutched the tambourine to my breast. Mary Lizbeth paled a bit as she reached for the back of her chair.

Mama half-stood and cried, "Your bride, chosen before birth, is ready." Her pupils contracted to a pair of black vertical slits before disappearing. All that remained were two sightless white eyes staring through our souls. Her head snapped back and forth as the strange guttural sounds of the Spirit took over her pink-smeared mouth. Blood seeped from her lips, staining her best Sunday dress like red wine.

Brother Everett stepped down from the altar and slowly made his way across the aisle. Mary Lizbeth stared out the window and waited on her groom.

The pastor stopped at each young girl and closed his eyes, listening for the sign. A few of the mothers burst into tears as their daughters were passed over. When he reached my sister's side he smiled.

The serpent's tail at last grew silent. Mary Lizbeth looked into its dead black eyes with a knowing certainty. Mama's voices screamed.

For appearance's sake, Brother Everett hurried to the last few girls and then returned to my sister. "Mary Lizbeth, you are the chosen one. Praise the Spirit."

Once again the church filled with song. The congregation pounded its chairs and cried. Feet stomped so hard I felt my body shake. Daddy wept into his hands and gave thanks in a choked whisper.

Mama led Mary Lizbeth up to the altar. "Lie down, child," she said, helping her onto the floor in front of the pulpit. "Didn't I always say this day of joy would come for you? The voices told me I was the guardian of the bride and I believed."

"Yes, Mama." Mary Lizbeth smiled, her wedding dress spread out like snow around her. Her tiny breasts rose and fell rapidly.

Mama returned to her seat, crying as she joined in the hymn. Daddy tried to pull her close but she pushed him away with a look of exasperation.

Brother Everett had to yell to be heard above the crowd. "Mary Lizbeth, do you come before us chaste and without sin?"

My sister's voice rang clear. "I embrace our serpent's union with reverence and in faith I give myself to the church."

The congregation grew still.

I shuddered as the pastor knelt between Mary Lizbeth's legs as if in worship. With a humble smile he raised her dress to reveal white, soft thighs. One gentle tug and her cotton panties were removed and folded with solemn care. Mary Lizbeth's eyes focused serenely on the water-stained ceiling and I wondered if Mama's voices were calming her.

"I christen thee Eve, the serpent's first bride," Brother Everett said as he spread her legs wide, exposing her to us all. "Take thee of thy viper, thy groom through eternity." The viper hissed and unfurled from the pastor's arm, gliding noise-lessly down to the ground. "Let the Spirit of us all be reborn in thee."

The pastor swallowed hard, beads of sweat gathering on his brow as the snake coiled up Mary Lizbeth's legs like a poison. Its slick tongue snapped against her skin.

"We are reborn," the congregation chanted softly. Outside, crickets sang to the summer night.

The viper's head reached the opening of its pathway. Its rattle vibrated vigorously. Brother Everett parted my sister's legs a little wider. With one swift thrust the snake entered her.

Mary Lizbeth raised her head and gazed down at the ser-pent's tail extending from inside her. She trembled, and I wondered if terror might replace her faith. The pulsating rattle was quiet as the snake was urged deeper into her womb. She pressed a hand to her lips to stifle a sob and her eyes glazed over.

I squeezed the tambourine until I felt it crack and the tiny cymbals fell through my clenched fist. I didn't dare breathe for fear I might scream instead.

Mama pulled at handfuls of her short gray hair till her scalp bled. "Thank you, Spirit," she mumbled.

The serpent had completely filled Mary Lizbeth as she arched her back and cried out. Her head turned, she gazed down at me with the black slit eyes of a snake.

"We are reborn," I whispered.

Brother Everett held her shoulders down. "Behold, broth-ers and sisters," he cried. "The Holy Union is at hand."

I watched as Mary Lizbeth's stomach expanded until the seams of her wedding gown seemed ready to burst. I could hear the faint rattle coming from inside her like a muffled scratching at her womb.

A young girl in front slumped over in a faint and slid quietly from her chair.

Mary Lizbeth's manic laughter filled the church with a nervous jubilation. She arched her back again as blood coursed from between her legs and streamed down the altar stairs like holy water. A few women in the front pew sank to their knees and wept as they licked the expanding red stain. Mary Lizbeth opened her mouth as if to scream but no sound escaped her pale lips.

Brother Everett bent back her knees so all could see the miracle—hundreds of tiny snakes slithering and twisting from her womb like black roots in a swamp. He gathered them up in piles as they squirmed around him, and placed them into the wooden box on the pulpit.

Mama rocked in her chair. "It is done, it is done," she whimpered.

The serpent's diamond head began reemerging from Mary Lizbeth as she gazed into an unseen eternity and died on the altar stairs, a look of horror frozen forever in her eyes. The snake slid easily from her poisoned womb and into the pastor's arms.

Brother Everett looked down upon his people. "Go with the Spirit in your soul, brothers and sisters, for we are reborn in the serpent."

The church broke out in a thunderous roar of joy.

Mama and Daddy smiled benignly as one by one the parents of the unchosen congratulated them.

The Heart in My Garden
Carol Queen

These days there's a lot of money to be made if you're in the right place at the right time, if you keep your shoulder to the wheel. That's how Mike and Katherine got their nice house, their cars (hers with that new-car smell still in it), an art collection, and a healthy nest egg. The house is close to San Francisco. Her car is a Mercedes. The art is mostly modern, up-and-coming painters you'll read about in *Art Week* any day now.

They're young enough that they don't have to worry about kids yet, so they don't—if you asked them, both would say, "Oh, kids are definitely on the agenda," though they'd sound a little vague. They're old enough that the honeymoon's over, neither of them quite remembering when it ended.

Seven years is a long time to be married. Still, aside from that, things are sweet. The rhythm of their weekdays, long-familiar now, has them clacking along toward the weekend like they're on a polished set of tracks. They fill weekends with rituals of their own.

It dawns on Katherine very, very gradually that she can't remember the last time they made love. She knows they did when they spent that weekend in Monterey—Mike's last birthday. In that romantic B&B, how could they resist the impulse to fall into each other's arms? And it's always a little exciting to be away from home. But they had to break it off in time to get in a day at the aquarium—the whole reason they went—so Mike could see the shimmery glow-in-the-dark jelly-fish, delicate neon tendrils floating in the black water. He had seen a special about them on the Discovery channel, had to see for himself. She lost her heart to them too: she and Mike stayed in the darkened room for almost an hour, silent, side by side with their hands clasped together so lightly that for minutes at a time she lost track of the sensation of his skin against her palm.

That's what she likes about being with him. It's so easy. They can drive together silently, not feeling as if a conversational black hole has swallowed them; they can spend Sunday mornings reading the paper and trading sections with a touch on the arm; they fill each other's coffee mugs without being asked and hand back the steaming, fragrant cups accompanied by a little kiss. After that they work in the garden, sometimes side by side, sometimes like her grandparents used to: Granddad in the vegetables, Gram in the flowers. She can imagine the next fifty years passing this way.

They must have had sex since Monterey—that's four months ago—but she can't remember it. Mostly now they do it late at night, right before sleep, but it's not on a schedule like practically everything else. Neither is it very predictable, tied to watching the Playboy channel or *Real Sex* on HBO; lately they don't watch those shows much anyway. If you asked Katherine, she'd probably say she doesn't really notice, nor does she notice being turned on, wanting sex, thinking about it very often. There was a time when she lived in almost constant arousal, but that was years ago. She and Mike had just met; she was so much younger then. She's always too busy now, tired all the time, except when they get away for a few days. And they haven't had time to leave town since that weekend in Monterey. Katherine's a lawyer; Mike's software company will go public early next year. And if you asked Katherine whether her friends have more sex than she and Mike, she'd probably tell you not much—everybody's so busy now. Everyone has to concentrate on reaching for the brass ring. How else could you afford a house with a garden, two cars, the basics?

Katherine masturbates sometimes after Mike has fallen asleep. Lines of code lull him into light snoring, while Katherine's legal cases keep her awake. She goes over arguments, making mental checklists of every point she'll have to hit when she's in court the next day. She considers this productive time, until she has it organized in her mind—then the arguments begin to repeat themselves and she's so wound up over them she can't nod off. When she gets to this point, she pulls her vibrator out of the nightstand. It's one of those quiet vibrators, barely audible—even though Mike sleeps right next to her, once his breath has evened and slowed she won't wake him.

If you asked her, Katherine would admit that this proximity feels erotic: a little illicit but comfortable too, like the comfort of being with him while they weed or watch glowing aquarium fish in companionable silence. She sometimes slows down her breath to match the rhythm of his, a lingering synchronicity within which they are alive, alone, together—it doesn't matter that he's not conscious of her; it calms her down. Her climax, when it comes, drifts up on her gradually, and its power always surprises her.

Sometimes she gently places herself against him: pressing against his back when he's turned away from her, or reaching out with just her toes to make contact with his soft-furred calf. It's funny that she doesn't necessarily think of making love with him during these times, but in a way she *is* making love with him. If you asked her, Katherine would say that Mike knows she's doing it, knows it in his sleep. (When she first developed this habit she used to ask him if he had dreamed about anything in particular, but he could never call up sexual dreams. Or if he knew, he never said so.) Katherine respects Mike's sleep too much to thrash or buck, and really this is more about her own tension than about passion. And a tension-tamer orgasm can be quiet, an implosion that rocks her to sleep without rocking her world.

She wakes up refreshed the next morning and goes to court.

Mike has his own private time a couple of days a week, after Katherine leaves for the courthouse. He works a flex schedule, a perk of having stayed at his job for over five years, and two days a week he works at home. He's just as efficient at the home office as at the one downtown, even though this one overlooks his and Katherine's garden. In fact, he's *more* efficient at home, getting at least as much work done in less time. He takes one if not two breaks to jack off, the first in the still-rumpled bedclothes right after Katherine leaves (she accepts without question that Mike will make the bed on the days he stays home).

The first one is his favorite, especially because the bed still smells faintly of Katherine; he buries his nose in the pillow and lets the scent keep him company as he strokes himself hard. It's his way of keeping her comfortably close, even though she's already halfway to work by the time he begins. He takes plenty of time, a slow hand-over-hand on his cock while his mind wanders; he's in no hurry. His eyes closed, usually, he drifts through a lifetime's worth of mental images until he finds the one that sends a jolt of heat through his cock, maybe makes it jump a little in his hand. That's the one he'll use, embellishing it into a fully fleshed-out fantasy. If you asked him, he'd say he doesn't feel that he guides the fantasy. He feels like he's along for the ride, almost like the folio of erotic images riffling inside his brain has a life of its own, each separate image, in fact, a separate reality that he's simply stumbled into the way Captain Kirk is thrust into a new dimension if his crew doesn't set the transporter controls just right.

For half an hour twice a week Mike drifts in and out of dreams that take him to all sorts of places, sometimes even out of himself. When his orgasm comes it almost always swells up like music at the climax of a movie, the place in the plot where you're supposed to just give yourself over to the story, cry if it tells you to, or clench your fists in fear. When he's done he almost always writes code for two or three solid hours before even thinking of making himself some lunch. When the weather permits he takes his sandwich out into the garden.

He doesn't always take a masturbation break in the afternoon. Sometimes he's on a roll and wants nothing more than to work—Katherine comes home at six or seven and finds him still at it, though on those days he falls asleep really early. But once every week or two he gives himself an hour or two to surf the Net.

He has his favorite sites bookmarked. On the Net he always travels with a tour guide, the sensibility of all his favorite webmasters leading him into cul-de-sacs of sexual possibility he hadn't even known existed. Katherine uses the Net for e-mail and shopping at Amazon.com—for her it's just a handy extension of the local mall—but Mike goes to the bad neighborhoods and stays there as long as he can.

He thinks about going in and never coming out. Only his work ethic stops him from spending all day in this perpetual peepshow. If he overindulges, he knows, he could get his telecommuting privileges yanked, so he doles out his Web visits, perks he allows himself when he's done a good after-noon's work.

In Mike's mind there's no infidelity in exploring chat rooms and cybersex sites as long as he stops before Katherine gets home, as long as she's busy doing something else. He's never told her about it but he doesn't think she'd mind, as long as he gets his work done and their marriage doesn't suffer. For all he knows, she has her own favorite bookmarks on her computer at the office. He wouldn't mind that; it's just play, nothing real. Virtual.

It isn't often that Katherine comes home early. Once in a while she can get out at midafternoon on Friday, usually because she and Mike have decided to go up to the wine country or to a spa weekend. In the eighteen months Mike's been working at home, she's never arrived home before 5:30.

He makes sure he's zipped up by then, either back at work on his code or in the kitchen starting dinner. They often cook together, and sometimes Mike has dinner waiting when she has to work late. She pages him and dials "7:30"—he knows that's when to expect her. He doesn't even call back unless he needs to ask her to swing by the store for bread or a bottle of wine. They shop on Saturdays, though, so usually everything he needs is waiting in the kitchen. Mike likes to cook. So does she, though she rarely makes dinner by herself.

Today, though, the judge continues Katherine's case because a prosecution witness didn't show up. She's out of the courtroom at noon. She usually eats with the rest of her team on court days, so they go around the corner to the little Italian place. It's so close to the courthouse that Katherine almost always recognizes most of the diners—judges, other attorneys, people from the jury pool.

She's working with Marla today, the newest member of the practice. Marla's just-married, still trying to balance an intense work life with being in love. She's never late, but Katherine has seen her come to work breathy and flushed—if you asked her, Katherine would say she remembers those newlywed days when once in the morning and once at night wasn't enough, when she and Mike would sometimes skip dinner because they were on each other the minute they got home, when once Mike even got them a motel room at noon.

Marla fishes around in her purse and shows off the set of cufflinks she's gotten Bill for Valentine's Day. They're porcelain ovals with tiny pictures painted on them: one has a bottle of champagne, one a can-can girl with her ruffled skirts thrown high. "Wine, women, and song!" says Marla gaily. "And I got him a really good bottle of French champagne, and I'm taking him to see *Cabaret*. Katherine, what are you doing with Mike?"

Katherine hasn't planned anything special with Mike because she's forgotten that today is Valentine's Day. Jesus, wasn't it just Christmas?

"Ummm, just a really nice dinner and some private time." This is the best Katherine can come up with without notice, but it satisfies Marla, who has very few brain cells to spare for thinking about Katherine and Mike. She's probably too busy imagining the way she'll tug Bill into an alley when they leave the theater, and give him a sneaky handjob right there in public, Katherine thinks, only a little sniffy about Marla's single-minded focus. You're only young once.

Still, with the afternoon suddenly free, Katherine decides to give Mike a Valentine's Day surprise. He's probably forgotten it too—he's been just as busy as she has—but thank goodness it's a holiday that lends itself to last-minute planning. Katherine detours by Real Foods on the way home, picks up a good wine, some big prawns for scampi, a couple of cuts of filet mignon. On the way to the register she passes the bakery and adds a little chocolate cake to her basket. "Strawberries too," she thinks, "if they're any good yet." The store has a heap of huge ruby berries that look like they were grown in the Garden of Eden. And right next to the flowers stands a card display. She picks one that looks like a handmade Martha Stewart crafts project, a slightly-out-of-focus heart against a sapphire-blue background, blank so she can customize its message. She stops at the coffee shop downstairs for a latte and writes "Dearest Michael, you are the heart in my garden. All my love, Kath."

She thinks about using the pager—"3:30"—but decides against it, decides instead to slip in and surprise him. If she can get into the kitchen via the back door, she might be able to start dinner quietly without interrupting his work. She parks the Mercedes a couple of houses down from theirs.

Her grandparents' house and garden were in Idaho: at this time of year the garden would be cut back and mulched, maybe even buried under a drift of snow. Katherine loves living in California because even in February the garden blooms with life. The roses are finally gone but the pink ladies, tulips, and irises are starting; in the corner calla lilies burst whitely out of a clutch of huge green leaves. When she picks them she always includes one of those big leaves in the vase; otherwise the sculptural, curved callas almost don't look like flowers.

Passing the window of the room in which Mike works, she glimpses him, so riveted to the screen that he doesn't see her. "Must be on a roll," she thinks, but then she sees that he is moving in a way that she wouldn't expect to see from a man writing code. Though his body is partly obscured behind the desk and monitor, it almost looks as if he is masturbating.

Katherine noiselessly lets herself into the house and heaps her shopping bags onto the kitchen work island. She lays the

store-bought roses carefully on top, drops her purse and briefcase beside them, slips off her shoes. She makes it to the door
of Mike's office without being heard.

He's on a roll, all right: onscreen Katherine sees not lines of
code but a tiny movie looping repeatedly, a naked man in a
blindfold lying on his back, a woman in a shiny black catsuit—it looks like it's made of rubber—crouching over him.
The suit encases her body completely, except for her crotch,
which is naked, shaved bare, and she engulfs the man's hard,
upstanding cock over and over with the shockingly exposed
pussy—at least, Katherine finds it shocking, but not in a bad
way, more like a shock to the system, cold water in the face,
waking her up to feelings she barely remembers.

Clearly, Mike has not forgotten anything. His hand pumps
his cock rhythmically, eyes riveted on the miniature tableau as
the catsuited woman thrusts down and down and down. He
times his hand strokes to the woman's down thrusts, just as
Katherine herself times her late-night strokes to Mike's slow
and even breaths.

If you asked her why she isn't upset, discovering him like
this, she might tell you it's like her own late-night forays, only
so much hotter: she's never seen Mike jack off in the daylight;
she hasn't seen his cock this hard in years; she's erotically
attuned to his deep breaths from all those nights lying next to
him, vibrator or no vibrator; she's fascinated by the tiny
couple on the screen, smaller than Barbie and Ken; and the
fact that Mike finds them so compelling makes her pussy wet.
That her pussy is wet in the middle of the afternoon is such a
welcome surprise that all she can do for a minute is touch herself through her fine cotton stockings, the black fabric
clinging to her almost as tightly as the tiny woman's shiny catsuit. Katherine's mind spins, looking for a way to incorporate
this unexpected scene into her surprise Valentine's Day cele-
bration. Silently she begins to unbutton her gray rayon suit.

Mike's erotic reverie has advanced him so close to orgasm that when he feels a hand stroke his thigh and replace his own hand on his cock, it could easily be a part of the virtual connection he's having with the woman onscreen. For a second he doesn't even look to see who is holding him. Then he's recognizes Katherine's hand, a touch he knows almost as well as his own, and sure enough, when he glances away from the screen, she is crouched beside him. She wears nothing but her black bra, which snugly cups her breasts, and her black tights.

Smoothly she stands up, pulling him by the cock, and pushes the office chair across the room. "Lie down, Michael," she whispers. "So you can see the screen."

The rug, fuzzy against the back of his neck, gives him just enough cushion. When Katherine stands over him the screen is obscured, but that doesn't matter because she is taking the crotch of her tights in both hands and sharply ripping, tearing a hole like the one in the woman's catsuit. Katherine's pussy is pink, swelling, her arousal beginning to form visible moisture like dew on the callas' broad leaves. Mike strokes her thighs, reaching for her.

Katherine crouches down over him, and as her pussy makes contact with his rigid cock the woman onscreen is visible again. Katherine's tight wet pussy sucks at him. He's aware of the rug under his back, Katherine's weight poised just above his pelvis, her thigh muscles pumping as she matches the catsuit woman's thrusts, again, again, again. Mike's hands rove her body as he climbs again toward the climax she had interrupted. Her hands rest on his chest for balance, for contact with him, and he feels their pressure through his nipples. On the screen, the blindfolded man is completely under the catsuited woman's control.

Mike thrusts up into Katherine, his eyes wide, flashing from her to the screen, from her to the screen. He slips one hand through her brown hair, pulling the clip that holds it back in its demure professional style. The thick silky hair falls through his fingers, into her face, curtaining eyes that are getting wilder and wilder. Her breasts fill his hands; he squeezes, remembering their ripeness. Now their pelvises grind together, his cock thrusts up into her as deeply as it will go, both of them climb toward climax: maybe not together, but close. She has slipped to her knees, straddling him, her weight on him now, and he lifts her like she's riding a bucking pony when he thrusts into her. Onscreen the catsuit lady and her blinkered paramour have not changed; their fuck can never escalate. But Mike and Katherine are leaving them behind.

Almost. Without warning Katherine moves her hands. She puts them over his eyes, a moist, fleshly blindfold.

"Fuck me, Mike!" she hisses. "Hard!"

If you asked him now, Mike would groan that he has missed her, missed this, before bucking involuntarily into a come that she has taken from him, imperious and powerful in her ripped tights, that he could not hold back from her, that she demanded.

He has barely stopped shaking when she slides up his body, threads from the torn stockings tickling his nose, her hot, swollen pussy at the tip of his tongue: the catsuit woman demanding service, Katherine demanding pleasure, letting him drink from her. He laps like a cat until she yelps, convulses against his tongue, collapses on him. For a few seconds he rests under her body like it's a tent and he's a kid hiding from everything.

They walk into the kitchen naked and steamed from a long shower. It still isn't quite 5:00—on an ordinary day she wouldn't even be home from work yet.

She'd intended to make him dinner, but he insists on helping like he usually does, and begins rinsing the prawns while she runs water into a crystal vase, slices an inch off the stems of the roses, arranges them. They're red for Valentine's Day; the store hadn't even bothered to order any other color.

"Put a little sugar in there," says Mike. "They're wilting."

By the time the filets are on the grill the roses are perking up.

"Look," Katherine says. "You were right about the sugar. Hey, what's that beneath the vase?"

He opens the card, reads the message, kisses her, and sets the blurry heart up against the vase. After dinner they put on jackets and take their wineglasses out to the garden.

After Loss
Tabatha Flyte

After the tears had been shed, the damp tissues were buried in wastepaper baskets, and we had all given up asking *why, why, why,* Robert said that he should go back home. My sister Sarah said no: she felt she should stay overnight to keep an eye on Mum, even though my brother was still living at home back then. (He moved out a few months later. He said it wasn't the same without Dad).

I couldn't bear to stay in the family house so I asked Robert if he wouldn't mind dropping me at my flat, even though it was way across town. My eyes were blurry from crying, and I hate night driving even at the best of times. Robert said it was no problem.

Saying goodbye wrung more tears out of all of us. My sister and I hugged each other unusually tightly and I promised to call early the next morning. As I left the house I had a sick feeling in my gut: *what if they died too?*

Robert drove so effortlessly it was almost as if he weren't driving at all. I watched his big hand as he glided through the gears. He was a cool customer but I knew he was upset too.

He and Sarah had been dating for eight years; as Mum said, he was almost family. In fact, he probably got on with each of us *better* than family. I don't think he and Dad had ever conversed deeply, but they'd laughed about a broad range of things, as men do, and together they'd teased Sarah and me, the crazy sisters.

"I feel terrible," I said desolately when we arrived at my place.

"I'll come in for coffee," he said, and I knew that he meant a talk. Robert had been trying to talk us around for the last few days. He was full of correct homilies, lines from books on bereavement counseling.

In the bathroom, my face in the mirror looked unfamiliar. My eyes were over-bright and my expression seemed new, but not fresh-new. Surely I didn't have more lines, more gray hairs than last week? I pinched my cheeks, trying to bring some color onto the pale palette. I changed out of my formal black clothes into a dressing gown.

In the living room Robert was sitting on the floor, cupping his mug of cocoa. When he saw me a sympathetic look crept across his serious face. It was too gentle. Annoyingly, it started me off.

"Robert," I dribbled, "I need a cuddle." The words just spilled out like a leak.

"It's all right," he said. I swear I would have killed him if he'd said "Let it out" or "Have a good cry."

I sat down beside him, and he put his arms around me. It had been so long since anyone, any man, had touched me that for a split second I almost didn't know what to do. I tensed. It was a shock, just to be there, to be held. Eventually I relaxed. I felt the stress leave my body, and my muscles all seemed to flop. With my family I had tried to be so strong; now, with Robert, I defrosted.

Robert didn't let go. He held me in his warmth. He was a big cuddly bear. "It's all right, 's all right."

Men and women hug so differently. When I am hugged by a woman I feel that the arms around me say, "Yes you can do it, you can." When I am held by a man I feel that I am being told, "No, you don't have to do it, you don't."

A sob, a groan—I didn't realize immediately that it was he who was sobbing, not me. He was crying into my shoulder. I remembered Sarah saying, almost contemptuously, that he couldn't even watch a romantic film without welling up.

"It's OK," I whispered. It was my turn to comfort. I patted him awkwardly. This was my grief, not his, yet I was proud; if *he* was this bereft, think what sorrow *I* was entitled to. His face had that comical look men sometimes get when they cry; he was trying to cheer up, but grief literally pulled the corners of his lips southward.

I felt the carpet beneath my dressing gown burning against my thighs, but I hung onto him, squeezing him alive. How good it was to comfort someone rather than have him walk on eggshells around me.

"'S OK," I whispered. He looked at me for a second and then his face was comfortably looming over mine. His mouth moved onto mine, tender, searching.

"It's OK," I repeated firmly.

We kissed, and our lips parted and our tongues peeped out, cautious at first, tentative. Then, as his lips warmed mine, I couldn't stop my tongue from prying into his mouth. His tongue felt so good, like an extension of our comfort, a sharing of our pain. His wet tongue inside my mouth was like transference, like a mother giving her baby food. It was sweet, soft nourishment somehow—well, that's how it felt at first. I cupped his face, his beautiful face, and I felt moisture between my legs, but it didn't feel wrong or anything, just friendly. We held each other tight. He was massaging my back, making big circular strokes, and our mouths were widening and our tongues becoming more adventurous. I made a little whimpering noise and he pulled me closer.

OK, we weren't being so friendly then, but the opposite of friends is enemies, and we were still friends—we'd just slid along the sliding scale. It didn't feel like a big change, or an abrupt turn. It felt warm playing with tongues. Arousal dampened my knickers. Rising heat. Maybe we shouldn't have, but it was nice, so nice, not to be alone. We were like kids too young to know any better, playing doctors and nurses. He kept pulling back and studying my face but I couldn't stand having him look at me. I wanted his tongue inside me, his mouth wrapped around me. I didn't want him to see me; I felt like my face was just fragile skin stretched over skull. People say faces are beautiful, but they are just mineral, just shells. I wanted him to squiggle in my hole, to blot away my anger. I was becoming exuberant, feeling good, physical, for the first time in weeks. I felt that strange twist in my sex, the reminder that I was not dead.

How can you be dead when you feel like this?

Somehow, I don't know how it happened, but my dressing gown was gaping and he was down lower, sucking at my tits. I remember looking at his face, his tufts of dark hair, pressed into my collarbone. I felt womanly, maternal. I knew I couldn't stop this. There was no reason to stop. This was the best way to comfort someone. If I could do this for everyone, every man, then surely the world would be a better place. Imagine on the subway, healing the soulless faces, touching their hands grimy from newspaper print, letting everyone who needed it suck me there, hold me tight. I would spread sustenance, warmth, fulfill some fantasies.

My nipples were hard and he was rolling them around in his mouth, sucking them like candy, pulling at them. I still felt tender toward him, tender toward everything—but I felt crazy too. Go lower, I wanted to urge, go south. I wanted him to suck my clit before I exploded.

He was kissing me again, little angel kisses on my lips and my chin. He was pulling me onto him, and I let him because he was so upset, and if I was making him feel just a little better, it would make me feel a hundred percent better. To see my nipples harden and pinken was something I just wouldn't have expected at a time like this.

At a time like this.

I was leaning over him so that my breasts kind of plopped into his mouth. I was thinking how lovely it was. Nothing else. I know that you are supposed to be wondering tortured thoughts—*Where will this go? How will this end?*—but I didn't wonder about any of that. In fact, I thought he, we, wouldn't go further. I thought this was it, a complete story. But then he yanked my dressing gown up at the back and his hand landed on the cusp of my ass. Fuck!

Jesus, it felt nice. The hole between my legs turned liquid from his hands toying with my butt. I was making little noises of approval. These fired him up: the next instant he was sucking my breast furiously, fiercely, harder than before. I thought, *What about the other one? What's wrong with that one?* Then he moved over and nursed my other nipple and I was controlling his head, urging him on. Even to myself I sounded like one of those women in the dirty movies, telling him to suck me, telling him how horny he made me.

I felt like he was taking possession of my body. He was really moving in, and I didn't know how I felt about that. At the same time I was thanking God that someone was taking control of me. It was glorious to let someone else be responsible for a change. I was sitting lightly on his hands, and he was massaging my naked buttocks. Biting my titties. Did he know how creamy my cunt had become? Did he realize that I would fuck him like a shot, bereavement or no? He looked me in the eyes again before another round of bruising kisses.

"Robert," I murmured, "what are we doing?"

I suppose my intervention came too weak, too late.

It did not take much for the poor man to slide one finger, just one culpable finger, between my legs. And it took just one exploring finger to change the way of the world and to make all of our decisions. His finger found my cunt, wandered up my creamy slit. I was wetter than the ocean. He groaned his surprise. Still, as soon as his fingers were slithering around in my moistness, I knew that this wasn't right.

Sarah will kill me.

I had never fancied Robert before, and I say that in all honesty. But I wanted him now. Oh yes. I wanted him to fuck me like I wanted nothing else in the world.

His finger filled my sex. And he had such massive fingers, and his other hand, the hand on my buttocks, was clenching me tight. Exploring where it shouldn't, gliding up and down the gap between my cheeks. Oh God, Robert, do it to me more.

Sarah will never find out.

More fingers were involved. One was on my clitoris, flicking gently, Oh God, Robert, you are going to make me come. I was burning up. I was reentering the earth's atmosphere, or maybe I was halfway to heaven.

Sarah taught you well.

I felt that he wanted me on top of him, but I wouldn't. I didn't want to straddle him but to be annihilated by him. *Fill me up.* Wasn't I the "victim" here? He pressed down on me—not questioning, not fainthearted, but assertive. *This is my right, my primitive right.* His cock grew huge against my thigh. *Yes, bigger you bastard, as big as it will go.*

My wetness coaxed him to be brave. In the tremors of our bodies, our grief was forgotten. He started kissing me again. Long deep dark kisses, knowing kisses, victorious kisses.

Sarah aged twelve asking Dad what erogenous zones were. "Places that are hot," he'd said, winking at me.

My dressing gown was parted and Robert was sucking powerfully on my nipples, yearning at them, serenading them with his pointed tongue.

I wanted to feel alive again.

Remind me that I am not dead. Show me that I am flesh and blood, and squealing cunt, and horny thighs, and breasts, and curly pubic hair. He went there, between my legs, with his lovely, clever tongue. He licked me there, my wet pussy, sucking out my loneliness the way people suck out the poison of snakebites. He pushed me down so I was lying with my dressing gown askew, legs open, bent at the knees, not caring what he did to me. My shutters were thrown open. He was fielding my pussy, soaking his face and rubbing it against me.

"You're so good."

I wondered how we compared sister to sister. Did we taste the same? Would we come the same? He licked and licked and I moved, rocking against him, making his face so wet that he had to pull away and wipe himself. And then he was back, determined, vibrating my clit, tongue and fingers, fingers and tongue, and I was cunt-up, eaten up, losing it, losing him. I thrust against his licking face, mad for it. The orgasm stole through me, big shudders following little ones. Embarrassed laughs of disbelief followed my roars of approval.

And then he was up; up and ready to insert his big cock inside me to blot out our pain. He fiddled between my legs and found my welcoming space. After the hors d'oeuvres, my cunt was hungry for the main course. He moved to enter me.

"Do you have a condom?" I hissed.

No.

Then we couldn't fuck, we can't fuck because tonight is definitely not the night the first grandchild will be conceived, not by him and me. I didn't trust him not to come the moment he entered me. I would, why wouldn't he?

Oh shit, the interruption, the aching, I needed fucking like I never had before. This emptiness had to be filled. *Let me escape just for a minute again into the oblivion of orgasm.* My body was still shaking from the tremors of the last one, the aftershock. *Do it again before it wears off and we wake up from this dream. Fill me up, fuck me up.* It had to be all of it, his hands on my tits, his mouth on my mouth, and his throbbing dick thrusting up my hole.

"Up my ass," I whispered. I knew Sarah wouldn't. I knew he wanted to, and I knew she wouldn't agree to it. "It's dirty," she'd insisted during one of our private sex chats. Well, I was dirty, a fucking whore. *So fuck me, hurt me, harder, deeper, go where you shouldn't go, come when you shouldn't be thinking about fucking, do it to me when you should be crying, or praying, or drinking sweet tea and eating plain biscuits.*

I got up on my hands and knees, doggy-style. I must have looked a sight with my ass up in the air, waving it about, jiggling it, at a time like this. I liked looking like this. He caught hold of my cheeks and pulled them apart, exposing me, wasting me.

His breath caught. "It's so tiny," he said cautiously. It was the first time for both of us, I think.

"Yes," I said, though I didn't know, how could I know? Dwarfed next to his rigid rod. His fingers sneaked their way around to my underbelly. He put his face forward and nuzzled me again. I clamored for more. I was bewitched.

I wanted it up there.

Things were not normal. Things were unnatural. Him here, me here, making out like teenagers on the carpet, fingering each other in places we didn't know. But I didn't want to be alone; I didn't want time to think. He was a bandage for my wounds, and, I suppose, I was for his.

He held me open and probed my hollow softly with his index finger. It wouldn't budge so he sucked his forbidden brother-in-law finger and put it damp in my forbidden sister-in-law hole. I was anxious, impatient, and terrified. The puckered valley was temporarily sated by the explorer. He entered me. I loved him entering me. I wanted to buck and shout and shudder. He was stroking my buttocks with his bigness, showing me what he was made of. Kneading me with his shaft of neediness.

"Are you sure?"

Sure? What was there to be sure about in this world; nothing would ever be sure again. I could only gulp my fucking willingness. My willingness to be fucked all over. I saw us in the mirror, his mesmerized expression, concentration and the work ethic etched on his lips. He was going to screw me like I needed to be screwed.

He pushed forward. I felt my insides tear and howled, "No, no, no!" We all make mistakes. To think I could do this with him was a big mistake. But he held steady, thank goodness he stayed still and waited for my expansion. I could accommodate him, yes I could. More than that. I wanted to hold him inside me, up me. I scrambled back against him, mashing and grinding. He wrapped his arm around me, perching his hand over my pussy. His hand looked like a diver poised to launch into the deep blue sea. He dove. I felt the trigger, the chase, the splash. All holes filled, all bases covered.

I slammed back again and again to feel his cock work up and down that new place, that uneven road. His hand worked magic on my clitoris and I slammed back, again and again, sighing and coming, and breathing hard, and promising I loved him, and I knew I was alive, I was really alive.

He sped up, and was groaning hot cunts and fucks in my ear, and we jerked against each other, together but not together, alone in our excitement, our exalted incredible comings. I couldn't stop myself from wailing as his cock sliced through me.

Afterwards he disappeared into the bathroom, where he probably examined his prick and tried to wash the guilt off him. *What the fuck have I done?* I knew he must have been feeling that, because I was. He dressed hurriedly, like a man who has overslept on the day of the big company presentation.

"Well, if there's anything you need..." he said, backing away toward the sanity of the street. The car sat loyally against the curb like a puppy faithful to its owner.

"You've already said that."

I watched him walk away. I watched him intently almost to convince myself that he *had* been there, inside my house, his head between my legs, his cock up my ass. As soon as the car drove off he seemed to erase, or vanish. But not completely. My skin felt different, touched, and the hole, the passage, felt used and unfamiliar. Later, no matter how I tried to contort and distort my memory, I could never drive out the events of the day. I realized I had simply exchanged one kind of grief for another.

Jack

Cara Bruce

I was thirteen the first time I met Jack. It was one of those stifling-hot Virginia days, the kind when the air smells like Budweiser even if there's no one drinking. All my carefully applied makeup was running down my face and dripping onto my faded blue cotton halter top. The beige streaks got caught up in the lacy neck and I was just about to pull the top off altogether when Jack came up behind me.

"Hey," he said, his southern drawl heavy, like he wasn't opening his mouth at all, just sort of pushing the words out with his tongue. "Sure is hot."

"Yep, sure is," I said and looked at him. He was scrawny. His white undershirt was soaked to the bone and sticking to him—you would have been able to see all his muscles, except for the fact that he didn't have any. "I'm Jack," he said, rubbing his sweaty palm across his chest before offering me his hand.

"I'm Ceilia, but everyone calls me Sissy," I told him. I used to hate the nickname but nobody ever paid mind so I had no choice but to get used to it.

"Sissy," Jack said, smiling. "I like that."

Suddenly we heard voices. I recognized the high, shrill laugh immediately—it was my older sister Janice. I crouched down behind the fence and Jack did the same.

Janice and her boyfriend came up the path, stopping just a few feet away from us. I held my finger up to my lips, signaling Jack to be quiet. We sat there hunched down and watched as they began to kiss. He was sticking his tongue down Janice's throat and she was making these awful moaning sounds.

Jack and I had to clamp our hands over our mouths to keep from bursting into laughter. They lay down on the grass and the guy rolled over on top of her. Janice started saying stuff that I guess was supposed to be sexy; Jack and I just sat there and watched. After a few minutes they were done and gone. I looked over at Jack, who was even redder then before. His eyes were as big as the dishes hanging on my Mamma's wall.

"You ever done that?" I asked him.

Jack shook his head no. "Have you?"

"Nope," I admitted. Then we both fell over laughing. We laughed so hard tears rolled down our faces, mingling with droplets of sweat.

"Oh, Jack, you are a man," I said shrilly, mimicking Janice's heated cries. Jack made a bunch of kissy noises and we laughed until our sides hurt. That's how Jack and I became best friends.

It wasn't until many years later that Jack and I ended up having sex, and I fell in love with him. Poor Jack, he never really filled out like his brothers or most of the men we knew. Maybe that's why he thought he had to act macho, always bossing me around: "Sissy do this, Sissy do that, Sissy girl, come here and get on your knees."

Oh sure, there were times I hated him, but for the most part I just couldn't help myself—I was in love with the man.

Jack was bossy, and he was rough in bed. It just made me feel sorrier for the poor guy—always feeling like he had something to prove.

Life was good. I made up names for the kids we were going to have and made plans for our wedding. Then one day out of the blue Jack seemed to lose interest. He'd come over and just sit there staring at the TV, watching soap operas and talk shows. Maybe it was because we were best friends before anything else—but a best friend never would have done what he did to me. I woke up on our wedding day and there was nothing in my bed except a letter on my pillow telling me he'd gone. He didn't write another word to me until the other day, when I got a letter telling me he was coming home and needed to see me.

I was sitting on my porch thinking of all the things I wanted to tell him: that he was a rotten bastard, that he'd messed up my life for years. It was a hot day and I held a glass of ice water to my forehead. The longer I sat waiting for him the angrier I got, until I'd almost made up my mind not to talk to him at all, just to give him a big smack across the face.

An hour later his big old truck came rumbling up the driveway, spraying dirt every which way and sending my flowers flying. Just like Jack—not even out of the truck and already messing up everything in sight.

The door to the cab opened and I saw his boots hit the ground. He stood behind the door for a moment and I walked over to give him my hand in greeting. He looked up at me and smiled. It was still Jack, except for one major difference: he was a she.

My mouth dropped open and I took a few steps back, almost losing my balance stumbling on an old tire.

Jack's head dropped. She stared at the dirt and said, "I'm sorry, Sissy. I should have told you but I was afraid you wouldn't see me."

I didn't know what to say. Jack was a beautiful woman. His cropped hair was now long and curly. He still had the same slim build, only with tits. There was no way I could hide my shock. I walked up to her and wrapped my arms around her 'cause I didn't know what else to do. Jack pulled me close and held me. Her new body fit perfectly against mine. She smelled like musky sweat. I laughed to myself, thinking of all the heartsick nights I had spent imagining Jack with another woman.

"Sissy," she started slowly, "I know this is probably a shock but I'm happy now. I had to leave."

I held my finger to my lips. She looked up and met my eyes. I smiled at her.

We went into the house and I fixed her a drink. She sat easily in the chair, her legs spread open in tight blue jeans. I wondered if the operation was complete. I wanted to pull down her pants, more out of curiosity than lust—or maybe even out of anger.

"Have you been to see your family?" I asked, keeping my cool.

"No, I wanted to get your reaction first," she said. "You know, Sissy, I really did love you."

"I know," I said, forcing a smile. "I loved you too."

We made ourselves comfortable in the living room and talked about old times. After a while I came over and sat next to her on the couch. Jack looked at me tentatively. Man or woman, I supposed the brain was the same—I used to be able to turn him on like a light switch. I didn't think it should be any different now.

"You want to take a shower?" I asked. "You know, to cool off?"

"Sure, Sissy, that would be great." I led her to the bathroom and handed her a towel.

"Do you mind if I join you?"

Jack looked a little uncertain but I didn't leave. She slipped off her sweaty tee shirt and black bra. I was surprised at how nice her tits were. She was hesitating, though, and I didn't want to give her time to get uncomfortable, so I stripped and stood waiting. Jack unbuttoned her jeans and slipped out of them. I looked at her crotch and smiled; I couldn't see any major differences between hers and mine—but I also couldn't wait to get down on my knees and find out. We got into my small shower stall.

"Let me rub you down," I offered, soaping up the washcloth and sliding it down Jack's back. She kept her back to me so I had to turn her around to get at her front. Jack kept her head down—the poor girl had no idea what was going on. I lifted her chin with my hand and brought her lips to mine. The kiss was soft and sweet. I opened her mouth with my tongue, a mouth I had known once before but without lipstick. Jack moaned: her voice was higher. Slowly I drew my hands over her round, wet ass. I groped it, pulling her closer. I pushed her back against the shower door and knelt before her.

My hand reached up between her legs, pushing them farther apart. My fingers slid easily up her dripping slit. She arched her back and leaned on my hand. If she were truly a woman then I knew what she would like; I thrust another finger into her and felt her created cunt tighten around me.

"Oh yeah," she murmured as I knelt before her. My tongue went from clit to cunt as my fingers pumped. I felt her knees weaken as she grabbed my hair.

"Do you want my dick?" I asked her, my fingers never ceasing.

"Your dick?" she asked, her voice surprised—but I detected a twinge of hope.

I led her out of the shower and pushed her onto the bathroom floor, then ran into my bedroom and got the harness and dildo I had gotten as a joke for my twenty-first birthday—which Jack had missed.

I strapped it on and sauntered back into the bathroom, feeling like a cowboy with my gun drawn. If she wanted to be a woman I was going to fuck her like one. She looked at me wide-eyed; I smiled as if this sort of thing happened to me every day, and lay down on top of her.

"How does it feel to be a woman?" I asked her, guiding my plastic prick into her hot hole.

"Good," she whispered. "It feels so good."

"Do you like my big cock?" I teased with the old Jack's own words. "Do you like my big dick inside of you?"

"Yes, oh yes, I do."

I thrust it in a little farther and began to pick up the pace. "Tell me. Say 'I like Sissy's cock.'"

"I like Sissy's cock," she whispered.

I brought one hand down and slid a finger up her tight ass. She bucked her hips against me and groaned. I fucked her hard and rough, the same way she had fucked me years before. Jack was clenching at my shoulders, digging nails into skin, trembling and whimpering.

I got my angle perfectly so my clit was being hit with each thrust. Her legs began to shake.

"Oh yes, Sissy, fuck me, oh yes." I pumped her harder and faster until she came, calling my name and writhing on the floor. My only regret was that I couldn't come first and leave her unsatisfied.

We got up off the floor and showered again. Jack looked at me now with those big post-orgasm doe-eyes. I fixed up some dinner and we sat down to eat.

"I'm really sorry I left you, Sissy," she said. "I've always loved you."

"I was sorry you left too, but I got over it," I told her with a smile. I had her right where I wanted her—still in love with me, and now in love with my dick.

"Maybe things could still work out between us?" she asked, resting her hand near mine.

"I don't know Jack, it seems like we've both been through a lot of changes." She laughed until she realized I was serious.

"Oh Sissy, you don't even know how much I've missed you," she gushed, tears forming in her eyes.

"Why don't you spend the night?" I said. "I've got a little game we could play."

I led the horny Jack into my bedroom and brought out my handcuffs. Once she was securely fastened to my bedpost I began to dress.

"What are you doing?" she asked, frightened.

"I thought I'd go get dessert," I said. "Don't worry, I'll be back."

I took the keys to her truck and walked out the door. Who knows—maybe I'll come back someday.

Branded

Rebecca Kissel

I'm terrified. And the funny thing is, I'm terrified by something I agreed to. Agreed to? *Suggested*. Ever since I read the Gor books (yes, yes I did, so what?) I've been fantasizing about being branded. A mark burned into my body that says I'm his. More his than a ring can say, or a collar, or even a tattoo with a heart and arrow and his name inked into my skin by some hairy guy named Big Ed.

We've talked about the branding, my lover and I, read Web pages, decided on the brand, bought supplies to keep the branding from getting infected. I wanted the whole experience. I wanted to be tied, gagged, and helpless. Remember the old saying, be careful what you wish for? I am tied, gagged, blindfolded, helpless, no safe word or grunt or gesture. I am going to have a brand like some cow in the pasture, only skin isn't leather and I know what the smell of burning metal means and even though I went to the bathroom before he tied me my bladder feels full. Sweat is pouring from my skin in droplets, soaking the bed.

He is standing over me, the cool alcohol swab feeling so good against my flushed skin. I am hot; it's the sweaty heat of absolute terror. Isn't this what I wanted, always pushing, always wanting more—more pain, more fear, his cock punishing me, ramming inside my throat, my unlubricated ass? Now I'm getting more—more than I can handle. I don't want to do this; the problem is, what I want doesn't matter. I have no way of screaming "stop"; the screams and whimpers and "NO, NO" coming out of my ball gag are incomprehensible sounds that could be pleasure. There is no backing out, and I'm helpless and afraid and wondering if I'll pee the bed or pass out. I'm hoping for passing out.

The smell of metal is getting stronger; I can hear the fire popping. We chose to rent a cabin in the woods. That way no one would call the fire department or any other potentially embarrassing thing like that. I didn't realize the potential embarrassment would be internal. I am going to shame myself because I've finally reached my limit. Only it's too late.

I have to be honest. In spite of the terror and discovery of a limit, the knots in my stomach are not all fear. No, there is the sexual tingling of finally discovering true helplessness. Poor lover, he can never rape me or beat me into oblivion because I always really want it. I don't want this, but I'm going to get it, and that total helplessness has me so turned on I could come with the simplest touch. But the touch I'm about to get isn't the kind I need.

I hear him walking to the fire; he is telling me what he is doing. "Pet, I'm walking to the fire, pulling out the brand, it's glowing red." He is talking softly, gently, about his red-hot poker, and I'm thinking I'm going to puke. Great, now I have three choices: puke, wet myself, or pass out. A few minutes ago I thought I had no choices at all.

"I'm standing over you now. I'm going to mark you as mine." He is purring, his brand of ownership to be on my body always, burned into my skin. I'm screaming, my throat hurts, my head feels as if it might explode. I'm thinking a stroke isn't a farfetched possibility. I'm not sure my body can hold such fear, such excitement.

I feel the heat before it comes close to my hip. I can picture the glowing red of the silver brand. Closer, closer, then pain. I am trying to struggle, but he has me tied really well—my lover knows his ropes. I'm screaming but all that's coming from behind the gag are whimpers. I am sobbing, my tears mingling with the sweat pouring down my face. He is counting the seconds we decided on to make the brand permanent, I can barely hear him over the roaring in my ears. I don't think I will pass out from the pain. I can't describe it, do justice to the pain, but I will try: it's intense, and it is the focal point of my life. I can feel my muscles bunched, knotted like the rope tying me down. My fists are clenched, heart pounding, and I am taking the pain. I have no choice as my hip burns and blackens and blisters. I think he's stopped counting and the branding iron is gone, but it doesn't matter because it still burns, still hurts. I can feel his hand touching between the folds of my lips, and yes I'm wet, yes I'm excited. Even through the pain I can feel his fingers probing inside me, and I know I am going to orgasm. I don't want to. I feel I've given everything I have to give and he wants more; I'm limp and ragged and my hip hurts.

Still, he wants something more, and it's something I can give him, because I can feel the coiling in my belly that tells me my orgasm is close. Suddenly my body stiffens and I scream into the gag, only this time in pleasure. When my orgasm finally subsides, he removes his hand. I feel his body weight press down on the bed in front of me, his cock pressing between my legs. He can only enter me shallowly, from in front—my legs are tied together but I'm wet enough that he can glide over my thighs and between my wet swollen lips. Belly to belly, I can feel his cock gliding in and out, his hand trailing along my body, feeling the sweat, the heat. His fingers stop right before the brand, my breath catches, I feel him gently trace his brand, barely touching, but the pain makes me squirm, the squirming pushing me closer to him. I feel his thrusting increase and I know I'm going to come with him as he suddenly grabs my hips, his fingers digging into the muscles of my bottom, the weight of his wrist against my brand making me scream and wiggle harder. I can feel him coming, the sticky wetness on my thighs and lips, my own orgasm answering him.

We lay there a moment, panting. I know he'll untie me soon, ask me if I'm okay. I also know I will probably laugh and tell him about the rush, the high, and not mention that I wanted him to stop. My reputation as a pain slut will stay firmly in place. In fact, I'm already wondering if we shouldn't put a matching brand on my left hip.

Pilegesh
Lisa Prosimo

"I have tried. You know I have tried," Rachel told God as she sat among the women in *shul*. "I'm twenty-six years old. If someone doesn't touch me soon, dear Lord, I will die."

She felt a slight poke in her rib. "You're swaying," Kippy, her best friend, whispered. Rachel took a deep breath and held her body still. If she wasn't careful, she would bring disgrace upon her family. Already her mother had warned her to be mindful of her deportment. "You must not forget you are an Orthodox woman. Do you want everyone to think badly of you?"

I would like someone, anyone, to think of me, period, Rachel thought.

She strained to see David Nussbaum standing on the other side of the partition separating the men from the women. It wasn't easy to penetrate the thickly veiled divider, but with a furtive gaze she was able to recognize him. Once, David had thought of her. "I think of you all the time, Rachel," he had said.

Young, strong, handsome, and from one of the leading families in the congregation, David had looked at her in a way that allowed her to dream of their being joined as husband and wife. Her parents had been pleased, of course, but her mother had warned her not to get her hopes up. "The Nussbaums' *yichus* is far superior to our own. David's lineage can be traced to a highly regarded dynasty of rabbis in Hungary, while we are of common Jewish stock."

Although Rachel's family was by no means destitute, the dowry that would have been demanded by the Nussbaums, had they found Rachel suitable, was a sum her parents would have found impossible to satisfy. Yet she had dismissed her mother's concerns. Surely, if David wanted her as much as his eyes said he did, her pedigree would be of little bother.

Rabbi Weisfogel's voice rose above Rachel's thoughts and she pulled her eyes from David's face. She had no right to look at him. Her mother's concerns had proved to be real. David had been married for two years now to a girl with a *yichus* as worthy as his own. He was the father of a year-old son, a baby so plump, red-cheeked, and precious that her breasts and belly ached when she was fortunate enough to hold him.

Rachel let her eyes return to David's face. Rights be damned! The child, as well as the father, should have been hers! David looked so unhappy these days. She never saw him smile anymore. *What is it that has taken your joy,* she wondered. *Do you ever regret not choosing me?*

"Rachel!" Kippy's harsh whisper pierced her ear. "You're like a billboard advertisement, for goodness sake. The way you look at him! It's a wonder the Rebbe has not reproached you."

"I can't help it," Rachel exclaimed as they walked down the boulevard behind Rachel's parents after the service. She stopped abruptly. "Kippy, am I ugly?"

"Of course you're not ugly. You're a beautiful girl. I'm ugly."

"No!"

But it was true. Kippy not only had a questionable *yichus,* she was ugly. Rachel sighed. Perhaps that's what bothered her most. If she'd been ugly like Kippy she could accept her status, go on about her life, content to render service to her family and community the way Kippy did. Perhaps then she would not feel cheated. She resolved to pray extra hard for God to take away her resentment, to be content with being Rachel Brand, the daughter of Chaim and Miriam Brand, good and loving parents; to be content with her job at Dr. Jacobson's office where she made appointments and billed insurance and kept meticulous records. And if God saw fit, He would send another man to take David's place in her heart.

"I have a ten o'clock, Mrs. Weissman," said Rachel into the telephone. "Dr. Jacobson can see you then. What shall I tell the doctor is the nature of your complaint?" She nodded. "A cold. All right." Rachel scribbled the name Chana Weissman into that morning's ten o'clock slot. "We'll see you then," she said.

Curious, Rachel thought, that Chana Weissman should take time to visit Dr. Jacobson because of a cold. The woman never stopped running. "She pours herself out like a drink offering," Rachel's mother had said more than once. "Have you ever seen a woman more service-minded? From Rabbi Weisfogel's mouth to Chana's ear!"

Ten o'clock came quickly. "I suggest more rest, Chana," said Dr. Jacobson as he walked Chana Weissman to the front counter. He smiled at Rachel. "I'll see Mrs. Weissman in a month."

"Yes, Dr. Jacobson." Rachel prepared an appointment card for Chana Weissman and handed it to her.

"Rachel, dear," said Chana, "we haven't spoken in such a long time. Perhaps you would take lunch with me today?"

The invitation took Rachel by surprise. She usually ate her lunch in Dr. Jacobson's back office, taking no more than twenty or thirty minutes with her sandwich and glass of tea. She smiled up at Chana Weissman. The widow was a *shadchan,* but if she had a match for Rachel wouldn't she have approached her father first?

"I am so hungry for Solomon's kishka," Chana said. "Get your coat."

When Chana Weissman used that tone, there was no protesting or questioning. Although it was only a little past eleven o'clock, Rachel shut down her computer and pulled on her coat.

Chana Weissman took a large swallow of tea and made a face. She reached inside her mouth to loosen a piece of food that had stuck to a back tooth. "Too dry," she proclaimed. "And to this much onion, I am violently allergic." She shrugged. "So, Rachela, your family is well?"

"Very well, thank you, Mrs. Weissman."

Chana Weissman pushed aside her empty plate and eyed the uneaten half of Rachel's sandwich. "You eat like a bird," she said. "Or, the brisket is dry, also?"

"No, no," Rachel assured her. "It's very good. It's just that my stomach is a little..."

"Upset?" She nodded. "Say no more. I understand. More than you know, I understand." She reached over and placed her hand over Rachel's.

"Excuse me?"

Chana Weissman lifted her hand from Rachel's and waved it before her. "The sad eyes, the droopy lips—I know these things, Rachel. And so does the Rebbe. And so does God."

Rachel felt her cheeks flame. Kippy was right. Her body was a billboard and Chana Weissman had taken her to lunch to reprove her. She lowered her head and tried to blink back her tears.

"No, no, my darling girl," Chana whispered. "Stop already. I am here to tell you that God has seen you suffering to no end. You have been chosen."

"I've been what?"

"Only two words I have for you. *David Nussbaum.*"

"Mrs. Weissman!"

"Should we know more than God? Than the Rebbe?" She put her hand over Rachel's again. "You love him."

It was a simple statement and Rachel could not disagree.

"The details are not my business, but the Rebbe has given David a *heter,* a special dispensation for a *pilegesh*. He and God have chosen you."

Rachel found it difficult to breathe. David Nussbaum wanted her to be his concubine! That practice had been banned since medieval times. These were the '90s! She stared at Chana Weissman.

"Have I taken your breath away, Rachela? Again I say, 'Should we know more than God?'"

Chana explained that should Rachel agree, like a married woman she would be expected to immerse in a *mikvah,* the ritual bath that would eradicate the effects of her spiritual impurity due to menstruation. "Of course, since this is a special situation between David, the Rebbe, and God, you will take your *mikvah* alone."

Rachel stopped listening. David wanted her. And God wanted David to have her. At that moment she didn't care why or how such a thing could be. It was. She wiped away her tears and smiled at Chana Weissman, God's disciple.

Rachel's mother was pleased when Chana Weissman took her daughter under her wing. "You can learn so much from Chana," her mother said. "Yes, by all means, go. Spend a few evenings with Mrs. Weissman."

Seven days after her period, Rachel completed her *mikvah* under Chana's guidance. Now she stood before the mirror in Chana's bedroom, adorned as a bride for her husband.

The floorboards creaked as Rachel moved from the mirror to the bed. An eerie silence had settled over the apartment since Chana Weissman discreetly slipped away. *Should David find her sitting on the bed or standing in front of the mirror,* she wondered. *Perhaps brushing her hair?*

Soon the door to the bedroom opened and there was David, his tallis bag in hand. Rachel recognized it as the gift his wife had made him for their wedding day. The embroidery was splendid. Embarrassment flashed over her and she tore her eyes from the bag. David set it down and walked to her.

"I have prayed and prayed," he said. "And God has seen fit to answer."

Ghosts of questions dizzied Rachel's brain, but she pushed them aside. She was standing before the man she loved. Better not to give the questions bones or meat.

David lifted Rachel's hand and brought her fingers to his lips. "So thin and delicate," he said. He kissed each one. Rachel closed her eyes, feeling the readiness in her thighs. Her body seemed to float upward. A brief, electric current pierced her belly. *Love is strong, love is potent,* she thought.

David's lips came down on hers, his hands following the curve of her breasts under the thin cotton gown. "Lovely," he murmured. Rachel's mouth opened to receive his tongue. She heard a sigh catch inside his throat. David stepped back and drew the gown up and over Rachel's head. His hands covered her breasts. "How long have these been waiting for my mouth?"

"Too long, David."

He leaned forward and sucked a nipple between his lips. She looked down at the curl of his lashes, the slant of his nose, the blush of his cheek. Her body loosened, her knees grew weak. David caught her at the waist and lifted her into his arms. He brought her to the bed and gently lay her down. Quickly he shed his clothes and joined her.

They lay face-to-face, touching and stroking. David reached between her thighs. His fingers slipped into her wet folds and found her clitoris. Rachel's body hummed with the wonder of his touch, each caress evoking a hunger that astonished her. He withdrew his fingers and replaced them with his mouth, his tongue making circles over the small nub that beat to the rhythm of her heart.

On his knees in the near-dark, David caressed Rachel's neck and then slipped his thumb inside her mouth. His silent invitation explicit, Rachel slid across the linen and grasped his penis in her hand. He moved forward and she opened her lips to take him in. He rocked back and forth, his penis slipping in and out of her mouth, and she marveled at its texture, like a water-smoothed stone. The sound of her moist sucking carried her further along the stream rushing inside her.

Abruptly, David stopped and rolled away, disturbing the carnal haze that enveloped her. She watched him fumble with the drawer of Chana Weissman's nightstand. When he turned back he had a condom in his hand. "There cannot be a child from this union," he said. His statement held the tone of apology, but she said nothing as he ripped the square open and removed the latex sheath. She watched him roll it down over his penis. The sight of him touching his own flesh sent sparks through the bud of her sex and she forgot the regret of having to be separated from his seed. She forgot everything except the length of his body against hers, his hands sliding beneath her buttocks, lifting and parting her cheeks as he drew her closer, his penis jutting forward, seeking to open her. Breast to breast, belly to belly, sweat-slicked and steamy, he pressed zealously to rupture the barrier of her virginity. His lips at her ear, he murmured, "Need...unbearable...so sweet...please, Rachel, please..."

Rachel could not speak. With each thrust she lost more of her conscious self, dissolved in a pool of pleasure, the craving finally answered, the appetite finally satisfied. How easily her body unhinged, threw off the years of modesty, etiquette, propriety. How easy it was to cast aside her privacy, her convention, her reason. Only with her body could she murmur, only with her flesh could she answer the need, relieve the unbearable, acknowledge the sweet. *Ah, yes, David, yes...*

Inside her now, deeper, his arm around her waist, his hand pressing into the small of her back, arching her upward, closer, his mouth feeding greedily at her breast, her legs askew, bouncing lightly against the linen, staining Chana Weissman's expensive linen, her arms flung wide, hands gnawing the air, clawing the bedpost, her mouth open. Dry, her sounds, a nest of birds cooing deep within her throat. That place within her, that sense of self, that last frontier giving way, obliterated by ecstasy, by flesh answering flesh.

David, drawing in and out of her, loosening and tightening, words mumbled and jumbled, licks and bites and cries..."Oh, God...oh, no...not yet...it's so good...so long...too long...I don't want to yet...oh, God...I'm...Oh, God, I'm coming!"

Later, lying in David's arms, Rachel marveled at how wrong the Talmud is in its description of what a virgin feels when she is deflowered. "The pain of hot water slowly poured upon a bald head," it says. Ridiculous. More like the balm of Gilead being rubbed into an aching muscle. Blessed relief.

"David?"

"Yes?"

"Am I truly your wife?"

"You are the wife of my heart." There were tears in his voice. "Life is not always fair, Rachel."

"I know."

"A man must have passion in his life if he is to feel alive."

"A woman, also. David?"

"Hmmm?"

"Listen. Do you hear it? Inside the silence?"

"What is it, love?"

"The sound of my happiness."

David buried his face in her bosom. His tears drenched her skin. "Before this night, I hated my life." David sat up. "Since the child, there has been nothing. Not even during *Shabbos* when there is an obligation to make love!"

"David! You mustn't tell me these things. I'm not made of brick."

"No, of course, you are right."

"I am here for you."

He sighed. "You won't think me dirty? You won't mind my words?"

"No, of course not. What words?"

"The words for lovemaking."

He tossed the covers off their bodies, pointed. "My cock. Your cunt."

Rachel ran the words over in her mind. Cock. Cunt. Intimate words. No, she didn't mind the words. "I like them."

He laughed and covered her body with his. "I love you, Rachel. This will be a good marriage."

In the months that passed there were other words spoken in the sanctity of Chana Weissman's bedroom. Fuck. Suck. Lick. K-Y jelly. Even innocent words took on erotic meaning when David and Rachel came together. Squeeze. Rub. Stroke.

She was bold. "Where do you want me?" she'd ask. Then he would reach over to her ass, stroke her crease with slippery fingers until she begged him to put his cock inside her.

He took her every way but one without a condom, entering her cunt with his unspoken apology. Each time she heard the words of their first meeting. "There cannot be a child from this union." They stabbed at her heart for a moment, until passion gripped her and they fell away.

Sometimes she used her mouth, kissing, licking, nibbling at his inner thighs until his cock grew rigid and he groaned her name over and over. Then she would tongue him, making small circles around the glans, slowly increasing the pressure before finally wrapping her lips over him and sucking slowly while she caressed his balls. She loved when he whispered "Suck me," a cry in his voice.

At *shul,* as she sat between Kippy and Chana Weissman, she would stare at the head of the person in front of her as if it were a television screen, watching herself and David. Limbs twisted, lips giving attention to each other's nipples, pelvises straining forward, cock to ass, mouth to cunt. Her breath would escape her lungs and she would feel the perspiration gather in slick desire as she struggled to shield her eyes from Kippy's curious stare and Chana's knowing smile. What did Chana Weissman think, coming home and smelling their hours of sex in her bedroom? What kind of reports did she give the Rebbe?

Rachel did not allow herself to look at David's other wife. Friends remarked on the cut of Mrs. Nussbaum's clothes, the richness of her furs, and the sparkle of her diamonds. She was well respected and envied as the wife of David Nussbaum, diamond broker, his booth on 47th Street a success, as it had been for his father and his father's father. Mrs. Nussbaum, whose husband's generous gift to the congregation's building fund had made a new library possible. Rachel knew if she were to give the woman even one glance, she would taste bile. Instead she concentrated on what she and David would do when they came together.

Next time she would ask David to tie her up. She would ask him to put one of Chana Weissman's pillows under her ass to give him maximum access to her cunt. She would watch as he slid his cock inside her; then she would bring her legs up and encircle his back and rock into him, feel him reach all the way through her body, burrowing into her, one long, then one short stroke, as was his habit. He could fuck forever that way, ringing her cunt with pleasure. Just before he came he would seek out her tongue and suck hard, muffling their moans of rapture. Yes. His other wife had his name, his child, his worldly goods, but Rachel was happier to have his cock and his soul.

Rachel sat in Dr. Jacobson's office, her embroidery needle poised over the square of practice material she had cut from a larger piece. She examined her stitches and frowned. Not nearly good enough. She had purchased the finest needle, one you could hardly see, and the most delicate silk thread, but her work still looked bulky and amateurish. She pictured David's tallis bag with its exquisite embroidery, and she wanted to cry. She might as well admit it. She did not have the same talent for needlework as David's other wife. She could not give him a gift of beauty from her hands, just as she could not give him a gift of beauty from her body.

Rachel sighed and stuffed the swatch and needle into her bag. She had to get ready to assist Dr. Jacobson with that afternoon's patients; Sheila, his nurse, had gone home sick. Thankfully, the doctor's schedule was light.

Rachel looked at the clock. The doctor would be returning from lunch in a few minutes. She walked into the front office and began to restack the magazines, pausing when she heard some sort of commotion outside in the hall. A male voice begged for quiet. The plea was met by a high female wail, a sound so sorrowful that it entered Rachel's bones.

The door flew open and Dr. Jacobson all but dragged Deborah Cohen into the office. Mr. Cohen, Deborah's father, quickly shut the door. Again, he begged his daughter to be silent.

She screamed an emphatic "No!" and broke free of Dr. Jacobson, ran to where Rachel stood, and grabbed a fistful of her sweater. "I curse God!" she hissed, her eyes wild, her spittle spraying up into Rachel's face. "He is a liar!"

Rachel stood speechless as Mr. Cohen and Dr. Jacobson wrestled the young girl away and into the nearest examining room. Even with the door closed, Rachel heard Deborah shouting curses, condemning the Almighty, the Rebbe, Isaac Gittleman, and others whose names became too slurred to decipher.

After a few moments she heard nothing. She tiptoed down the hall and stood outside the examining room, listening. She couldn't help herself. What could make a lighthearted young girl, barely eighteen, behave in such a manner?

"Yes, I understand," Rachel heard Dr. Jacobson say. "A wild story, yes, but where could she have heard such things?"

Mr. Cohen, his voice anguished and weary, answered, "I don't know. We are losing our minds, my wife and I, listening to these ravings, is all I know. My daughter has gone mad. She is screaming in the night, seeing hands and other body parts I cannot mention. *Oy,* I tell you, Sol, we are beside ourselves."

A quick shuffle and the door opened. Rachel, caught like an infidel at the altar, felt the blood drain from her face. Dr. Jacobson stared at her for a moment then walked past her and into his private office. Mr. Cohen stood in the doorway.

"I didn't hear any more screams," Rachel explained, knowing she didn't sound convincing. "I was wondering..."

"Dr. Jacobson gave Deborah a sedative. As you can see, she's resting."

Indeed, the girl was asleep. Her body lay in a relaxed heap upon the examination table. Rachel nodded and attempted a smile but Mr. Cohen shut the door in her face. Her heart pounded wildly. "I want to know what you heard," said Dr. Jacobson when the last patient had gone.

Rachel couldn't bring herself to admit that she'd heard nothing. She wanted to know more. So instead of telling him the truth she said, "I heard everything."

Dr. Jacobson ran a hand across his eyes. "Rachel...I don't have to remind you that what happens here must be held in the strictest confidence."

"Yes, Dr. Jacobson. You don't have to remind me."

"You should not have listened at the door. It was wrong of you to do so."

"I was worried about Deborah," she said, realizing that her excuse was partially true. "No one we know has ever behaved that way."

Dr. Jacobson leaned forward. "No. And I'm sorry you had to see it. Listen carefully, Rachel. The girl is very ill. Her accusations are the ravings of a lunatic."

Answer carefully, thought Rachel. "What if she's not a lunatic, Dr. Jacobson? What if she's telling the truth?"

The impact of her question colored the doctor's cheeks, letting her know that he had considered the same possibility. Rachel concentrated hard on keeping her composure.

"Come now, Rachel. Surely you don't believe a person of Isaac Gittleman's integrity would force himself upon Deborah, then tell her that God had seen fit to give her to him."

Rachel's mouth went dry. "It could happen," she whispered.

Dr. Jacobson sighed and leaned back in his chair. It seemed as if he would collapse under the weight of his shoulders. "For once, the soup was just right. Not too hot, not too cold. A pleasant lunch. Then I get Meir Cohen and his daughter for dessert. And now you, Rachel, give me a hard time."

Though she'd known Dr. Jacobson all her life and respected him as she did her own father, she felt an urge to reach out and slap him. Instead she pulled a chair over to his desk, sat down, and leaned toward him. "Everyone loves the Rebbe, Dr. Jacobson, yet Deborah cursed him. This comes from the sky, this hatred?"

"In one who is delusional, why not?"

"A strange rainstorm, no?"

Dr. Jacobson slumped down even further. "We should not even speak of such things."

"I thought I heard her yell Chana Weissman's name," Rachel pressed.

"Yes...a woman who has been very kind to Deborah. Like a second mother."

Rachel nodded. "She is like a second mother to me, also."

"So, see? Who knows where such things come from?"

Rachel dropped her eyes and stared at a nick in the desk's polished mahogany. After a few moments, she stood up. "Maybe you're right." She pulled the chair back to its place in front of the desk. "I have to close up the office." She turned to leave.

"Rachel?"

Rachel faced the doctor and forced herself to smile. "I won't say a word. You have my promise. And I know you'll do all you can to help Deborah."

"Of course."

"Good night, Dr. Jacobson."

On the bus ride home Rachel tried to push the image of a hysterical Deborah out of her mind, tried to concentrate on her next meeting with David, tried to picture him kissing her all over, murmuring his love into her ear, reminding her how happy he was now that she was part of his life. But she couldn't forget the girl's feverish eyes, her terror, her look of utter despair.

She gazed out the window. This neighborhood was her life. Her whole world. Rarely had she ventured from the confines of its traditions and mandates. There had been a few forays into the forbidden—a couple of trips by herself to the New York City Library, seeking written words that might validate the feelings and changes taking place within her body. She had pored over volumes and volumes that allowed her to glimpse worlds where people expressed and even, God forbid, celebrated their feelings. The excitement and guilt of her secret excursions had lasted for weeks. What she had learned served her well. Hadn't she proved it in David's arms?

Although Rachel could not pretend to know what might be taking place within the congregation, she could not go beyond her gut reaction to Deborah's desperation or to that look of fear in Dr. Jacobson's eyes. Did the Rebbe give Isaac Gittleman a *heter,* also? Had God made Deborah his *pilegesh?*

That nothing would come of Deborah's plight was certain. Her father and Dr. Jacobson would see to it that she, along with her ravings, would disappear. She would be cared for, of course, but until she was "cured" she would cease to exist.

What about Rachel? What would have happened if she had rejected her arrangement, questioned Chana Weissman's proposition? What if she had gone to her father and told him everything? He would not have believed her. Perhaps she would have been sent away to be "cured" as well.

Rachel knew that there were men who sold women to other men. Pimps. But their Rebbe was not a pimp. He was cherished and revered by the community, heir to an almost infallible approbation by God through his forefathers. Who would dare challenge his authority? If, for instance, their arrangement became public, could David not simply point to his Rebbe and the *heter,* written proof that their union had been sanctioned? Or would he just deny their arrangement even existed? Within the congregation, how many would protest? Perhaps no one. Except David's other wife—wouldn't she have the right to demand a divorce if she did not see things the same way?

Rachel had never allowed herself to think about the particulars of her and David's arrangement. Now her head hurt from thinking of all the possible consequences. David could have divorced his wife for the same reasons he had been given a *heter* in the first place. Technically, he would have been within his God-given rights. So, then, had God given him a choice? And where, in all this, was *her* choice? Where was *her* hope for the future?

Stop, she told herself. *Stop. Admit that your choice was to have David Nussbaum between your thighs, for whatever reason.* Perhaps this was God's way of answering the prayers of women who long for the men of their dreams. Who could question His reasons for favoring one person over another, the way he favored Jacob over Esau, Esther over Vashti? Were not all God's ways a mystery, and His people merely instruments put on this earth to work out His will?

Enough thinking already. In just two days she would be with David and he would make her body shudder with God's blessing.

Rachel sat on Chana Weissman's bed waiting for David. She placed her hands on each side of her head and squeezed. If only she could squeeze out all of her questions, drop them to the floor, kick them under the bed!

Questions demand answers. *But what answers do you want, stupid girl? Do you want your answer to be: never touch David again?* God forbid! Had she the power, she would have David Nussbaum crawl up inside her womb, where she would lock him in and keep him forever.

David walked into the bedroom. He tossed his tallis bag aside and did not bother to tell her he had prayed before coming to her, did not seem anxious to include God in their union. Instead he tore at his clothes, freed his cock, and quickly pushed it deep inside her. "All month I dreamed of this," he said. She exploded around him, coming with a force that left her legs shaking. She felt him, still hard within her. She squeezed his cock with her muscles but knew he would not come, not without protection.

"I love to make you come quickly," he murmured against her ear. Their pleasures had become familiar, yet this familiarity seemed in no way to diminish his hunger. Rachel was proud of this.

She pulled away, dipped her head, and covered his cock with her mouth, gave it a few sound licks up one side and down the other, then stopped. Silently, she stripped off his clothes. Shoes, socks, pants, jacket, shirt. Between his legs again, she took him inside her mouth once more, slowly inching her lips over him until her nose came to rest against his soft, hairy nest. She breathed in his spicy smell and felt her moist sex swell. Rachel groaned deep inside her throat, an animal sound. His scent, the taste of his cock slick from her saliva, the questions swirling around in her head, called up a wildness she could not tame. She drew him deeper into her throat and rotated her hips slowly, silently begging him to reciprocate. He reached down and grabbed her legs. With his strong arms he swiveled her body until her legs came to rest near his shoulders. His lips clamped down over her steamy cleft, licking and sucking and smearing his cheeks with her dew.

Rachel felt as if she were drowning in perfection. A perfect fit of man and woman. A perfect union of flesh. Perfect, blessed lust. She formed the words in her head. *Are we not perfect together, David Nussbaum? Am I not your perfect wife? Am I not worth more to you than your other wife?* And to God: *Do I not deserve this man? Have I not proved worthy of him?*

Her orgasm followed his, so exquisite it seemed to liberate her from her body. She lay on her back, panting as sweat poured down her sides and between her breasts. David slipped his arms around her and held her tight. Her long hair stuck to his skin. "My God, Rachel," he whispered. "You are incredible."

She felt the tears gather in her throat and tried to keep them secret, but couldn't.

"What's this?" He turned toward the nightstand to snap on the light, but she begged him not to. She didn't want him to see her wretchedness, as much a part of her passion as her wantonness. "Why are you crying?"

Rachel tried to harness her sobs, swallow them as she had swallowed his semen moments ago, but it was impossible. She grabbed for David, pulled at the hairs on his chest, balled her fists, and pounded weakly.

"Sometimes...sometimes...I don't know who I am!"

David wrapped his arms around her and rocked gently, whispered that she was Rachel, beloved of David, the woman who owned his heart. He crooned into her ear that she should never doubt, that she was blessed, hand-picked by God, chosen to be with him forever. "Rachela, Rachela, my beautiful bride, my jewel," he hummed. Words pretty and soothing. Like a song. He held her close to his heart for a long while, until her breathing found its peace.

"David?"

"Yes, my love?"

"I was chosen for you."

"Yes. Chosen."

"By God."

"Yes. By God."

"We are working out His will."

"Yes, love. We are."

"Whatever we do together. Whatever I do, whatever you do, is because it is God's will."

"Yes, yes, Rachel. God's will."

She sighed. "I love you, David. I love you so much."

"And I love you, Rachel. I always will."

"That's good."

"And you feel better?"

"Yes. Much better."

David gathered Rachel's long hair into his hands and caressed her scalp. "You have the most beautiful hair." He ran his lips along her cheek. "And the smoothest skin." He dropped his head to her breast and licked a nipple. "And you are delicious." He pulled back slightly.

"Don't stop," she said.

"I have to go to the bathroom. But I'll be back. I'm not finished with you," he teased. He slipped out of bed and bent to turn on the light. "You're sure you're all right?"

Rachel squinted against the glare. She nodded. She watched him cross to the bathroom and go in. She sat upright, her arms clasped around her knees, rocking back and forth, the same way David had rocked her in his arms. "I am here to do God's will," she hummed softly. Like a song.

She heard David run water into the tub. Ah, they would have a bath. He would make the water very hot. Later it would be just right. Rachel slid off the bed and padded across the room to the chair where she had put her clothes. She tossed aside her neatly folded sweater and skirt and reached for her bag. She opened the flap and took out her practice embroidery swatch. She shook her head. Terrible stitches. Just terrible.

Rachel walked back to the bed, to David's side, and sat down. She opened the drawer, removed the lid from the box of condoms, picked up several, and tenderly pushed her delicate embroidery needle through each foil-wrapped square.

The Survey
Mary Anne Mohanraj

So this guy walks up to me on the street at something like 8
P.M. on that deserted stretch over by the park, y'know? I'd be
scared except he's just a kid, and he says, "Hey, you wanna do
this survey?" And I say, "What's in it for me? I'm a busy
woman." And he says, "Five bucks—and if you answer the
long form, fifty."

Well, fifty bucks is not something to sniff at, y'know?
There's a lot I could buy for fifty bucks. There's this long
black velvet coat over at Goodwill, only twenty bucks, and a
nice pair of rhinestone heels I've been eyeing, five bucks, and
that leaves twenty-five for the kids—half for them, half for
me. That's fair, right? And that sounds so good I can see the
money's already spent, so I'd better answer his questions. So I
tell him, "Shoot." And he says, "Do you masturbate?"

So I reach back my arm and I'm gonna belt him a good one
right there, only he ducks and hollers out—"It's for the
survey!" And I drop my arm and I say, "What the fuck kinda
survey is that?" And he says, "It's a fucking survey, see? The
university is doing a survey on fucking. I got stuck with asking

women if they masturbate, which is not making me popular, believe me. My roommate, he gets to ask guys where the best places to get a blow job are, lucky bastard. You wouldn't believe how many women have tried to hit me already today, lady. Look, one of them got me." And he shows me this bump on his forehead, under where his greasy hair falls in his face. So I say, "What the hell kind of school do you go to that does a fucking survey? Never mind...I don't wanna know."

So he's standing there, waiting, and I'm standing there, thinking. "Do you gotta know my name?" I ask him. He says, "Well, we have to put down a name and an age, but you don't have to give me your real name. They won't know." And I think it over, and finally, I think, Sure. What the fuck. Give the kid a thrill. "Put me down as Esmerelda. Esmerelda Valentino, age twenty-eight." Ever since I watched *I Dream of Jeannie* as a kid, I've liked the name Esmerelda. "And the answer to your question is 'Yes.'" The kid scribbles something down on the clipboard he's holding, and then reaches into his pocket and hands me a five. And I say, "Where's my fifty?" And he says, "That's only for the long form, Miz Esmerelda. Nobody wants to answer the long form." And I say, "Show me."

So he hands over the clipboard, and there's this sheet of paper with big words at the top—*How Do You Masturbate?*—and a long list of questions below. Questions like "How many fingers do you use when you masturbate?" and "Do you prefer clitoral or vaginal stimulation?" and "Have you ever inserted foreign objects into your rectum?"

I hand back the board. "That's what they want to know? They got this list—that's supposed to tell them how we do it?" The kid nods his head, looking embarrassed. And I laugh. 'Cause it's just too damn funny, y'know? And I say, "Siddown, kid. Grab a patch of sidewalk. That little list of yours won't tell you nothin'. I'll tell you how I really do it." So we sit down on the sidewalk and I stretch out my aching

230

feet, 'cause it's been a hard day at the diner, and I close my eyes and start talking.

"It all starts with Johnny, see. Not Johnny Stepanino, that lousy no-good bum that I've been seeing for the past six years, who keeps promising me a ring but do you see it on my finger? Not him—he's got stringy hair and doesn't remember to bathe half the time unless his mama tells him to; I wouldn't give him the time of day 'cept he's got a good business and could really take care of me and my kids. But he's never gonna get up the nerve, 'cause his mama don't like the idea of him marrying a girl who's only a little bit Italian, mostly mutt, and dropped out of high school when she got knocked up at sixteen. His mama don't like that idea at all.

"Anyway, the one I'm thinking of is Johnny Viaggi. Johnny Viaggi with the long black hair that falls into his face so cute—kinda like yours, kid. He smells clean all the time, clean as spring, with the smell of new bread hanging heavy over him—that's 'cause he works at Cantalini's bakery over on Fourth.

"That Nina Cantalini! How that little shit managed to snag Johnny Viaggi I'll never know—oh, she's all-right looking, I'll give you that, with that tight ass and those big tits. But them Cantalini women are all drinkers, which is why the men run the shop, and I swear that before she's thirty Nina will be drinking up the profits and lettin' her body go to hell. She's gonna swell up like a balloon and those big tits are gonna droop over the beer belly she's gonna have. And that tight ass is gonna loosen right up, and Johnny Viaggi is gonna be damned sorry he married such a worthless drunken lump of a woman when he could've had me.

"You're wondering why I'm telling you all this. See, when I'm getting off, I'm not alone. No, I close my eyes, and Johnny Viaggi is right there next to me. It's his big thick hands that lift me up and move me to my bed, his hands that unbutton my blouse and push it down my shoulders and off my arms. Slender arms, and a slender body, and if my tits aren't as big as that damn Nina's at least they'll still be standing up straight in ten years. I don't fucking care if I'm only a 32A—my nipples are sensitive as hell, and that's what counts. That's what Stepanino says, anyway, and for once the scumbag is right.

"I've got great little tits, and when I unhook the front of my cherry red bra and pull it off, that's Johnny's fingers doing it, and his big hands cupping my tits so that they disappear under his rough touch. Then my nipples stand up hard, so hard they poke out between his fingers, and he starts playing with them, rolling them between two fingers, squeezing and pulling a bit, all the while whispering words of love, '*Mi amore, cara mia,* darling Angie.' And I'm moaning under Johnny's touch 'cause it's so good, and my nipples are so sensitive, and his breath is soft against my ear, against my neck—I'm almost ready to come right there, but he likes to take it slow.

"Then his hands slide down my body, unzipping my skirt and pushing it down, so he can see the red silk garter belt and black stockings I wore just for him, just like he asked me to. No panties, and Johnny's fingers trail down and down, almost tickling but not quite, sliding over my shaved pussy until they're barely touching my clit. And he touches me then, and it is so sweet, so fucking sweet that I moan Johnny's name, oh yeah. I'm lying in my bed with his body warm beside me and his mouth on my nipple now and his fingers sliding into my pussy, warm and wet and slick and hard, pumping harder and harder until I'm almost about to come and it's then that he whispers, 'Angie, will you marry me?' and that's when I scream 'Yes, yes, yes!' and I'm coming hard and fast like you wouldn't believe.

"*That's* how I masturbate. You got all that down, kid?" He's staring at me with wide eyes, like he's never heard a woman come before.

Maybe he hasn't. And I'm standing up and shaking the dust from my ass, and he comes alive quick and reaches into his pocket, fumbling a little, and then counts out nine more fives into my hand. He's still not saying a word so I smile at him and turn away, walking down the empty street and not caring that my feet still hurt 'cause I've got fifty dollars in my pocket and a sopping-wet pussy.

Take *that,* Nina-fucking-Cantalini.

About the Authors

TRACEY ALVREZ lives and writes in the historic Ahipara Gumfields of New Zealand. Besides loving writing fiction, she enjoys helping other writers through the Web site she maintains, nzwriters.com, and is the coeditor of a New Zealand magazine that deals with environmental and lifestyle issues.

HANNE BLANK is a saucy broad who writes a lot. Trained as an opera singer, she decided that writing about sex was a logical next step. She lives in Jamaica Plain, Massachussetts, and in cyberspace at hanne.net.

MICHELLE BOUCHÉ is a writer, artist, teacher, consultant, rugby player, and all-around rabble-rouser who loves New Orleans for all the wrong reasons. She has held such varied jobs as production manager for an opera company, signing publicity pictures for a famous mouse, and being an extra in the movie *Animal House*. She is currently working on her second novel. "I would like to dedicate this story to my teacher Liz, who not only got me to write it but yelled at me that it wouldn't sell sitting in a drawer."

CARA BRUCE is the editor of *Viscera: An Anthology of Bizarre Erotica*. Her short stories have been published in many anthologies, including *The Oy of Sex: Jewish Women's Erotica, Best Lesbian Erotica 2000,* and *Best Women's Erotica 2000.* She is also the editor and founder of the online magazine *Venus or Vixen?*

KATE DOMINIC, a Midwestern transplant to Southern California, has a fondness for cats, organic gardening, and Frappuccinos—all of which have inspired her writing at one point or another. Her erotic stories appear in *Best Women's Erotica 2000, Best Lesbian Erotica 2000, Herotica 6, Lip Service, Wicked Words, Strange Bedfellows,* and dozens of other publications under various pennames. Kate's first book, *Any 2 People Kissing,* will be published by Down There Press in spring 2001.

TABATHA FLYTE has written erotica for various publications, including, most recently, an anthology of water-based erotica edited by Mary Anne Mohanraj. Her first novel *Tongue in Cheek* was published by Black Lace in 2000 and her second, *The Hottest Place,* is forthcoming.

LISA GLATT'S work has been published in literary journals and anthologies, including *Columbia, Indiana Review, Crab Orchard Review, Gargoyle,* and *The Bust Guide to the New Girl Order* (Viking/Penguin, 1999). She currently teaches in the writers' program at UCLA. Her books of poetry include *Monsters and Other Lovers* and *Shelter.*

SACCHI GREEN lives in western Massachusetts. She writes some science fiction and fantasy, but the erotic side of the force is often more seductive. Her work can be found in *Best Lesbian Erotica 1999* and *2000* as well as in *Zaftig: Well-Rounded Erotica* and the upcoming *Set in Stone*.

KRISTINE HAWES has played with words for twenty-plus years and has finally decided to toss them into pieces of fiction. All scenes have been thoroughly tested to meet rigorous quality standards. Just ask the cat. When not testing written acts of carnal pleasure, Hawes is editing other hot stories as a *Clean Sheets* webzine fiction editor.

Emma Holly is a sucker for a good vampire story, and has written a number of erotic novels. Her first sexy historical romance will be out sometime in 2001.

DEBRA HYDE maintains a sexuality web log at pursedlips.com. Her erotica has appeared in numerous Web and print publications. In her experience, you can sometimes tell a Tourettor's thoughts or feelings by the nature of the tics.

SUSANNAH INDIGO (susannahindigo.com) is a writer and consultant living in Colorado. Her fiction is published in *Best American Erotica 2000, Best Women's Erotica 2000, Herotica 6,* and on audio for Passion Press. She is also published in many magazines and online journals, including *Libido* and *Clean Sheets*.

REBECCA KISSEL'S story "Branded" was the first she ever submitted for publication. When it was purchased for *Viscera* she was flattered; when it was chosen for *Best Women's Erotica* she was flabbergasted! Rebecca's dark side is well taken care of by her husband and lover of eighteen years, Jim.

MARY ANNE MOHANRAJ (mamohanraj.com) is the author of *Torn Shapes of Desire,* editor of *Aqua Erotica,* and consulting editor for *Herotica 7.* She has been published in a multitude of anthologies and magazines, including *Herotica 6, Best American Erotica 1999,* and *Best Women's Erotica 2000.* Mohanraj serves as editor in chief for the erotic webzine *Clean Sheets.* She also moderates the EROS Workshop, co-moderates the newsgroup soc.sexuality.general, and is a graduate of Clarion West '97. She has received degrees in writing and English from Mills College and the University of Chicago, teaches writing at the University of Utah, and is currently starting a new speculative fiction magazine, *Strange Horizons.*

G. L. MORRISON is a righteous, leftist, white, working-poor, omnivorous, vitamin-deficient professional poet, amateur mother, publisher of the zine *Poetic Licentious,* editor, writing teacher, reluctant journalist, and sometime scrawler of fiction, essays, and bathroom graffiti. Her work appears in *Early Embraces 2, Pillow Talk 2, Burning Ambitions,* and other print and online anthologies.

MADELINE OH (eclectics.com/rosemarylaurey) is a transplanted Brit, retired LD teacher, and grandmother now living in Ohio with her husband of thirty years. She has sold erotica to *Vavoom* and *Blue Food,* and writes romance under the name Rosemary Laurey.

LISA PROSIMO is a freelance editor and writer for several online publications. She will soon follow her muse to northern California, where she will live and write surrounded by grapevines. A native New Yorker, Prosimo can't wait to develop purple feet. Lisa's stories have appeared in *BWE 2000, Herotica 6,* and Lonnie Barbach's *Seductions.*

CAROL QUEEN has a doctorate in sexology, which she uses to impart more realistic detail to her smut. Her work has been extensively anthologized (for a complete bio, see carolqueen.com). She is the author of *The Leather Daddy and the Femme, Real Live Nude Girl,* and *Exhibitionism for the Shy* and coeditor of *Best Bisexual Erotica* (with Bill Brent), *Sex Spoken Here* (with Jack Davis), and *PoMoSexuals* and *Switch Hitters* (both with Lawrence Schimel).

NATASHA ROSTOVA is an art historian and the author of several novels from Black Lace Publications. She is currently working on a collection of short stories about the parallels between art and sexuality. Her Web site, Venetian Blue, is located at hyperlinx.net/~blue.

HELENA SETTIMANA is the pen name of a Toronto artist and writer who shares a home with one husband and four exuberant cats. Her fiction and poetry have been featured in the webzines *Scarlet Letters, Dare, Clean Sheets,* and the *Erotica Readers Association,* and on her own site angelfire.com/on3/helenasettimana.

MICHELLE SCALISE has sold well over one hundred poems and short stories to such magazines as *Carpe Noctem, Pirate Writings, Dark Regions, Talebones, Mindmares, Roadworks, Enigmatic Tales,* and the anthology *Viscera.* She was nominated along with Tom Piccirilli for the 1999 Rhysling Award for their poem "Badges of Eithers Woe."

ANNE TOURNEY has published erotic fiction in various journals and anthologies, including *Paramour, Best American Erotica 1994* and *1999,* and *The Unmade Bed.* She lives in the San Francisco Bay Area.

About the Editor

MARCY SHEINER is editor of the *Best Women's Erotica* series and *The Oy of Sex: Jewish Women's Erotica* (Cleis Press, 1999). She is also editor of *Herotica 4, 5, 6,* and *7* (Plume; Down There Press). Her stories and essays have appeared in many anthologies and publications. She is currently working on a novel.